The Rainbow Man

And Other Stories

by

David Gardiner

MERILANG PRESS
Bodyfuddau
Trawsfynydd
Gwynedd
LL41 4UW

Second Edition
Copyright © David Gardiner 2010
First published in Great Britain in 2003 by Boho Press

A CIP catalogue record for this book is available
from the British Library

ISBN: 978-0-9555430-6-7

9 780955 543067

Dedicated equally to:

The members of the Storyshed Writers' Group for their invaluable criticism and advice,

Sue Booth-Forbes of the Anam Cara Writers' and Artists' Retreat in Co. Cork for her role as midwife in The Rainbow Man's birth, and

Andrea Lowne and Richard Harris of UKAuthors.com for everything they have done to support and encourage aspiring authors like myself on the right-hand side of the Atlantic.

You pick up this book with its charming exterior thinking you are going to read a collection of equally charming short stories, seasoned perhaps with a little grit to raise it above the tame, but what you actually get are jawdropping vignettes of the sort of lives only a writer of David's calibre could relate with such vivid and at times disturbing realism, and all this whilst at the same time managing to avoid the usual, the jaded and the hackneyed to ensnare your attention. Nothing is as it seems and the more mundane the surface, the more layers there appear to be; we are talking about a true literary onion here, multi-layered and quite able to bring tears to your eyes.

In their way, short stories are the hardest of all genres to write, for it is in the very economy of words that volumes are spoken. David is masterful with his word budget; he can induce more impact, chill the blood and widen more eyes in half a dozen pages than some authors could ever dream of doing with 30,000 words. It is a gift, and one rarely offered to the reading public in this Godforsaken age of heinous, ghost written, celebrity dross which is laughably called literature, and the steady, gentle voice of a true storyteller is often sadly too hard to hear with any clarity over the cackling of a cash-fuelled mediocrity. But when you hear it, you will hear a voice which will remain inside your imagination long after the book is closed, set aside, and that whatshisname mediocrity has grown too unlovely for the public at large.

Binnacle Press Book of the Month Review
© copyright 2004 Binnacle Press

Table of Contents   Page

Introduction 7

The Rainbow Man 9
Inseparable 13
Collateral Damage 21
Blind Date 35
The Lies of Sleeping Dogs 43
Knight Errant 61
Letting Go 69
Ellen and Aubery 87
The Oracle at the Adelphi 93
The Dragonslayer 109
The Battlefield Philosopher 117
Cinderella's Slipper 129
Services to the Community 135
Muskie's Big Break 151
The Summer of Dust 167
Letter to Mammy 183
Imbalance 189
Lettie 199
Immaculata 207
Personal Services 225
Celia's Shrine 235
Witchcraft 241
The Go-Between 247
The Debt Collector 253
The Hand of God 265

Publication history 273
About the author 275

Introduction

Bluechrome/Boho, publisher of the first edition of *The Rainbow Man and Other Stories*, is no longer trading, so this book has been unavailable in the normal way for the last three years or thereabouts. This new edition forms a companion volume to my second collection *The Other End of the Rainbow*, also published by Merilang Press (2008) which I hope you will read as well if you haven't already.

Revising a book presents an opportunity to correct errors and include newer material, and in the present case I have added two new stories but removed none of the original ones, giving this edition a total story-count of 25. I have also modified somewhat the wise words of The Rainbow Man introducing each of the tales. Don't take his pronouncements too seriously, he would never do that himself.

Although in appearance almost a children's book, this collection contains some fairly dark material, so be careful how you go.

Short stories and poems make more demands of their readers than novels do, or at least demands of a different kind. In order for these tales to work you must join with me in the creative process, use your imagination to fill in the little sketch that is the story on the page. Remember that a short story does not even set out to be complete in any sense, it's merely one half of a collaboration with the reader whose aim is to create a meaning or an insight of some kind. All go to the well but each draws something slightly different. My hope is that each story will have something to say to whoever reads it – it won't be the same thing in every case, and that is exactly as it should be.

The Rainbow Man

Children have many worlds through which they are free to roam. It is an ability that rapidly fades with age in most of us, for it is feared and discouraged by the adult world. Yet occasionally if it is properly nurtured and exercised, this faculty can survive in a person for as long as life itself.

My childhood was spent in a little market town named Ballyrowan on the border between Northern Ireland and the Irish Republic. It was also a smuggling town and a recruitment and training centre for the IRA, but none of that mattered to me. Ballyrowan was simply my world, the only place of which I had any direct knowledge. It had a river where you could swim in the summer and woods where you could play chasing games and cowboys-and-Indians, a graveyard where you could play ghosts-and-vampires in the winter evenings and lots of derelict and abandoned farmhouses on the outskirts where you could play king-of-the castle or knights-and-dragons or "house" if you were a girl. There were a few adults around, including my father and mother, but they didn't count for very much and we only interacted with them when we needed something or when they had demands to make of us, such as going to school or going to bed or looking after little brothers. They weren't of any real significance in our lives. All, that is, except one, the old man we called the Rainbow Man.

It was no great mystery how he got that name, because he was to all outward appearances a walking rainbow. He had an obsessive love of brightly coloured pieces of cloth, the brighter the better, and gaudy costume jewellery of all kinds, and knowing this people would give him their unwanted garishly coloured curtains or chair covers or scraps of fabric, or the play-jewellery that their children had out-grown; partly out of kindness and partly out of curiosity to see what use the Rainbow Man would find for them. For the Rainbow Man was an artist, and his canvas was himself. He would find ways to wrap gaily coloured pieces of old fabric around his head to simulate a Maharajah's turban, and ways to turn discarded beach-towels and chair coverings into elegant kilts and togas and flowing caftans. Nothing was wasted. A thin left-over strip of some lurid purple artificial fibre would find a role as a belt or a scarf or a headband or an accessory worn around the ankle or the wrist. Every day the Rainbow Man would wander the streets and surrounding lanes of Ballyrowan wearing a new ensemble, each one more dazzling and inventive than the last.

Families driving through the town would alert their children in advance to look out for him, and if they were lucky enough to spot him, the youngest child would be handed a threepenny bit or a sixpence to give to him. Offer-ings of this kind he always accepted with a polite "God bless you", and nobody saw any harm in it, the notion of slightly deranged adult males posing a threat to children having yet to enter the public consciousness.

The Rainbow Man was a local tourist attraction, like the monument to William Allingham in the town square or the carving of the Fiddler of Dooney on the Sligo Road.

As children we were able to get to know the Rainbow Man a lot better than the adults, and to listen in to the complex one-sided conversations that he carried on with his ever-present invisible companions.

"Oh, youse won't be laughing tomorrow, when they crown me king," he would tell them, or "Only one of youse is coming with me when I go to Mars" or "I know youse have got my son's head in a bucket, but I don't care, what did that boy ever do for me?" and so on. The mere contingencies of reality were never allowed to impinge on the conversations between the Rainbow Man and his voices.

As we followed him around we joined in these conversations with enthusiasm, either inventing our own unseen respondents or attempting to contribute something to the Rainbow Man's dialogues. Occasionally he would acknowledge our presence also, and he was never lacking in courtesy even to the youngest of us, but usually he was too preoccupied with some more ethereal exchange of his own to pay us very much heed.

With the passage of time and under the influence of his fine example we developed our own techniques of communication with the unseen world, and tried to create voices with particular interests and attributes and consistent personalities. The people I spoke to included St. Francis of Assisi whose life we had been learning about at school, a robot space traveller from a remote galaxy, and a beautiful fairy princess who could sprinkle me with star dust that enabled me to fly like Peter Pan and Wendy.

The fashion for children to carry on conversations with their invisible companions spread rapidly through the four-to-eight-year-old age group in Ballyrowan.

Fathers and particularly mothers started to become alarmed and the phenomenon became talked about in the local Women's Institute and obscure sub-committees of the Roman Catholic Church. Inevitably, the Rainbow Man became ostracised, no longer to be accepted or encouraged by respectable society in Ballyrowan. Unwittingly, our mimicry of the Rainbow Man's interesting affliction had sewn the seeds of his destruction. Madness in a (literally) colourful vagrant might be viewed as quaint, but if it was of a contagious kind that infected the children of the town then it had to be viewed as an evil.

Alarmed mothers forbade their offspring to talk to the Rainbow Man, or to themselves, or to have anything more to do with him. The flow of threepenny bits and sixpences diminished to a trickle, as did the gifts of cloth and baubles from previously well-meaning members of the adult community. Of course there were children who still managed to smuggle scraps of food to the Rainbow Man, rather in the manner of Red Cross parcels for political prisoners, and sometimes they even managed to get him what he seemed to hunger for most of all, his beloved scraps of brightly coloured cloth. But with the odds so heavily stacked against them, those responsible for these kindly acts of insubordination were quickly brought into line.

The Rainbow Man was seen less and less frequently in the streets of Ballyrowan. When he was he seemed subdued and less colourful, his retinue of children missing, his dazzling attire slowly fading into pastel hues due to non-renewal and the slow accumulation of dust and grime. He spoke more quietly to his voices and walked more slowly, unable to comprehend the reasons for the sudden change in his fortunes.

Then came the inevitable. Late one Saturday night, down a narrow alley by the side of the local cinema, two old men who had gone down to have a pee discovered the body of the Rainbow Man, small and crumpled and faded to a neutral grey. From the loudspeakers behind the screen powerful and distinct voices filled the night air, but the Rainbow Man was no longer able to hear them.

"Why are you always talking, Mr Rainbow Man?" a grubby-faced urchin asked as the small group of children followed him down Ballyrowan High Street.

"It's important to keep in touch with your friends and family," The Rainbow Man explained. "They're all we've got in the end."

Inseparable

"Come in, boy. Sit up there by the fire. Take that coat off. I'll get you a cup of coffee. You look like a High School kid. How old are you?"

"I'm twenty-eight, Ma'am."

"Twenty-eight. I don't think I can rightly remember being twenty-eight. How did you hear about me?"

He made himself comfortable on the wicker armchair and balanced his briefcase carefully by its side before he replied.

"Well, Ma'am, my grandfather died about two months ago and I inherited a lot of his stuff. He had a record collection – easily fifty, sixty years old, some of them – and when I looked through I found this one here." He withdrew it carefully from his briefcase. "It was recorded by a couple of local girls. It says they came from Redwood County, Vermont."

He handed her the delicate old 78, which she slipped out of its faded paper jacket. She put on her glasses to read the label. He could see that it choked her up slightly. "You drove all the way up from Burlington because of this?"

"It's not all that far, Ma'am."

"Forty-six miles and a hundred-and-fifty years, we always used to say. I was born in this house, you know."

"Yes, I do know, Ma'am. I've been reading up a bit about the twins. I was surprised I'd never heard of you. You were pretty famous people... back then."

"Back then is right. And back then is a long time ago. What makes you think anybody'll be interested now?"

"Well, most folks are interested in local celebrities. Burlington – even the whole state of Vermont – doesn't have all that many famous people to boast about."

"Famous people? Famous people are presidents and Nobel Prize winners and astronauts and film stars. We were never famous like that."

"Your records sold pretty well. You played the Grand Ol' Opry. Got a bit of film work. Quite a lot of stage work. That's famous enough for Vermont."

She laughed. "The two easy roads to success – aim low or get yourself born in Vermont. Yeah, we done alright for a couple of country girls from out here. People used to ask us if we would've done so good if we hadn't been twins. We used to say: How the hell would we know? It was a way of putting us down, really. Saying we had no talent, just looked cute. Anyway, who cares? Being twins was our gimmick, and if that's what got us the bookings then thank the Lord for it. I ain't going to look no gift horse in the mouth.' She gave him back the record and went over to the wood-stove. "Here's your coffee. Want a bit of stew? It's all I've got."

"No thanks, Ma'am, I ate before I set out."

"Can we drop this 'ma'am' thing? My name's Tillie."

"Sure. Is that your real name?"

"Are you kidding? Our agent gave us those names. Millie and Tillie. Millie really was Millie – her name was Millicent – but Tillie? Nothing like my real name. It was made up. I always resented that she got to keep her real name but I had to have a made-up one. Real name's Theresa. At least it begins with 'T'. I haven't used it since I was about fifteen, so best call me Tillie or I may not know who you're talking to."

He nodded. "Is it okay if I take notes?" He slid a spiral bound pad out of his briefcase as he spoke.

"Sure. I'm glad it ain't a tape recorder. Those things make me nervous as hell."

"Would you say that you and Millie were very close?"

"Name me a set of twins that wasn't. When we were little we were almost one person with two bodies. It never occurred to us to be selfish, or to keep secrets from one another, or to do anything on our own. There was us, and then there was the rest of the world. It's something you probably can't understand if you haven't lived it."

"And did that closeness last for the whole of your lives?"

Tillie hesitated. "You want cream in that? I got some. Sugar maybe?"

He shook his head. There was a pause, but he wouldn't be sidetracked. He waited for the answer.

"No relationship of any kind stays the same for a whole lifetime. You're too young to know that but you'll find out." She sat down wearily at the kitchen table and rested her head in her hands. He couldn't see her face any more so he came over and sat nearby. His reporter's instinct told him to say nothing, simply wait.

"We used to take advantage of people because nobody could tell us apart,' she said quietly, not looking up. 'I guess most identicals do. People used to think they could, but we could easily fool 'em. Millie was a bit more shy and quiet than me, so if I wanted to be Millie I would act a bit more timid and everybody would be sure it was her. We used to play tricks on our beaus – maybe Millie would go out on a

15

couple dates and then she'd tell me to have a go and I would go out on the next one pretending to be her, and tell her afterwards how we got on and what I thought of the guy. We never got caught out, not once. Well... maybe once." She hesitated. "You know, I don't think I ought to be telling you this here stuff. This has nothing to do with our career."

He sensed that he had struck a nerve. If he could find a way in he might have a story here. A real story. "You know, Tillie, a reporter doesn't have to put everything in when he comes to write his piece. There's an ethical code – sometimes we get told personal stuff that people don't want to go any further. And it doesn't. It's as simple as that. If it did folks would stop trusting our profession, stop talking to us. So I want to give you my absolute assurance that you'll have a chance to see whatever I write, and if there's anything whatsoever that you're not happy with then it doesn't go in. Simple as that. That's the way I work."

She looked him straight in the eye but remained silent. He closed the notebook and put away the pen, making sure that she saw him do it.

"This is something you haven't talked about before, isn't it? I can tell. Sometimes it's good to talk, you know. It's a cliché but it happens to be true."

"It was in the early 1950s," she said in little more than a whisper, turning to watch the glow from the wood-stove, "all the guys were going off to the Korean War. If you volunteered you got a better posting than if you waited for the draft. America had never lost a war back then, it was all like a bit of fun. Couple months and it'll be over, we all thought. Go in there, wipe 'em out, come home heroes. We didn't understand why we were fighting – didn't care – it was a war, America was fighting it and so America must be right. Simple-minded times, eh?" He nodded.

"We were at the height of our career then. Those were the Grand Ol' Opry days. And radio of course. Radio was big back then. Bigger than TV. We were good Republicans, like all our folks, like most people in Vermont. We volunteered to go out and entertain the troops. Us and a thousand like us. We thought it might be a little bit rough, didn't know what to expect, but what we found out there scared the hell out of us. Young boys getting hauled into field hospitals with limbs hanging off. Bits of blown-up bodies that they couldn't even identify. Trophy gook bodies cut up so that more than one guy could claim a kill. You think that only happened in Vietnam? That was invented in Korea. You've seen it all on MASH – but I've seen the real thing. That's a bit different. And I was only about twenty-five. Younger than you are now. Hadn't even been overseas before."

"I know a little bit about it, Tillie. My dad was in 'Nam. I've been lucky, so far. My generation has been mostly lucky. Not the ones in the Middle East, of course…"

"Well, you can imagine how it was, we were two young good-looking girls in amongst a few thousand combat troops, no chaperones, no holds barred. We had a pretty good time, romantically-speaking. I hope that doesn't shock you. I know each generation thinks it invented sex. Not true, kid. Not true."

She paused for a long time. He wondered if he should say something. His instinct told him that he shouldn't and it was right.

"We were playing that little prank I told you about – switching roles, swapping dates, comparing notes, giggling about it all when we were on our own. Only…this time it went a bit too far. You see, there was somebody Millie really did care about. Somebody from near home, as it happened, quiet type, not much confidence, hated the war and what he had to do...

"Millie and me – we didn't understand anything really. About our own feelings, I mean. All our songs were about true love, betrayal, jealousy, broken hearts – but the truth is, we didn't know a thing about that side of life. The only relationship we gave a damn about was the one between the two of us. Everything else was just a big game. We were two kids playing with matches in a barn full of dry hay.

"Jace – that was his name – sent Millie a note to say that he'd got a new posting and he wouldn't be able to see her after tonight. I happened to know she wouldn't be around that night, but I guess she would've cancelled whatever it was she was doing to see Jace. Anyway I didn't tell her. I went in her place. Jace was pretty keen. Things got a bit physical. Jace and me went all the way. I know Millie and him had never done that. Like I said, we always told each other everything. Or at least we did up to then."

"So that was the first secret you'd ever had from Millie?"'

"Guess so. And it was a pretty stupid one to try to keep. As soon as he wrote her from his new posting she found out what had happened. I'd betrayed her and that would have changed everything even if there had never been anything else."

"But something else did happen, didn't it?"

Tillie sat back in her chair and sighed. "You can probably guess what it was."

"You got pregnant?"

She smiled. "No, we weren't that stupid." The smile vanished. "Something worse. Her next letter got returned. Soldier boy Jace had got himself killed in action. He only lived a few days after... Well, let's talk about something a bit more cheerful, can we?"

There was a longish pause.

"You didn't stop working together though, did you?"

"No, of course not. That was our living. The only thing we knew. We stayed together for years after that. But something had gone out of the act, you know what I mean? That closeness that you talked about, that was what made the act special. Just looking like a pair of bookends wasn't enough. People knew something was wrong, something had died. Our career went down after that. Quite slowly, thank the Lord. We had time to ease ourselves out of the music business. If things had gone different we might still be together now – like the Beverley Sisters. Must be ninety if they're a day. I even tried to go solo for a little while. Now that was a mighty stupid move. Millie got out of the business – moved down south somewhere."

There was really only one question left to ask. He wondered if he should – if he even wanted to know the answer. "What happened to Millie?"

The colour drained from Tillie's face. "You mean you don't know? I thought you said you'd read up about us?"

He wriggled in his seat. "I didn't find any reference to that," he said.

"Millie swallowed a month's supply of sleeping pills and washed them down with a bottle of Southern Comfort. Nobody knew how she got hold of either of them. She did it sitting on a bench at The Korean War Veterans Memorial in Washington DC on July 27, 1995 – just after it was dedicated by President Clinton and Kim Young Sam. Nobody noticed that she was dead until the following morning."

"...People...didn't even notice?"

"I guess folks don't pay too much heed to an old bag lady, out cold on a park bench with a bottle in her hand.

"Now – is there anything else you would like to know?"

"Don't tell me I killed you just because you were a German," The Rainbow Man sneered. *"If I killed you you'd know all about it 'cause you'd be dead!"*

Collateral Damage

He had no idea where the rest of the squad was now. Mickey Levitt had obviously bought it, he'd felt the blood splatter his own face when the side of Mickey's head exploded. At least it had been quick for him. The sergeant had shouted something but his voice had been lost in the numbing thud of a shell behind them. By the light of the same shell he had seen them veer off to the right, maybe towards a bunker that he hadn't spotted himself. If there was a bunker he hadn't been able to find it.

Moving blindly forward he trod on something soft and yielding. It was a human arm inside the sleeve of a uniform. It might still be connected to its owner's body, there was so little light it was difficult to tell, and in any case it made no real difference. He paused and looked furtively from side to side into the darkness, every inch of him trembling, as he tried to come up with a sensible course of action.

Two enormous flashes lit up the horizon ahead of him, momentarily throwing into silhouette the shapes of running soldiers and illuminating the pitted brown earth strewn with the scattered bodies of countless others. As the image vanished the sound of the two explosions reached his ears, a crushing double thunder-clap that left him momentary isolated, his ears suddenly filled with imaginary cotton-wool, aching and sending to his brain the familiar phantom high-pitched whistle. A huge goldfish-bowl had descended from the black sky to cover him up. He could still see, in so far as anyone could in the depths of a misty and starless night, but the sounds of the battlefield had been diminished to the distant clatter of marbles falling into a biscuit tin.

As he dropped down into a crouching position some of the debris thrown-up by the massive explosions began to rain down on him. He felt falling stones sting his back through his uniform and clatter against his tin hat.

Now he had a purpose. A destination. Where those two large calibre shells had just fallen there would be a crater of some kind, and a crater meant cover. Almost as good as a trench. And even if it had been part of the German front line five seconds ago, there sure as hell weren't any living Germans near it now. The heavy guns behind him had put two shells there, they weren't going to waste a third on the same spot. It was the safest possible place to head for.

Pleased with his own logic, he straightened up and started to jog clumsily in the direction of the flashes, rifle at the ready, left hand circling the handle of the bayonet in his belt-sheath. He was headed straight towards the German defences now.

He woke trembling and feverish to darkness and the sound of distant gunfire. Voices were shouting too, some of them female, and the explosions were punctuated by strange whizzing and whirring noises that he could not identify. The voices sounded oddly happy, celebratory even. What could this be? VE Day? Soldiers returning? It didn't make any sense.

He pulled himself up into a sitting position and rubbed his eyes with the palms of his hands. Familiar objects in his bedroom began to fade into view. The wardrobe and the dressing-table with its big oval mirror. The door with his jacket hanging on the hook, and the window with the thick lined velvet curtains that his daughter had made for him to let him sleep through the early summer dawns. But the sounds were still there, the gunfire and the voices...

Getting to his feet with more than a little difficulty he walked shakily to the curtains and opened them enough to see out. It was the middle of a cold and starless night, and yet lights were on everywhere in the houses across the road and eerie flashes of coloured light were turning the whole scene to daylight, not just white but red or green or blue daylight: like the bursting of multi-coloured artillery shells. People seemed to be out in their front gardens, laughing and drinking and – yes – kissing each other! He distinctly saw two men kissing the same girl, one after the other! Must be what they called "swingers", he thought. Wife-swappers. But imagine doing it right in the front garden, in the middle of the night, with glasses of booze in their hands. My God, what was this street coming to? Is that what he had fought the Germans for?

Well, yes, he smiled to himself, in a way it was. If young people wanted to live a different kind of life it wasn't really anything to do with him. In a way that was exactly what it was all about. As he looked for his dressing gown in the wardrobe he remembered a radio programme, narrated by Richard Dimbleby. How many years had Richard Dimbleby been dead, he wondered. It had been a sort of reverse news-cast, a long list of all the things that hadn't happened that day. "This morning," Richard had begun in his fruity, pompous old voice, "No British citizens were arrested for failure to produce their identity cards. No workers were dispatched from any British town to the factories of Essen or the mines of Northern Germany." And so it went on. No Jews had been transported to the gas chambers of Auschwitz or Bergen Belsen. There had been no Hitler Youth rally in

Regents Park. No bodies had been found on the streets of British cities with bullets in the backs of their heads A whole litany of abominations had not occurred. And why not? For one reason and one reason only, Richard had told them. Because about thirty-five years ago countless tens of thousands of the finest and most idealistic men and women of this nation and many others had laid down their lives to insure that these things wouldn't happen. It had been a very powerful broadcast. The memory of it still stirred him to pride, straightened his back a little.

The source of the coloured lights was obviously somewhere behind his own house. He made his way downstairs to the French windows. Yes, as he had guessed, a fireworks display in the park. The mighty waving columns of shimmering multi-coloured dots, almost too bright to look at directly, snaked and cascaded from somewhere behind the distant line of low yew trees, soaring all the way to the cloud-base, lighting up the clouds with emerald, orange and blood-red incandescence. Rockets like tracer- bullets sped in great arcs to the very interior of the low clouds and exploded noisily, turning the clouds for an instant at a time into great bulbous multi-coloured mini-suns.

For a few seconds the landscape of his dream replaced the clutter of little streets in the dip between his garden and the rear of the park. A sea of corpses, craters, mud, discarded rifles, crumpled uniforms, disembodied bits and pieces of human beings, the stench of sulphur and of the exposed contents of human intestines... then it was gone. Just a fireworks display. A harmless, pretty display of fire-crackers in a public park.

He slid open the French windows and felt a cold fresh breeze on his face. He rather liked its coldness, and he could detect on it that ever so faint but oh so familiar odour of freshly detonated gunpowder. With the window open the sounds were much louder, not overpowering, but sharp and crisp, full of the drama of battles long ago.

He walked out into the garden and stood on the path, the fresh breeze ruffling his hair, the sky in front of him alive with cascading lights.

"My goodness, Mr Dempsey," came a patronising female voice in an affected accent, "what on earth are you doing out in your slippers and robe, on this of all nights? You'll catch your death of cold outdoors in December dressed like that. Well, January actually, come to think of it. I thought I was the only person in the whole of England seeing-in the new millennium on my own. Happy New year, Mr Dempsey. Happy new millennium!"

"Thank you, Mrs Nugent," he returned with forced politeness. "And... happy... millennium to you too." So that's what it was all about, he thought to himself. New Year's night. A lot of poppycock. When you had seen in as many new years as he had you didn't make as big a fuss about it.

"You aren't going to leave me here on my own are you?" she coaxed, "I mean, I had lots of party invitations, but I'm just not a party person. Ever since Sid died, I've kept myself to myself. He was the outgoing one. I don't like parties. Never have done. But you'll help me celebrate, won't you? You'll have a glass of sherry with me?"

He hesitated, trying to think of a polite way to refuse, but it was too late. She was on her feet now, opening that little interconnecting gate that his son-in-law had made, at his daughter's suggestion, so that if "anything happened" Mrs Nugent would be able to come in and interfere.

"Come along, Mr Dempsey. May I call you Robert?" He shrugged. "And you have to call me Doris. I won't hear of anything else."

She led him to her own French windows, which were in the same position as his but older in design, wooden framed and rickety. His daughter had replaced his a couple of years back, thought it would make the house more secure. Everybody seemed to think they had to protect him, to organize his life. A bloody impertinence. He knew how to look after himself. He had demonstrated that for once and for all, about sixty years ago in a field in Northern France.

He noticed without a great deal of interest that she had altered the interior of her house at some stage. What was the lounge in his own was a kitchen-diner in this one. He didn't approve of people doing that. It destroyed the character of these little Victorian terrace houses. Pretensions. Delusions of grandeur. Typical of Mrs Nugent. Of all the Mrs Nugents.

He sat down on one of the armchairs by the coffee table. She went to find him a glass, and for a few moments he looked around at the crass imitation-everything of his surroundings. Kitchen units made of some kind of plastic simulated stripped pine, with make-believe varnished wooden work-surfaces and bottles of cheap wine stored on their sides in a rack beneath the counter. Impractically big kitchen knives and cleavers with stainless steel blades and black imitation ebony handles dangling from a special wooden rack above the sink. A string of garlic, purely for decoration he was certain, slung over a vacant hook by the side of the knives. An early-morning-television studio set of a French provincial kitchen.

"It's a... very nice kitchen," he lied as she handed him the sherry.

"Thank you Robert. Good health and happiness in the new millennium. And lots more New Years to you as well."

What was that supposed to mean? That she thought he was about to keel over and die? Not for a while yet, my good woman, he thought contemptuously. "Thank you, Doris," he said mildly, "and a good long life to you too." He sipped from the glass. It was a bit sickly sweet, he thought, like Doris herself. She sat down, slightly closer than he would have wished.

"Mr Dempsey... I mean Robert, you and I have got off on the wrong foot, haven't we?"

Damn it. She didn't want a heart-to-heart did she? It was the last thing he wanted.

"You don't have to say anything," she went on, sensing his discomfiture, "I know exactly what you feel about me, and I understand why you feel that way. You are a proud and independent man, and I admire you for that. So does your daughter. You wouldn't believe the respect she has for you, the way she talks about you. She worries about you. Maybe she doesn't need to, maybe you're as indestructible as you think you are, but you should be very happy that somebody cares about you that much. Not... not everybody has some-one who cares for them like that..."

He realized that she was fighting back a tear and felt a momentary impulse to put a hand on her shoulder. Then they both pulled themselves together.

"Robert, there's no disgrace in growing older. Nobody can live the same life at eighty as they can at twenty.. or at fifty."

Fifty. That was probably her own age. It was young to be a widow. Wonder how Sid died? Not the best time to ask.

"Isn't it wonderful that you've lived to see the begin-ning of a whole new century? Aren't you thrilled about it? Surely it's time to let somebody else do a little bit for you? You've nothing left to prove, Robert. It's time to relax. Let other people carry a little bit of the weight. Do you know what I mean?"

"You think I should go in to some kind of funny farm for old incontinents who can't remember their own names? Well, I'm not ready for that yet. I can stand up straight, I can see straight and I can think straight. A few years back, I got lost in the car in the city traffic and she made me stop driving. How many times have you got lost driving around this city? How many times has she? What kind of accident record have you had in the last twenty years? Do you want to know how many I've had?"

"Robert, it wasn't a question of accidents or of getting lost. You weren't able to pass the eyesight test any more. That's all there was to it."

"Doris, if you want to get a few things straight then let's get a few things straight. I don't say things behind people's backs. I say them to their faces. I resent the way you watch me and report everything back to Karen. You watch when I go out and when I come in. You count how many times I take a bath in the week. You tell her what time I go to bed at night and what time I get up in the morning and how many bottles the milkman leaves at the door. You tell her if I miss a Saturday at the club, or if I have a visitor. Now is that any way for a grown man to live? A man more than old enough to be your father? Would you like to be spied on and reported on like that?"

"But don't you see that it's because she cares? She doesn't want anything to happen to you. She wants to know that you're eating properly, and getting your sleep… and looking after yourself."

"All right. Tell her thanks. I'm looking after myself. I've looked after myself for a long time. If I want any help I'll let the two of you know."

"Don't be upset, Robert. Don't be angry with your only daughter. She deserves better."

He lay back in the chair and thought for a moment. "Yes," he said at last, "You're right. But there's nothing wrong with me. I wish the two of you would get that through your heads. Being old isn't a disease. I haven't gone soft in the head. Some people do, granted, but I haven't. So can you just leave me alone to live my own life in my own way. That isn't too much to ask now, is it?"

"No, Robert, it isn't. So are we okay now? Are we friends? Do we understand each other?"

"You and Joyce mean well. I know that."

Doris smiled and filled their two glasses again. "Did you realize you just called your daughter Joyce? Joyce was your wife, wasn't she?" Robert felt a twinge of annoyance, mostly with himself, but did not answer. "I'm glad we had this talk," Her smile softened. " I was going to sit outside and watch the fireworks. I would invite you but you would catch your death of cold in that thin robe."

"It's all right. You go outside and I'll just turn my chair around. I'll be able to see perfectly well from here."

She touched his hand, smiled, and returned to her seat in the garden.

The display was building up to some kind of grand finale. The rockets were going up thick and fast, bursting into globes of falling yellow, blue and red embers in the sky, one every second or even less, and behind them a huge fan of deep violet light moved from side to side across the clouds. It was pretty damned impressive he had to admit. The local council weren't doing things by half measures. He sipped his sherry and lay back in the chair.

It was impossible to judge how far away that crater might be. Maybe as much as a mile, he reckoned, but probably less. He tried to keep his back bent and his head down as he ran, to present as low a profile as possible to the stray machine-gun fire. In the near darkness he stumbled many times over bodies and shrubs and rocks and discarded backpacks, but paid them no heed. He knew where he was going now, he would not be deflected.

Just in time, the explosion of a distant shell back-lighted a huge tangle of razor-wire directly across his path. He managed to stop just before plummeting headlong into it. "Jeez Christ!" he heard himself mutter as he ducked low behind it.

"Are you British, mate?" said a faltering Cockney voice from almost directly in front of him. The wire seemed to twitch slightly as the voice spoke. He stared down and saw the round wide-eyed face of what seemed a young boy, so drenched in blood that in this light he could distinguish nothing but the eyes and the teeth. He was wearing a British uniform but no helmet, and his body seemed to be bent double beneath the wire.

"I'm Bob Dempsey, private in the Royal Engineers," he said as though introducing himself at a polite cocktail party. "What happened to your helmet?" It was a ridiculous question but simply the first thing that had come to his mind.

"Len Farrow is the name. Sixth Infantry. Had to take my helmet off. Took a bullet. I'm not sure if it went right through. Can you see if my head's okay?" He bent right down and examined the other's head as best he could in the faint glimmer of light from whatever was burning up ahead. He could have lit a Lucifer to see better, but it would probably have signed both their death-warrants. Anyway there was no need. It was the first time that Robert had seen an exposed section of the human brain.

"I think it's quite bad," he said as cheerily as he could. "If I was you I would stay here and wait until I come back with help."

"Whatever you say, Doc. I wasn't really planning any journeys anyway."

He touched the fallen man's hand. "Hang on in there, Len. You're going to be just fine."

"Of course I am. Say, Bob, I've got a girlfriend up north. Name's Joyce Bennett. 19 Sharrow Road in Hull. If you're ever up that way you might like to drop in and give her my love, would you?"

He felt himself choking up. "I'll do it Len," he promised solemnly, "if it means coming back from the dead."

He got out his wire cutters and started working on the coils. "19 Sharrow Road," he shouted back as he continued on his journey, "I'll tell her you love her a lot!" There was no reply. Len didn't seem to be moving any more.

The razor wire, he knew, would mark the outer boundary of enemy lines. He moved more cautiously now, tried to listen for the least movement. Another shell-burst lit up the landscape for a fraction of a second, like the flash-bulb of a reporter's camera. It told him that there were very few bodies in this area and the ground was relatively flat, but it also picked out an odd human sculpture a couple of hundred yards ahead of him. It looked like the back view of a man sitting on something with his hands held out slightly from his sides, palms upwards, almost as if he were checking to see if it was going to rain.

Robert slowed down even more and approached the weird seated figure as silently as he possibly could. It was difficult to make out the man's form, but the faint glimmer from the fires up ahead let him see that the man was wearing a German helmet. He was keeping his hands still, but his head rocked very gently from side to side like the bough of a tree in a soft summer breeze. Exactly like a scarecrow in a field of rippling corn. Anybody could see that he was out of it, he probably didn't even know which way he was facing, because he was staring mindlessly at his own lines, with his back to the advancing British.

But he could still be dangerous. Where was his rifle? Robert couldn't see it, which meant that he might have it between his legs. German officers and NCOs carried pistols as well. Nutter or not, this was an enemy soldier and Robert wasn't going to take any chances. He reached down for his sheathed bayonet. Not there! Impossible! It had been there a few minutes ago. Could it have slipped out while he was cutting the wire? Ridiculous, the clip was still buttoned across the sheath. He stopped moving and feverishly went over the events of the last few minutes. He was sweating now, all that he had was his rifle, and if he fired that he was going to draw attention to himself in a big way.

Behind him, somewhere along the British lines, a flash of light gave him one more still image of his surroundings, and to his vast relief the bayonet was on the ground beside him. Not questioning Providence he grasped it in his right hand.

He stepped up soundlessly behind the seated figure and sliced the bayonet across the soldier's throat with all the strength at his command. With a skilled encircling move-ment the man's head was all but severed from his neck, and blood gushed upwards to drench Robert's torso and arm. The whole thing had taken perhaps two seconds, and made less noise than a single footfall. Robert gently guided the limp body forwards on to the ground.

He looked down at it and noticed a strange rippling effect around the helmet. It was as though he were seeing it from a long way away, through a shimmering heat-haze. Sometimes it looked like a German helmet and sometimes it looked like a grey woollen scarf tied around a woman's head. The light was getting better, he noticed, and an occasional peculiar whizzing noise seemed to have mixed with the rattle of the distant machine-gun fire and the stomach-wrenching booms of the exploding shells. He held up his bayonet and noticed that it had an imitation ebony handle with a hole drilled through it for hanging it up on a kitchen rack.

He stopped shaking and looked up. That crater couldn't be much further away now. Time to carry on. He recovered the bayonet, shoved it into the belt of his dressing- gown, and set out at a brisk pace towards the bursting shells behind the line of yew trees.

*"I only said I loved 'ye for a bet," The Rainbow Man
taunted. "The only person who could love a critter like
you would be yer own mother, an' that on a pretty dark
night as well!"*

Blind Date

When Lisa had first arrived at the shopping centre, fifteen
minutes early, her worst fear had been that he was going to
stand her up. She knew that it would hurt if this happened,
it would make her feel ridiculous... and pathetic... and...
cheap, she had thought. Like the kind of girl who has to
throw herself at a man, who has to use classified advertise-
ments, who doesn't get asked out. But of course that was the
kind of girl she was, wasn't it?

The reason that she had chosen somewhere so public
and so ordinary, a wooden bench by a fountain in the foyer
of a City Centre shopping arcade, was in case this might
happen. If she had had to sit by herself in a restaurant or a
bar, and he hadn't turned up, all those eyes would have been
watching her, judging her. But here – why here she could sit
as long as she wished, or simply stand up and walk away.
Nobody would pay the slightest attention. She could be
waiting for a girl friend, or just resting her feet. She felt
almost... invisible.

Now that she had been there for a while, and the actual
agreed time for the meeting was drawing near, she began to
worry that he *would* show up. She was by no means at ease
with herself about what she was doing. Rationally she knew
that it was a very sensible and honest thing to do: to take
control of her own life and go out and find somebody, to
simply say what she wanted and see if anybody was willing

to offer it. But in her heart of hearts she felt a kind of shame. She was beginning to wish that the whole thing was over and done with, and she was on her way home to her own little room and her own comfortable, single bed.

An even more appalling thought had occurred to her. What if he came to have a sneak preview before committing himself? What if he was one of these men standing around, reading their newspapers, searching for their credit-cards, rearranging the shopping in their carrier-bags, waiting for wives and girlfriends to return from the shops or the toilets or who-knows-where...? He could easily pretend to be passing the bench and take a little peek. Then if he didn't like what he saw he could walk on... she would never know. It was horrible. Maybe at this very moment she was on display, like a cow at a cattle-market, being assessed, weighed-up, considered as a worthwhile prospect... very likely being rejected.

She looked at her watch. Two minutes to go. No, more like one-and-a-half. She wondered if the device was really as accurate as that. Probably not. The moment might have come and gone already, or it might be three or even five minutes into the future...

She stopped herself. This wouldn't do. She was becoming paranoid. She must calm down and try to relax, try to approach the situation like an adult. It was only a first meeting with someone who had sounded perfectly all right on the phone. She hadn't been nervous then. He had been easy to talk to. What was she worried about? She was being silly. She made a deliberate effort to make her breathing slower and deeper, and to stop fidgeting with her handbag. That's better, she told herself. That's much better.

"Lisa?" The voice came from behind her, almost next to her ear, and it made her start. "Lisa Cooper?"

It was a kindly voice, and when she looked around it was a kindly face that met her gaze.

"I'm sorry. I shouldn't have sneaked-up behind you like that."

"No, not at all, it was silly of me... my mind was miles away..."

As she spoke he made his way around to the front of the bench and smiled down at her. She realised that her heart was racing slightly now. He was a lot better looking than she had imagined him! Taller, thinner, younger, better dressed... better in every imaginable way! Now she began to worry that he wouldn't like her... Stop it, she commanded herself. This is ridiculous.

"Sam Levin" he introduced himself, although of course she already knew his name, "May I join you?"

"Oh yes! Of course. Please do."

Now I'm sounding too keen, she said to herself. Oh, why can't I just relax and be natural?

For a brief moment, neither of them spoke. They were looking at each other eagerly, with barely concealed fascination, but trying to do it tastefully, without seeming to stare.

"Am I... as you expected?" he asked with a broad smile.

She was flustered by the question. If she told the truth it would sound too forward... "Yes," she replied hesitantly, "pretty much. What about me?"

"Better in every way. Younger, more attractive, more vivacious... a bit daunting, to be honest. You're better than I deserve."

She laughed. "Oh, please! We've only just met... you're embarrassing me!"

"Sorry. I take it back. You're fat and ugly."

She laughed again. He was charming. So charming. And so natural! Why couldn't she be natural like that?

"I... I've never done this before, you know," she said hesitantly, then instantly regretted having said it. It sounded such a cliché, and he probably wouldn't believe her anyway, and besides – what did it matter to anybody whether or not she had done it before? It only mattered if she was ashamed.

"I have," he replied, breaking her train of thought, "but nothing ever came of it. They really were fat and ugly. No, that's unkind. And it isn't true. They just weren't for me. I told them so. I was quite open about it. I mean, the chemistry is either there or it isn't, don't you think?

"So... you can decide as quickly as that? After one meeting?"

He paused and seemed to consider the question. "I think I come to decisions quite quickly about most things. Whether or not they are always good decisions is another matter."

She paused. "And... you've already decided about me, have you?"

"I've decided that you're beautiful, charming, desirable... but of course, as you say I don't really know you yet. You might be a mass-murderer or some kind of raging Neo-Nazi. But I would be willing to compromise on things like that." She laughed a little too loudly, then the embarrassment flooded back.

"Why don't we go somewhere and eat?" he suggested with a smile that would have made her knees buckle if she had been standing up, "Somewhere quiet, where we can talk?"

He offered a hand like a knight in a fairy-tale, and she stood up and accompanied him out towards the car-park while he held her elbow, Prince Charming leading Cinderella onto the dance floor.

Lisa arrived home a little earlier than she would have predicted, poured a glass of plain water at the wash-hand-basin and sat on the edge of her bed to drink it. Her head was swimming with a strange and unfamiliar mixture of emotions. She would not have been able to put names to all of them if she had tried, but among them were elation, excitement, anxiety, and a deep, painful vein of sadness and self-pity.

She sat for some minutes, quite motionless, then she noticed that her bedside telephone answering machine had a little flashing red light, indicating that someone had phoned and left a message while she was out. She played the tape.

"Hello, Lisa? It's Yvonne. Look, sweetheart, I don't care how late you get in, I want you to phone me straight away and tell me how you got on with that man! Even if it's tomorrow morning!" She giggled suggestively. "I mean it. Don't let me down now! Bye."

Automatically, she lifted the phone and touched the "memory" button to dial Yvonne.

"Hello, Yvonne... Yes, I know, it is quite early. Well, no, nothing happened. It was... quite incredible, really. He was tall, and very handsome... and he had lovely teeth... and I really liked him. Yes. He was a perfect gentleman... Yes, I know it sounds great... It's just that..." she found herself choking with tears, "it wasn't real, Yvonne. Do you know what I mean? I mean, he was just being nice to me. He was sorry for me. I could sense it. He's way out of my class, Yvonne. Honestly. Like a film star. I've never spoken to anybody as... as perfect as that. He tried to make me feel okay, but it was all silly nonsense. He almost told me he loved me as soon as we met! It was over the top, Yvonne. It was just embarrassing. I don't know why I let him go on with it. Why I didn't just go home... I suppose I was flattered. I suppose I wanted to believe it. But it was no good. I couldn't. No, I just said: You've got my number, give me a call. But I know he won't. Oh, Yvonne, I feel so stupid!" Finally she could hold back the tears no longer.

Sam didn't go straight home. He parked his car in the usual place outside his house, then went for a long walk across the flat stretch of parkland that bounded his back garden. He sat on a bench by the side of the lake and watched the play of the moonlight and the distant streetlights on the water's surface.

He felt deflated. To have come so close, and to have failed. Why didn't she like him at least a little when he was so bowled-over by her? The only girl since Trudy who had actually made his heart leap when he laid eyes on her, who had brought the sweat to the palms of his hands, who had left him tongue-tied. That must have been it. She must have thought him a total fool, babbling with all that nonsense about how wonderful she was when they'd only just met. It was a ridiculous way to behave. She must have been laughing at him inside. She must have felt something close to contempt. Somebody as beautiful as that already knows she's beautiful. She doesn't need a half-witted totally ordinary person like himself to go on and on about it. It must have been such a let-down for her when she saw what he really looked like. She was so careful to hide it too, to protect his feelings. She must be such a lovely person, to humour him like that.

He took the little piece of paper containing her phone number out of his pocket and looked down at it, held it against his chest for a moment like a talisman, cupped it between his two hands.

He was going to have to be a bit more realistic, he told himself. Lower his sights a little. Stop dreaming impossible dreams.

"Ugly ducklings shouldn't go bothering swans," he announced to any resting water-fowl that might be within earshot. Then he crumpled-up the piece of paper, flicked it neatly into the rubbish bin beside him, and started back towards the house.

"Why is youse Americans always over here pokin' about at yer roots?" The Rainbow Man demanded. "Don't yez know that if ye' go pokin' about at yer roots ye'r goin' te fall over?"

The Lies of Sleeping Dogs

Through the little rivulets of water running off his umbrella, Liam Norris watched them lower his father's coffin into the damp Donegal earth. As the priest's muffled blessing came to an end, the pall-bearers, unhitching the ropes from the now invisible handles with just a fraction too much haste, started back up the hill towards the church, followed by the priest with his own large black umbrella, and the two rain-soaked altar-boys who hurried ahead with little pretense of reverence. The mourners, a group of seven or eight rather shabbily-dressed men of his father's generation, ambled over to Liam and Francie and solemnly shook Liam's hand one by one, looking him up and down curiously as they did so, telling him that they were "sorry for his trouble". Liam thanked each of them for coming and for their kind wishes, but in reality all that he felt towards them was a mild unease, mixed with guilt at his own lack of emotion throughout the entire ceremony.

After all, the old man had lived with Liam and his family for the best part of forty years. Surely there should be some sadness, some genuine grief? Perhaps he was merely numb. That was what people often said, that it doesn't hit you until afterwards. But he was pretty sure that that didn't apply to the present case.

When he was honest with himself he had to acknowledge that he and his father had been merely polite to one another during their time in America. There had been no real bond of affection. Connie had liked the old man of course, had been very close to her grandfather, but not Liam and not Ella. Ella hadn't really wanted him there at all, Liam was almost certain – after all, why should she? – but she had never said anything, even in private, and she had treated him with the utmost courtesy. His father's real life had not been lived at home anyway, it had been lived down at the Irish Center, where he spent his days telling stories to all his old cronies and to anybody else who would listen to him, about his life in Ireland as a celebrity and his wonderful boxing career.

The little group who had accompanied the coffin, none of whom Liam really knew, drifted away like the priest and the others, up the wet gravel path towards the gray stone church and the tree-lined road into Ballywellan. Liam paused a moment to let them get out of earshot, then strolled slowly after them, trying to hold the umbrella so that it would protect both himself and the bare-headed Francie by his side. "Thank you, Francie," he said quietly, "I'm really grateful for the way you handled the arrangements at this end. You did a wonderful job."

"Och, that was the least I could do. Sure me an' yer dad were never apart when we were little. We were like brothers. An' you had the hard part anyway. Getting the body over from California."

"Oh, that's quite common now. Lots of Irish Americans want to be buried in the old country. It's no big deal."

"I thought it all went very well," Francie ventured after a pause.

"Did you?... No, sorry, I'm not criticizing. It's just that... I thought the atmosphere was a bit strange."

"Och. I know there weren't that many people walkin' behind the hearse, but Pile hadn't been back in Ballywellan for near forty years. The most of the people he grew up with are already here," he waved his arm across the sea of head-stones.

"I wondered if it had anything to do with those two tragedies before we left Ireland. Do you think maybe they see us as... an unlucky family?"

Francie seized eagerly on this explanation. "Aye! Just so! An unlucky family. That makes people cautious, you know."

The walk through the town had felt like a somber, surreal circus parade. Hundreds of people out to watch the little procession, standing silently at the street corners, or sheltering in doorways and under awnings, hats and caps in hand, perfectly silent, their faces completely unreadable. Net curtains at upper windows discreetly pulled back as they passed. Front doors opening a crack to reveal pale intense faces that followed their progress down the street. The unease in Liam's stomach growing steadily every step of the way.

There had to be more to it than just a silly superstition about an unlucky family. The people of Ballywellan knew something that Liam didn't. There was something in the air that he didn't understand. Whatever it was he was going to get to the bottom of it. Of that he was determined.

They had reached the funeral limousine now, and the gaunt, top-hatted driver, a figure straight from a Dickens novel, held open the rear door to let them in. "I'll take you back to where you're staying, Sir," he announced quietly to Liam as he climbed into the driving seat.

Liam found himself thinking in camera angles again. Lighting, background music, shots and where the cuts should come. The funeral would have made a marvelous sequence in some low-budget horror film. He often perceived the world as a movie that he was making. It was a habit no longer subject to conscious control.

"Tell me," he asked as they moved off, "why did you decide to bury him so far away from my sister and my mother? Wasn't there any space left in the family plot?"

"Oh, yes Sir. But the thing was, he wanted a totally new headstone, all to himself, so that meant a new plot. And the one next to your mother's, even though it might look like empty ground, is what we call a mature grave. That means that if you dug down there you'd be uncovering old bones in no time at all. And nobody wants to do that. Wouldn't be proper, Sir."

"No, no, of course not. I just wondered."

The headstone. That was another thing Liam didn't really approve of. The old man had done the drawing himself. It was to be a long, low slab of Connemara marble with just the words:

Peter "Pile-Driver" Norris – Undefeated
Heavyweight Champion of Ireland

and underneath the dates of his birth and death. Just that. No "sadly missed by", no "Rest in Peace". He tried to picture what it would look like. It would be more like a boxing trophy than a headstone. But that was what the old man had asked for and Liam wasn't going to make a fuss.

"Say, would you mind if I got out here?" Liam suddenly asked the driver.

"It's raining, Sir," the driver reminded him, pulling in as he spoke.

"That's okay. I feel like a walk. I'll see you back at the hotel later, Francie."

"So this would have been your bedroom, would it, Mr Norris?" The old lady gently pushed the door open. "It's my son's room now. He's a sergeant in the Guards in Dublin. Doing very well for himself."

"Delighted to hear it, Mrs Rowe. Yes, this was my room... with the little balcony over the stairs. The bed was the other way around then, facing the window..." As he told the old lady about how it had been, he began to feel himself a child again, back in that big untidy bedroom that over-looked the hall. He began to think back to the night that Loretta had walked out the front door, never to return. He could hear the storm again, the rush of the wind and the scraping of the branches against his bedroom window. Then, for the very first time, he remembered something else. He remembered that there had been voices in the hall: raised, agitated voices. Pile and Loretta, arguing. That was very unusual. Pile had often shouted at him, but almost never at his sister. He had heard some of the words, now they came drifting back from some lost recess of his ten-year-old brain. Loretta's voice was high, almost hysterical. "I don't care," she was shouting, "I'm going to see the doctor!", and Pile was thundering back: "I'll see you in Hell first!" It probably didn't mean much of course; Pile often talked like that when he was angry. But Liam was intrigued. What was it all about? Why had Loretta wanted to see the doctor?

His train of thought was interrupted by an insistent query from his hostess.

"I said, did you want to look at the master bedroom, Mr Norris?" she repeated, the words forcing their way into Liam's thoughts.

"Oh, sorry, I was miles away. No, that will be absolutely fine, Mrs Rowe. It was very kind of you to let me look around. And thanks for the tea..."

"Och, sure wasn't it little enough, and all the trouble you've been through... And, it was a great thrill to meet a big Hollywood film producer."

He smiled as he made his way thoughtfully towards the front door, "I'm a director, Mrs Rowe, I work more in the artistic end. The producer's involvement is more financial and administrative..." he lost interest in explaining himself. "Tell me, Mrs Rowe – did you live in the town during my father's time?"

"Oh, I did indeed. I knew your family very well. Your mother was a lovely woman, Mr Norris, a lovely woman."

"Kind of you to say so. Tell me – who would have been the doctor in the town back then?"

"The doctor? Oh, that would have been old Dr O'Neill in Sheen House. He's retired this long time."

"Dr O'Neill. Yes, I think I remember that name. Do you have any idea where he went when he retired?"

Liam stood outside the back door of Dr Kieran O'Neill's big double garage and hesitated. He could hear someone whistling inside, together with the occasional rattle of some metal object. He knocked. After a brief pause the door was opened by an elderly, thin and fit looking man with longish wispy gray hair and a trim beard. He wore a pair of clean blue overalls and beamed a smile at Liam from behind his owl-like perfectly circular brass-rimmed spectacles.

"My God!" he greeted his guest, "I know you! You're Pile Norris' son, aren't you? The Hollywood picture man?"

"Yes," Liam replied, pleasantly surprised by the immediate recognition, "your wife told me I would find you here. I hope I'm not interrupting anything."

"Interrupting only what was well due for interruption. Come in, come in! Take a...." he looked around at the furniture of the little workshop, the two benches, the storage racks, the power tools, the upturned packing-cases, "seat," he finished at last, motioning to one of the wooden boxes.

As Liam sat down he noticed the project on which the doctor had been working: upside down on a piece of cloth in the center of the garage, it resembled at first an elaborate odd-shaped antique table, but further examination revealed it to be a beautifully crafted small musical instrument resembling a piano, its internal workings laid bare by the removal of a large painted bottom panel. Beside it, neatly arranged on another piece of cloth, were the tools that the doctor had been using, for all the world like a row of clean surgical instruments by the side of an operating table.

"It's a virginal from the mid-Tudor period," his host explained, "basically sound but in need of some serious restoration... This is the third one I've done. It's for the Berlin Conservatory. It's going to be played! Imagine that! It's going to come to life again. Now that's something I couldn't do for my human patients. It's beautiful. Isn't it?"

Liam nodded, deeply touched by the old man's reverence for the ancient object.

"That's the best relationship you can have with the past. Pick out the bits that were beautiful and worthwhile, nurture and preserve them, don't dwell on the sordid and the squalid. When I leave this world, which must be fairly soon, I want it to be just that little bit the better for my having visited. That's the only ambition I have left now."

49

Liam merely nodded again, he could think of nothing to say. Dr O'Neill closed the door and sat on a box opposite his guest.

"Did my wife offer you anything to drink?"

"No, nothing for me thank you. I just wanted to have a talk with you, if you can spare a few minutes."

The Doctor smiled. "You know, when I was in medical practice I never worked as hard as I do now, but I think I can spare you a little while. What did you want to talk about?"

Liam paused for a moment to collect his thoughts. "Well – you know that my father... passed away..."

"Oh yes. I heard he was to be buried in Ballywellan. You have my very deepest sympathy."

Liam told the old doctor about the funeral, the odd reaction of the townspeople, his feelings of unease. O'Neill listened without comment or interruption. "It just seemed like all those people were in on a secret that I knew nothing about," he finished. "The way they watched me was almost.. intimidating. Old Mr Nair – Francie – he was fine, but the others seemed odd. Almost hostile."

"Did you speak to any of them at the funeral?"

"No, not really. Except the old man in the wheelchair, of course. Pedro McLaughlin. The last man my father ever fought. He sent a note to say that he wasn't well enough to come to the ceremony, but he would like to meet me before, at the hotel. His son came along with him to push the chair, and to interpret."

"Pedro didn't have very much speech then?"

"He could only talk in vowels. No consonants. It sounded a bit like Chinese. The son told me what he was saying. He said Pile didn't mean it, that it was okay. He came to issue some kind of forgiveness. Jesus that poor man was in a mess."

"Pile turned his brains into strawberry jam with one punch. Sorry, I didn't mean to be offensive."

"No, please, that's what I've come for. A bit of straight talking. I need to know the truth. Everything. I was only ten when we left Ireland, and I don't remember very much about our life back then. Most of what I know is what Pile has told me. I want to know what really went on: the bits he didn't tell me. I want the truth."

The old Doctor's smile melted away. He clasped his hands together over his tummy and looked Liam straight in the eye. "Truth is very strong medicine," he said quietly, "it should be administered with great caution."

"I really need to know. For myself, and for Connie."

The Doctor did not reply straight away but started to slip out of his overalls, revealing a scuffed pair of brown trousers and an old pullover. "Do you fancy a walk?" he inquired.

As they strolled along the twisted, overgrown path that threaded its way between the trees by the side of the little river, Dr O'Neill at last returned to Liam's question. "So now. You want to know all about your family. Or at least all that I know about them. Let me just say that I don't advise it. It's the kind of thing that's much better left in peace. You and your daughter have nothing to gain from raking over Pile Norris' ashes."

"I'll take that chance. Believe me, I won't give up until I find out about it. Whatever it takes."

"Please yourself. A few less secrets for me to carry to the grave. I'll be loaded heavily enough without those particular ones. Where do you want me to begin, then?"

"Right back. When my father started boxing. Did you know him back then?"

"I knew him all his life, more or less. He was a couple of years younger than me. He started boxing – if you can call it that – around about the year I went to Medical School. He was a great big bruiser at seventeen. Looked like Desperate Dan out of the Dandy. He started fighting in a booth at the fairs around Letterkenny and Donegal. You paid half-a-crown to fight him, and if you were still standing after three rounds you got a certificate that you could frame and a five-pound-note. He used to say that nobody ever stayed the three rounds, but it wasn't entirely true. One or two did, not many."

"You mean... he was a fighter in some kind of freak show?"

"He was a fairground booth fighter. There were lots of them back then." He looked at Liam's expression. "Are you sure you want me to go on with this?" he asked gently.

Liam ignored the question. "How come his family allowed him to do that? They had stud farms. They weren't poor. How could they let their son do that?"

Dr O'Neill scratched his beard. "The Norris family had stud farms," he confirmed, "but Peter wasn't really a Norris. He started to use that name when the fight promoters in Dublin took him on. They were trying to build up his image. His real name was Nair."

"Nair." Liam stopped walking. "That's the same name as that old man. Francie. His friend."

"They were more than just friends. That old fellow Francie Nair, if I'm not mistaken, would have been a full brother to Pile Norris. Mind you, it's hard to remember. The breeding efficiency of the Nairs put the local rabbit population to shame. And they didn't live in conventional family groups. More... extended families."

Liam tried to cover up his shock, tried not to admit to himself how repellant he found the idea that that peculiar old man, with his dreadful clothes and his faint smell of urine, was his full blood uncle.

"Who are they then, these Nairs?"

"Travelers. Tinkers. Well known all around Donegal and Letterkenny. They're decent enough people, the most of them, but they weren't the kind of family that Pile wanted."

"I see. So he disowned them."

"Disowned them. Rejected them. They didn't forgive him for a long time, but judging by what you told me about the funeral, they came to say their last goodbyes."

"So that's who all those people were... on the street corners..."

"I would think so. Good of them to come at all, really." He looked around and motioned towards a fallen tree-trunk. "Why don't we sit down?"

They made themselves comfortable. Dr O'Neill noticed that Liam had grown pale. "Enough truth for one morning," he urged, "or do you want to go further?"

"Further," Liam whispered, "Everything."

"You have to admire Pile in some ways," the doctor continued, "He came from nowhere and he went a very long way. He invented himself, really. Learned to read and write when he was twenty-five years old. Learned to speak grammatically. Got rid of that awful West Donegal tinker accent. Started giving interviews to the Press and getting seen in all the right places. It's the American Dream, isn't it?"

"I suppose it is," Liam agreed doubtfully. "Okay. We're going all the way. There's more, isn't there?"

"All the way? Well... when he married your mother, she was already pregnant with your sister. He was very displeased about that, she didn't fit in with the image he was trying to build-up. He had wanted to marry money, prefera-bly old money, and your mother certainly wasn't that. They got off to a very bad start."

"I can remember arguments. I didn't know what they were about though."

"Do you remember your mother's death?"

"More or less. I can remember the funeral. She died of a fall, didn't she?"

"That's what Pile said."

"You didn't believe him?"

"I assisted the Coroner. We thought the injuries were suspicious, but we didn't say anything. It wouldn't have held up in court."

"What are you saying?" Liam could feel a cold sweat breaking out on the palms of his hands, "That he killed her? That my father murdered my mother?"

"It's only speculation. Manslaughter would be nearer the mark. You did know about your father's temper, didn't you?"

"I knew... that he could lose control at times... "

"Exactly. That was how he won his fights in the ring. Sheer temper. As soon as his opponent hurt him, Pile would get mad and lash out with a blow that would fell an elephant. That was all he had really, that mad-man's punch. He couldn't box for nuts. He'd never have won anything on points. He used to break bones in his right hand quite regularly, through the bandages and the glove and every-thing. Now, I think your mother offended Pile in some way and he let fly. Knocked her into eternity. That was what we all thought but there was no way to prove it. I'm telling you this in the strictest confidence, you understand."

Liam nodded, his head reeling. "But, he never hit me," he whispered, "or Loretta... he shouted at us, but he never hit us..."

"Without meaning to sound melodramatic, if he had hit you I don't think you would be here today telling me about it." The Doctor glanced at Liam who was beginning to look quite ill. "Enough?"

"Is there more?"

Dr O'Neill hesitated. "Why did you come to see me? I mean, why me in particular?"

Liam had forgotten that part. Now he remembered. He told the Doctor about Loretta's parting words on that fateful night.

"Going to see the doctor," the old man repeated. "I wish to God she *had* seen me. I think I could have saved her life."

"So, you knew what was wrong with her? What it was all about?"

O'Neill picked up a twig and started poking among the fallen leaves at his feet before he replied. "There were things we didn't bring out into the open at her inquest as well," he said quietly. "For example, at the time of her death, she was about three months pregnant."

"Pregnant?" Liam's face was blank, "I don't think that's possible. She was only fourteen years old. She didn't have a boyfriend..."

"Liam, before your mother's... accident... she came to talk to me about Loretta. Now, it isn't easy for me to tell you this, but she suspected that Pile Norris was interfering with Loretta. I asked her to bring the child along for examination the following day, after school. Your mother never lived to keep that appointment."

Liam's head was reeling. He was no longer really comprehending what was being said. "But in the year that my mother died," he whispered hoarsely, Loretta would only have been... twelve years old."

"I'm afraid it happens, Liam. Younger than that sometimes."

Suddenly the churning mass of emotion that was sweeping over Liam resolved itself into a searing anger. "God damn it!! Didn't you feel any responsibility for... for whoever was going to be his next victim?! I let that man baby-sit my daughter! They've been alone together... from the day she was born he's... How could you do that? How could you say nothing and let me trust that goddamn pervert?!!" Liam felt like doing exactly what Pile would have done; lashing out and pounding O'Neill's bones into little pieces.

"Now take it easy, Liam. I did everything that I could. I had a word with the Guards, and with the priest, and of course the nuns at Loretta's school. But since we didn't have anything that would stand up in court we had to be discreet. We couldn't just wade in with a vague suspicion of your mother's. It might have been nothing at all. It could even have been malicious. She could have been saying those things to get back at Pile for some grievance."

Liam's initial blind fury was spent. "But you didn't think it was nothing, did you?" he whispered.

"Honestly, Liam, I wasn't sure. The nuns didn't spot any of the usual signs either."

"The usual signs! My God! Just how usual is it for a man to rape his twelve-year-old daughter?!"

"I'm a doctor," O'Neill replied quietly and sadly. "I have had my innocence surgically removed."

Liam waited for his breathing to return to normal before he said anything else. "Loretta's death?" he whispered.

O'Neill hesitated. "You've filled-in one detail that I didn't have before. Here's what I think happened. She left that night in the middle of a howling gale to come and see me. Pile chased after her in a foul temper. In a blind panic, most likely. I think he hit her – either with his fist or just with his open hand. He broke her skull like an egg-shell. She would have died instantly. He threw the body into the sea and walked to the Garda Station and reported her missing. That's what I think happened. I can't prove a word of it. Two days later the body was washed up on the shore at Drumallan."

Liam's voice had almost deserted him. "The wind was supposed to have blown her over the cliff," he rasped.

"That's right. And it has happened once or twice. You can get freak gusts up there on a stormy night. But there was only one impact injury to the girl's head and no abrasions. Anybody who falls over that cliff hits the rocks on the way down, they get torn to pieces. That didn't happen to your sister. Either the wind blew her fifteen or twenty feet out from the cliff so that she missed all the rocks on the way down, or else..." he lowered his voice, "or else Pile Norris held the body up over his head and flung it out to sea with all the power of those great tree-trunk arms of his."

Immediately the scene manifested itself to Liam as a helicopter shot taken from over the sea, just below cliff-top level, lightning bolts and driving rain in the background, the camera tilting down to follow the body as it fell. What a shot! What a bloody brilliant shot! He jumped to his feet and just made it to the relative cover of the nearby bushes before the contents of his stomach discharged themselves on to the yellowing leaf-mold. O'Neill completely ignored the incident, waiting for Liam to return before he continued.

"I know you think we should have said something," he went on quietly, "but we didn't have any proof at all. There was no DNA testing back then, you know. We couldn't have proved that it was Pile Norris' baby she was carrying. We couldn't have proved that he had hit her, even if we could prove that somebody had. It was all circumstantial. All that would have happened would have been a nasty trial, a good year or two for the lawyers and the newspapers, ending no doubt in an acquittal. I think that would have affected your life a bit more than a few dirty looks from the Nairs at Pile's funeral. What would have been the point?"

Liam was silent for a long time. "At least I would have known," he managed to say at last, "I would have had some kind of warning."

"That's true. We had to balance that against the harm it would have done. It was... a matter of judgment. What we decided to do was to take Pile aside and put the fear of God into him. He knew that if he ever did anything remotely like that again it would all come out. Every bit of it. We made sure that he understood." O'Neill paused. "So – he took you over to America, got a job looking after the horses for one of the big Hollywood studios – the rest is your own life, I don't have to tell it to you."

A few minutes passed in silence, then the two men got up and started to stroll back towards the road. Liam seemed a little unsteady and the old doctor took his arm. "You know," he said, conversationally, "Pile Norris had no right to put that on his gravestone. He wasn't the undefeated heavyweight champion of Ireland. He lost to Pedro McLaughlin on a disqualification, for failing to obey the referee and for throwing an illegal punch. That was the last punch he ever threw as a professional. It mashed-up Pedro McLaughlin's brains. The promoters didn't want to have any more to do with him after that. Neither did the fans. Pedro isn't going to be very pleased when he hears about that gravestone."

For the first time ever the gleaming chromium-and-glass concourse of Los Angeles International Airport felt cozy and welcoming to Liam. It was a world of shallow commercial crap, but it was his own world and he was comfortable in it.

Ella and Connie were waiting for him, just beyond the customs barrier. They seemed to radiate normality with their beaming smiles and bright, pretty dresses. As soon as he had dragged his cases through, and they had kissed and exchanged a few greetings, Connie wanted to hear all about Pile's funeral. Liam did not reply at once. He looked at her lovely young, expectant eyes and thought for a few moments.

"I wish you could have seen it," he said at last, "the whole county came out to walk behind the hearse. The head of the Irish Boxing Federation was there, and the Minister for Sport. There were people running up to the hearse with flowers and trying to load them on to the hood..." As he warmed to his theme he began to hear the background music, to see the camera angles, the lighting, the dolly shots, the crane shots...

"Ye think yer somebody because you've slain a dragon or two?" The Rainbow Man scoffed. "I've done for more dragons than you've had hot dinners!"

Knight Errant

It was my father who first told me about Sir Lancelot and King Arthur and all the rest of them, and I was just a little boy the first time that Sir Lancelot came to visit me. I was in bed, in the big bedroom at the top of the stairs, and he rode right up the staircase on his horse, with his lance and his armour and everything, and stood at the end of the bed, with the horse rearing up every now and then, and making that kind of gargling sound that horses make, while he talked to me. He kept his visor down so that I couldn't see his face, but his voice was very clear and powerful. He said I was never going to see his face, and he was right, I never have. He said he would always be there to help me or any maiden in distress that I might happen to hear about, and that if I liked I could come along with him on some of his adventures.

Well, you can imagine how I felt about that! I couldn't wait! I said I wanted to go and have an adventure right away, and we did! We went to Camelot first and he showed me the castle and the moat and the drawbridge and the round table, and I met Merlin and Guinevere and Sir Galahad and I watched them practising sword-fighting and jousting and having feasts, and Sir Lancelot introduced me to some of the maidens in distress that he had rescued. They had all fallen in love with him of course and would never leave him, but his heart belonged to Guinevere and so he wouldn't let them give him a hug or a kiss. I said they could hug me instead, but they didn't seem very interested in that. After we'd been in Camelot for a while we went riding, with me sitting behind Sir Lancelot on the back of the saddle, and we found a maiden who was being kept prisoner in a tower by a horrible one-eyed giant about ten feet tall. Sir Lancelot told him he had better let her go if he didn't want to be put to the sword. That's what knights do to you if you're bad, they put you to the sword. Needless to say, the giant wouldn't let the maiden go, so Sir Lancelot had to put him to the sword. Then the maiden fell in love with Sir Lancelot and wanted to stay with him forever. He didn't want her, of course. He didn't seem to want to live with maidens, just rescue them. Like I said, his heart belonged to Guinevere. Speaking for myself, I would have been content with one or two of the maidens.

Even though we'd been away for days and days we were able to get back to my bedroom by morning. That was because Merlin could do magic, of course. My parents never knew that I had been away.

He came back other nights and we went on other adventures. Sometimes he rode right up the stairs like he did on the first night and sometimes he would leave the horse out on the driveway. I used to look down at it in the moonlight, a beautiful pure-white stallion, nibbling the lawn and making that little gargling sound again.

We fought and killed a dragon – put it to the sword because it had been eating virgins, which are a kind of maiden. It was a very big dragon, bigger than a red London bus. Another time we found a witch who was casting evil spells that made women give birth to dead babies, and stopped the cows giving any milk. We had to burn her at the stake, like on Bonfire Night, because that's the only way you can kill a witch. If you put them to the sword they just come back to life again.

Even after my father left my mother, Sir Lancelot kept coming to pick me up at night and taking me out on adventures. In fact I think he came even more often after Dad left. He never wakened my mother, she never heard the armour rattling or the feet on the stairs or the horse making that little gargling sound. And I was always back in my bed before the morning.

Then Larry came, and started visiting my mother. He had a very loud voice and didn't treat her very nicely, but she seemed to like him nevertheless. They used to go out drinking, and they would come back, him talking loudly and laughing quite a lot, and sometimes he would stay until the morning. I noticed that he used to hold her quite tightly by the shoulder, and once I saw him throw her down on the sofa very roughly. And he wasn't laughing that night. Dad was never rough with Mum like that. He knew how you were supposed to treat maidens. I was worried about Larry. I didn't like him.

The next time I saw Sir Lancelot I asked him about my mum and Larry. He agreed with me. He said that Larry sounded like the kind of man who deserved to be put to the sword. So I reminded him that he had said he would help me if ever I needed help, or if ever I came across a maiden in distress, and this seemed to fit both descriptions. I know my mother was a bit old to be a maiden, but Sir Lancelot said that that didn't matter and it was definitely a case for putting to the sword. But he couldn't use Excalibur because that was a special sacred sword. He would need an ordinary sword for Larry. I had a look in the kitchen and found a small sword, about nine or ten inches long. Sir Lancelot said that would be all right. So we waited for them just inside the door that night and Sir Lancelot did what had to be done.

My mum didn't see Sir Lancelot putting Larry to the sword because it was so dark, and she just ran out screaming and screaming. She couldn't really remember anything about it afterwards, and because of this people seemed to get the idea that it had been my dad who had put Larry to the sword. I told them it wasn't, that it had been Sir Lancelot, but they wouldn't listen to me. They said I had just been in bed and had dreamt about Sir Lancelot. So there was nothing I could do. I couldn't stop them from putting Dad in prison.

My mum started to cry quite a bit after that and she let me sleep in her bed a lot of the time. I didn't like it when my mum cried. Sir Lancelot couldn't come of course while I was in her bed.

My mum and I went to visit Dad in prison about once a month. I sometimes managed to get a few minutes on my own with him while she went to the toilet or something, and when I did I tried to explain to him about Sir Lancelot. It was no good trying to talk about Sir Lancelot while Mum was there because she didn't approve of me talking about Larry's death. She thought it was too upsetting for me and I should try to forget about it. But Dad listened, and as time went by I think he began to understand more about what I was trying to explain to him.

He made some kind of arrangement with the people in the prison, for me to explain about Sir Lancelot to a woman named Dr Sherman. Dr Sherman was the first adult who really listened properly to what I was saying about Sir Lancelot. She asked a lot of questions and she wrote everything down. I had several talks with Dr Sherman, and then she sent me to another doctor, a man-doctor named Nigel Barry. He asked me to call him Nigel, which was strange for a doctor. Nigel believed me about Sir Lancelot. So did Dr Sherman. They were like Sir Lancelot, they rescued Dad from the prison. He was allowed to go home to Mum, and they're still together, living happily ever after.

But they haven't let me go home. At least not so far. They've put me in prison instead, in a tower in a big house, a kind of castle, where they have a torture chamber in the cellar, and lots of people, both men and maidens, in little cells like this one.

I've been here a very long time now. Longer than any of the others I think. I can remember a lot of Christmas dinners, so that must mean I've been here a lot of years. Five or a hundred years. Something like that. Mum and Dad used to visit me a lot at the beginning, but I don't see much of them now.

The people here have told me that I may be allowed to go home some day, but it doesn't sound to me like they think it's going to be very soon.

There's something extremely odd going on in this place. Nobody's allowed to leave, and the doctors and nurses torture them all day long, so that some of them have gone completely crazy. My mum and dad say that they're trying to help me, but I can't see it. The only help I need is help to get out of here. You'd think Dad would understand, having been imprisoned himself.

Of course what they don't know is that I can get out of here any time I like, because there's someone who really will help me – Sir Lancelot! He can come and visit me again now, because I have a bedroom all to myself. It's just one floor down from the very top of the tower. But he says it isn't time just yet. He wants me to spy for him first, find out what's going on here, what the doctors are doing to people. That's all right with me. I'm a very good spy.

The Head doctor, Dr Karl Leeman, is an evil wizard who scares everybody and makes them go mad sometimes.

He made Cecil kill himself by cutting his wrists while he
was having a bath, and he made Lorraine have a fit and crack
her head on the wall of the laundry room. Lots of stuff like
that happens here. Nurse Gunn, the one who talks with a
funny accent, she's a witch and she's in charge of the torture
chamber in the cellar. There's a maiden named Judith who
lives just above me – in the top room in the tower – and
Nurse Gunn takes her down to the torture chamber every
time she cries. And Judith cries a lot. They tie her up and
chain her to a table and then they give her electric shocks.
After she's been down there you don't see her for a while.
You don't hear her either. She's probably too frightened to
do anything but lie in bed after she's been down there. I've
told Judith that if she doesn't cry then maybe they won't
give her electric shocks, but she doesn't want to talk about
it. Judith has long brown hair and big dark eyes and she's
very pretty. She's so pretty I think she might be a princess
instead of a maiden. Yes, I'm certain she's a princess.
Maybe that's why she won't let me kiss her. I've tried and
she doesn't like it. Not everybody is allowed to kiss a
princess. Just princes, I think, and knights. I'm sure she'll
kiss Sir Lancelot all right.

I've got a whole list of people now that Sir Lancelot is going
to have to put to the sword. There's Dr Leeman of course,
and Dr Patel and Charge Nurse Robinson and Nurse Fowler
and Nurse Gunn... Of course Nurse Gunn is a witch so she'll
have to be burned at the stake. Maybe some of the others as
well, it's hard to be sure. Sir Lancelot will know the right
thing to do.

When the men were here painting the corridors I stole
this little plastic container of something called "turpentine
substitute". It says on the label that it's "highly flammable"

and there's a little picture of a flame, and a stake. I have it hidden in my secret compartment behind the piece of white stuff that they used to block off the old fireplace in my room. If you know where to pull it it comes right out and there's a space behind it like a little cupboard. I'm the only one who knows about it. I've got other things in there as well. There's a sword that I made for Sir Lancelot so that he wouldn't have to use Excalibur. I made it out of an iron bar that the workmen left behind the time that they had the scaffolding at the back of the main building. I got a hard black stone as well and I've been sharpening it with that. Both edges. It took a very long time, but it's ready now. It's ready for Sir Lancelot when he needs it. And I've got matches, and old newspapers and dry twigs and bits of wood. Things that Sir Lancelot will need for burning witches. I think it might be best for him to burn everyone here after he's put them to the sword, just to be on the safe side.

He'll rescue Princess Judith of course. I'm not sure if he's rescued any princesses before, but he probably has. That's even better than rescuing maidens. After she's rescued, Princess Judith won't have to cry any more. Maybe Sir Lancelot will marry her instead of Guinevere. I think she's prettier than Guinevere.

Hey! Guess what! I've just heard Sir Lancelot's armour rattling somewhere near by and I've had a look out the window. His horse is down in the car park, chewing at some of the leaves in the flower-bed. You can see it by the light of the big lamp in the middle.

Sir Lancelot must be just outside on the stairs, waiting for me. I'd better get the sword, and the turpentine substitute, and all the other things... he's got a lot of work to do.

Don't worry Princess Judith! Don't cry any more! It's almost over now. We're going to be free! And happy ever after.

I'm ready, Sir Lancelot! It's time for all this evil to be swept away!!

"Ye know the trouble with youse northerners?" The Rainbow Man interjected. "Yer memories is too bloody long."

Letting Go

Henry knew who it was as soon as he saw the little figure in the distance between the slender boughs of the palm trees that leaned lazily across his field of view. He watched him as he turned off the dirt-track that twisted its way across the dry cactus-sprinkled scrub land to walk up the rocky path towards his house. It was the way the man walked that gave him away: the purposefulness, the tightness of the gait, the disregard for the hazards of the bleached dusty stones that made up the path's surface. Henry had always imagined that he would be younger, somehow. An earnest young academic from some Polish university, dripping with anger and self-righteousness. This man wasn't all that much younger than himself – twenty years his junior, perhaps, a pale-skinned European in his mid-sixties, perversely dressed for the merciless heat of Thailand in a neat dark grey business suit, his figure long and gaunt, his silvering black hair thinning to near baldness beneath the little circular brown *yarmulke* that clung precariously to the top of his head. In his right hand he clutched a well-made black leather brief-case, held rigid against the rhythm of his long regular strides, like a precious icon carried in a religious procession.

Now that this moment had arrived, the moment he had imagined so many times, dreamed about so often, it seemed almost an anticlimax. Henry was surprised at how little he felt. Just a dull resignation, and a sadness. He had hoped that he might have been permitted to leave the theatre before the final act, but now he could see that it was not to be, and he knew that it was an indulgence he had no right to expect. In a way it pleased him that the issues were going to be addressed. Not put right of course, that lay far beyond his gift. No atonement was possible. All that he had to offer in reparation for his crimes was his miserable eighty-five-year-old life, a trinket so insignificant in the face of what he had done that its forfeiture would be almost a further affront to his victims. But at least the matter was going to be tidied up. That was better than nothing.

The man had reached the foot of the wooden steps leading up to Henry's veranda. He stood there for a few moments without speaking, staring into Henry's face with cold grey eyes that betrayed absolutely no emotion. It was Henry who broke the silence. "Why don't you come up? Take a chair?" he entreated politely.

The man climbed the three steps and lowered himself stiffly into the more scuffed of Henry's two wicker arm-chairs. Still staring blankly at the older man, he paused almost a full minute before he said anything.

"Do you know why I have come here?" he said at last in a voice that was as flat and emotionless as his stare. Henry noticed that he had an American accent. He felt a momentary crazy impulse to make a joke, to answer something like: You've come to read the water-meter. Or: You've come to read the gas-meter. That would be better! Oh yes, the gas meter: that would be suitably sick! But he didn't say anything. Instead he merely nodded.

Before he said anything else the newcomer opened his briefcase and carefully withdrew several neatly labelled manila folders, which he placed on the cracked glass top of Henry's coffee-table. "My name is Saul Abrams," he said quietly, "and you are Dr Wolfgang Heinrich Muller. Or do you intend to deny that?"

Henry exhaled heavily and felt his shoulders drop. "Wolfgang," he mumbled abstractly, "yes, I knew him once. It was a very long time ago..."

The newcomer showed a trace of emotion at last. He spat out the question: "Do you deny that you are Wolfgang Heinrich Muller, a former Major in the SS at the Experimental Medical Facility at Treblinka?"

He paused so long that Abrams was on the point of repeating the question. "'Major' was an honorary rank," he said at last, "I only held that rank for the last few months of the war."

"So... It was you..." the man with the manila folders whispered, "It really was you..." He said it in the tone of someone who had waited for this moment almost as long as Henry himself had waited. He said it as though he hardly dared allow himself to believe that it had actually happened. "It was you," he repeated, so quietly it was almost inaudible.

Henry shrugged. "Well, Wolfgang was a clever ambitious young man in his twenties with a straight back and strong arms, and bright eyes... and a lot of bad ideas in his head. And that young man grew into me. I wouldn't even recognise him now. I wouldn't know him if I bumped into him in the street. I don't remember a great deal about him. But despite all that, it is true that I am the man that he became. What do you want me to do? Should I cut my wrists? Will that make it all right?"

"No, Dr Muller. That will not make it all right."

"I didn't think it would. I'm going to pour myself a drink, Mr Abrams. Do you want one?" The other shook his head. "It won't be laced with poison, by the way," the old doctor added, "I'm not a great one for dramatic gestures."

He made his way to the modest cocktail cabinet and poured a generous quantity of brandy into a glass. Then he sat down again, nursing it on his knee. Abrams had taken a document from one of the manila folders and was holding it stiffly before him, but he was still looking at Henry. "Do you remember the total number of people who passed through the facility at Treblenka during the years 1944 and 1945?" he asked in a tone that was almost conversational.

Henry shook his head. "It's a long time ago, Mr Abrams. A very long time ago."

"We have estimated about seven hundred and fifty. Does that sound to you like the right kind of figure?"

"If you say so." Henry's voice had become very quiet and his eyes, almost unblinking, were fixed on those of his guest.

"It's the best estimate we have been able to arrive at. And of those seven hundred and fifty people, or thereabouts, all ages, both sexes...... how many, would you like to estimate, are still surviving at this time?"

Henry shook his head. "I have no idea."

"Six, Dr Muller. Just six, that we know of. Five women and one man." Abrams handed Henry the document that he had been holding. "These are signed and sworn statements from each of the six. You will notice that they have been translated into English. If you prefer I can let you see them in German or in the original Polish. Would you prefer one of those other languages?"

"It makes no difference," he said almost inaudibly, "I am acquainted with all of those languages. Although my Polish may be a little rusty." He fumbled around in his inside pocket to find his reading glasses and put them on. Such a cosy little scene, he thought to himself. For all the world like two old friends seated on the veranda, one showing his holiday snapshots to the other. How very civilised it all was.

"The allegations contained in these statements," Abrams continued in that same impenetrable monotone, "are of two kinds. There are specific allegations against you, and descriptions of the regime that these people witnessed at the Treblenka facility. The witnesses describe experiments in which human subjects were deliberately infected with life-threatening diseases, including typhoid fever, syphilis and hepatitis, and then used as guinea-pigs for the testing of novel drugs and treatment regimes. They allege that the percentage of subjects who survived these experiments was of the order of two or three per cent. Three of the women witnesses have also made allegations against you personally of repeated sexual assault. Are these allegations true, Dr Muller?"

"Would it make any difference if I said no?"

"Not a great deal." He put the piece of paper down on the table and Henry picked it up and held it carefully, moving it in and out in front of his face to find the best distance.

Abrams watched him read the first sheet, turn the page, watched his head nod very slightly as he hurried to the end. "I suppose you want me to sign this?" he asked passively.

"These statements are legal documents," Abrams continued quietly, "I shall witness your signature. After you have attested to the truth of each statement it shall be lodged in the War Crimes section of the Holocaust Museum and Archive at Yad Vashem in Jerusalem. It shall become a public document and shall be admissible in evidence if any of your surviving victims or the families of the dead should wish to bring criminal proceedings against you. And the State of Israel shall support them fully in any such prosecution."

"I see." Henry fixed the other's eyes once again. "So the State of Israel does not intend to bring any proceedings itself?"

"Not if you sign. You are no longer young, and, frankly, not all that important. It's the truth that we are primarily interested in in your case, Dr Muller. Nothing more."

"That's all you want of me? The truth? A small thing like that?"

Abrams did not reply. He merely produced an expensive-looking grey fountain pen and handed it to Henry. "How very... thoughtful of you," the other mumbled.

It took Henry about five minutes to read and sign each document. As each one was completed Abrams silently took it, carefully countersigned with the same pen, and placed it back in the manila folder. When they were all done, the two men's eyes met once again. Henry tried to read Abrams' expression but found that he still couldn't.

"Is there nothing that you want to say, Dr Muller?" Abrams asked at last. It was some time before Henry replied.

"You're a good man, Mr Abrams," he said at last, "a man who fights for justice. A man who has devoted his life to... finding out the truth. You can't understand somebody like me, can you?" Abrams said nothing. "And you're young! You weren't even born when these things were going on, were you?"

"Barely," Abrams admitted.

"It was a strange time. More strange than you can even imagine. A time of certainties, Mr Abrams. No shades of grey. National Socialism or Communism. Jew or Aryan. German or foreigner. Comrade or enemy. Men marching, drums beating, flags waving, organisations you had to belong to, slogans you had to chant when everybody else did, anthems you had to sing, things you had to believe, things you had to agree to. There was no middle path. Nobody could hold out against it. Nobody could get away from it... was a young medical graduate, with a new wife. I needed a job. I needed to eat. I needed security. Do you think I could have held out against all that? What was I supposed to do, for God's sake?"

Abrams studied him like a specimen under a microscope. He waited for the old man to continue. "I was weak, Mr Abrams. I was frightened. I was a coward. I took the path of least resistance. Maybe I could have done something else. I don't know."

"I have spoken to people whose circumstances were just as difficult as yours," said Abrams very quietly, "who *did* do something. I have spoken to people who were not Jews, who had no part in the fight, and yet risked their lives and suffered ruin and torture and imprisonment because they did something. I have spoken to people whose husbands, wives, brothers, sisters, parents, friends *lost their lives* because they did something. Lost their lives because they would rather die than do nothing."

"I told you, Mr Abrams, I was not a hero. I... cannot change things that have happened in the past." He paused. "Would you like to see what my wife looked like, Mr Abrams?" Without waiting for an answer he got up and went to a little shelf above a display cabinet in the lounge. He took down a sepia-tinted framed photograph of an attractive young woman with long dark hair. He returned with the picture and handed it to Abrams.

The girl in the photograph wore an embroidered dress of a light colour with a low square neckline, and she was smiling and lifting a hand towards her face, as though embarrassed at the idea of having her picture taken. Behind her were trees, and just visible behind them what looked like a wooden tower of some kind raised into the air on four rigid stilts. "She was very beautiful, was she not, Mr Abrams?"

Abrams nodded. "Yes, Dr Muller. She was very beautiful. Where was she standing when this was taken?"

"Where...? I don't think I can recall..."

"No? Perhaps I can help you. That is one of the Treblenka look-out towers in the background." He turned towards Henry but the old man made no response. "What became of your wife, Dr Muller?"

Henry took the picture back and laid it on the table before answering. "Near the end... when I knew it was all about to end... I sent her to Switzerland with false papers. We were to meet in America."

"And did you meet?"

"I never went to America. I came here instead. They... you... would have found me too easily in America."

"So you lied to her. You deserted her."

"Don't you think she was better off without me? Don't you think I did her a favour?"

Abrams shrugged. "So you've been here all this time? Did you practice medicine?"

"Never."

"Any particular reason?"

"I... Lost the stomach for it, I suppose." He thought for a moment. "Have you ever heard the legend of the dogwood tree, Mr Abrams? No, I don't suppose you would have. It's a bit of Christian mythology – folklore. The dogwood tree grows in North America. It's one of the most twisted-up, deformed little things you can imagine. The branches turn around, twist back on themselves. But the legend says that the dogwood tree was once tall and straight. It was the tree they used to make the cross to crucify Jesus. And when the tree saw what it had done, how its virtues had been misused, it decided that it would never grow tall and straight again. It would twist itself up into a little wooden knot, so that it could never be used to make another cross. That's what I have done, Mr Abrams. I have twisted myself up into a little knot and hidden myself away so that... Forgive me, I'm talking nonsense. An old man, rambling." He stood up and carefully carried the picture back to its place above the cabinet.

Abrams waited for him to return. When he had sat down again he looked quizzically at his guest. "You've studied my case for a long time, haven't you, Mr Abrams?"

Abrams nodded.

"Do you know anything about my wife? Anything about what happened to her? Anything at all?"

Abrams was silent for a long time. At last he decided to speak. "She reached America," he said very quietly. "In fact she claimed to be a Jew fleeing persecution. Was that your idea?" Henry did not reply but his expression answered the question for Abrams.

"There's more, isn't there, Mr Abrams?" Henry urged.

Abrams watched him fixedly. "Did you know that she was pregnant?" he asked very quietly. Again Henry's face answered the question. His eyes widened in startled disbelief.

"Pregnant... no, I never knew..."

"Would it have changed anything?"

"Well... yes... Of course... A child... changes everything. What happened to the child...?"

Abrams shrugged. "We never traced the child. Frankly, it wasn't your wife we were interested in. It was you."

"So... I might have a child... grandchildren even... in America?"

"Dr Muller, you might even have a wife in America. That isn't our concern. Your wife has committed no crime, as far as we are aware. To bear a child for a... a man like you is not a criminal act. To love a man like you... no crime. A mistake, but not a crime, Dr Muller."

Henry's head sunk a little lower into his chest. "All that," he said weakly, "was part of the price I paid. Part of curling myself up into that little knot. I know it isn't much, weighed against what I did, but if you think about it, it was all that I had. I've given everything that I had, Mr Abrams..."

"I apologise for stating the obvious, but you are alive, Dr Muller. You have good health for a man of your age. Your body is undefiled and whole. You have all of your limbs, you have not been castrated, your internal organs have not been mutilated, and you have apparently retained your sanity. Please spare me your self-pity."

It was the nearest that Abrams had come to a display of emotion. He said it coldly, without raising his voice, but the contempt and the condemnation sent a shiver down Henry's spine.

Abrams collected his papers off the table, gathered them neatly into the briefcase, and left without another word.

He walked briskly down the path to the road without looking back at Henry's house. Exercise was what he needed, a bit of brisk physical exertion to clear his system of the bottled-up anger and the tension that was making his heart pound, his head throb in time to his furious strides. As he made his way down the narrow road between the overhanging coconut palms towards the harbour, the tension gradually seeped out of him and he began to regain control of his seething emotions. He slowed his walking pace and began to look around. The hills were dotted with little ornate, gaudily-painted farmhouses whose steep-pitched roofs ended in flamboyant twists and scrolls that existed for no other purpose than to express something of the joy of existence. A gaily painted pick-up truck swept by him, its two occupants waving cheerily and shouting a Thai greeting as they passed. It was a happy, warm, friendly place, but Abrams had armoured his spirit against it and none of it made contact with his troubled psyche.

In the distance, near the village and the harbour, he saw a thin sloping ribbon of white smoke rising from somewhere behind the local Buddhist temple to vanish among the wispy grey clouds that drifted ponderously across the sky. As he drew a little nearer he could make out the sound of men's voices chanting: there was a ceremony of some kind in progress. He glanced at his watch. The ferry did not leave for almost two hours. There was no point in hurrying. He slowed his pace to a gentle stroll and, for want of something to do, made his way towards the temple and the rising plume of smoke at the far end of the village. The temple was a long, low, highly-decorated building, red and gold being the dominant colours of the scroll-work on the outside walls. Above the structure was a traditional highly ornate orange-tiled Thai roof of a dizzy pitch, ending in decorative coils at its four corners. Rising from the centre of this to dominate it all was a high silver *chedi* like an elongated metal cone standing on its base, the equivalent of the steeple on a Western church, a shape that he knew was repeated on Thai ceremonial headwear to symbolise the god-quality that the Buddhist faithful believed to reside to at least some degree in everyone.

The chanting was quite loud now, and as he entered the gate and circled around towards the rear of the building he came upon the outdoor service that was in progress in the field behind. He approached slowly and respectfully, sitting down near a small family group who were gathered around a rug on the grass. The rug was spread with food and some small vessels containing flowers, as though in preparation for a very formal picnic. Other similar groups were scattered among the tall carved burial stones that dotted the space between the temple and a crackling funeral pyre that had been built at the far end of the burial ground. Atop the neatly stacked firewood was a woven wooden burial basket, in which the body of a very slightly-built man reclined, draped with a vivid yellow shroud. Young Buddhist monks, their heads shaven, their bodies cloaked in robes of the same bright striking yellow stood solemnly in a semicircle around the base of the pyre, chanting their prayers with a calm dignity and rocking very gently in time to the rhythm of their chant. Every few moments someone would slowly approach, bowing low as they walked, and place something within the smouldering sticks. Abrams strained to see more clearly but it was a bit too far away for him to make out exactly what the offerings were.

"Welcome to this holy place," said a very quiet voice by Abrams' left ear, causing him to start despite its calmness. He turned to find a very old, wizened Buddhist monk sitting cross-legged by his side, smiling serenely, his fingers entwined on the lap of his yellow robes.

"Thank you," he replied in a similar hushed tone, "I hope I'm not intruding…"

"It is I who am intruding. I am an old man and very inquisitive. It is a dreadful vice."

Abrams found himself smiling. "There are worse vices," he assured the old man. "Who is the… deceased?"

"Khun Chaub. A very kind and good man. A farmer who worked hard for all of his long life, who loved his wife and his children and gave food and garments to the poor. It is a happy day for him, I hope I can meet my own death with so great a store of merit."

Abrams nodded. "And the things they are putting in the fire. What are those?"

"All kinds of things. Flowers. Food. Things that Khun Chaub may need in his next life. And messages for the souls of other dead people. And things that… that belong with the dead and not the living."

"What do you mean?"

The old monk seemed to find this a difficult question. "In this life," he began ponderously, "we form attachments. We cling to things. Especially to evil things. Things that are not good for us. Do you agree?"

Abrams nodded.

"And when someone dies… moves on to another life… that can be a good time for the people who are left behind to stop clinging to things that are no longer good for them. Things that are hurtful, damaging, things that put limits on the growth of the human spirit. Do you understand?"

Abrams was not sure that he did. The monk seemed to pick up his hesitation.

"Take yourself, Mr..?"

"Abrams."

"Mr Abrams. You carry a case made of leather. I observe the way you hold it. The case is black but your knuckles are white with the strain of the grip with which you hold that case. Is it not so?"

Abrams grinned somewhat sheepishly. "What's in there is very important," he said defensively.

"Is it? Is it something that makes you happy?"

"Well, no, not really."

"Is it something that makes other people happy? Something that makes the world a better place? That adds to the total sum of human happiness?"

Abrams looked at him strangely. "I'm not sure," he whispered.

"But you said it was very important?"

"Yes," Abrams agreed hesitantly, "that much I know. It is very important."

The old monk smiled. "Have you any knowledge of the South Indian monkey trap?" he asked with a mischievous sparkle in his eye. Abrams' blank expression told him that he had not. "Well," the monk began, obviously pleased to have Abrams for an audience, "I always think that it completely proves that the Lord Buddha passed that way, because it could only have been invented by a person of our faith. You see, the trap is nothing more than an empty coconut shell that is fixed to a branch by a strong rope. There is a small opening into the shell, and inside is placed a small piece of fruit, let us say a lychee. Can you see how the trap works?"

Abrams thought for a moment but was baffled.

"Oh, it's amazingly simple, Mr Abrams. The monkey puts its hand into the coconut shell for the lychee, and grabs it – like that!" The old monk made a fist to show Abrams what he meant. "Now can you see how the trap works?"

"Oh yes. Of course. When he has the fruit in his hand, he can't get his hand out any more."

"Exactly, Mr Abrams! The monkey wants that lychee very badly, and he will not let go. Because he will not let go, he is a trapped monkey. He has lost his freedom. He has given up everything that life has to offer a monkey, because he can not bring himself to let go of that lychee. Don't you think that he is a very foolish monkey, Mr Abrams?"

Abrams sat very still and looked into the face of the monk. Minutes passed. "May I ask you what you are thinking, Mr Abrams?" said the monk, no longer able to contain his curiosity.

"Oh, just about the monkey. It's a very sad story, isn't it. When all he has to do to get free is just..." Abram's voice faded out. The monk held up his hand which was still in a fist and slowly and gently opened it. Abrams said nothing but a calmness and a serenity seemed to spread slowly through his body. He felt himself relax, felt the tension drain from his features. He sat for several minutes in silence and complete peace. He suddenly realised that he was no longer holding the briefcase, it was lying on the grass by his feet.

"Would you... would you put that on the fire for me?" he whispered so quietly that he was surprised the other heard.

"Oh no, Mr Abrams. You have to put it on the fire yourself."

Abrams tapped gently on the hotel-room door. It was opened by his wife, an elegantly dressed slightly over-weight American lady of late middle age. She seemed mildly surprised at his appearance but greeted him warmly and ushered him in.

"You're back early, Saul. You look pleased. Did you get a result?"

He took off his jacket and threw it over the back of a chair before he replied. "What do you think?" was his laconic answer.

She looked him straight in the eye: "I don't know. I thought you looked... different some way, when you came in. That was the last lead, wasn't it, Saul?"

"The very last one," he confirmed, lowering himself on to the wide soft bedspread as he said it. He held out his two hands and his wife took them and allowed herself to be drawn down to sit beside him on the bed.

"Why do you look so pleased then?" she demanded, still eyeing him strangely.

"Ruth, I've wasted too much of my life on this search. Too much of yours as well. I want to apologise."

"Don't be silly, Saul. Of course you had to look for him. For your mother's sake." As she spoke she lifted the framed picture from the bedside table and handed it to Abrams. He took it and stared at it, an expression on his face that Ruth had never seen there before.

"I… I suppose he must have died then?" she probed, still convinced that there was more to the affair than Saul was willing to say.

"Ruth, we've got to stop talking about this thing. Stop thinking about it. Our grandson gets married in four days' time. We've got to get out of here. Back to the 'States. This isn't where we belong. We've got to start thinking about the future, not this stuff. Not what's over and done with…"

Ruth could hardly credit the change in her husband. "You've finally admitted it then. That he's dead. That you're not going to find him?"

He put his arm around her waist and pulled her towards him in a gentle embrace. "He died a long time ago. I know that now."

Ruth smiled and kissed him on the cheek, which embarrassed her as soon as she had done it. "I think I've got myself a brand new husband today," she laughed.

"I think you have, Ruth," he smiled. "I think you have." He looked down at the yellowing picture of his mother. It showed a young attractive woman with long dark hair, wearing an embroidered dress of a light colour with a low square neckline. She was smiling and lifting a hand towards her face, as though embarrassed at the idea of having her picture taken. Behind her were trees, and just visible behind them what looked like a wooden tower of some kind raised into the air on four rigid stilts...

"Have a bit of sense, woman!" The Rainbow Man scolded.
"If he's knockin' ye around ye'll get the hell out of there, if
you've any respect for yerself atall atall."

Ellen and Aubery

I arrived at London University, my first time away from
home, shy, awkward, embarrassed about my Belfast accent,
a cipher in a vast transit-camp of displaced overseas students. Too inhibited to speak to anyone, too proud to admit
that I was lonely, I listened to the creaking of other people's
beds and the groans of pleasure and occasional barks of
anger through the paper-thin walls of my tiny cell in the
austere Halls of Residence. Self-pity and homesickness
engulfed me.

A card appeared on the notice board advertising a room
in a shared flat nearby. Sparse details, but I could afford the
rent, and it offered the prospect of human contact, flatmates,
friendship-networks.

It was a two-bedroom conversion in a large crumbling
Victorian house. Aubery, the lease-holder, was not much
older than me, but dressed like a sixty-year-old: three-piece
suit, starched white shirt, dismal grey tie, big signet ring on
his right hand. His voice conveyed a sneering condescen-
sion, and an inability to pronounce the letter 'R'.

Aubery's girlfriend however was a delight. Strikingly
pretty, with long dark hair and a musical Welsh lilt in her
voice, she lit up the whole room with her smile. Her name
was Ellen. I was captivated at first sight.

I left expecting little of the interview, and was over-
joyed when Ellen phoned the following morning and told
me I could move in. I knew instinctively that she had

wanted me and that Aubery had not, but she had somehow prevailed.

Ellen was a first-year student at my college. Aubery was a junior accountant, but earning good money. I soon realized that he was a total fake. His superior accent and manner, his name, his vaguely aristocratic background, probably even his lisp, were entirely fabricated.

Aubery's working day was elastic. Sometimes he would arrive home before the five o'clock rush-hour, sometimes late at night.

Ellen kept similar hours to myself. In the mornings she would kiss Aubery goodbye, then we would walk together to the campus, and at lunch meet again and chat some more. In the evenings, before Aubery got back, we would often sit together studying, talking, or simply watching TV.

Our friendship blossomed. The only topic we avoided was Ellen's relationship with Aubery. She somehow knew that I had a low opinion of him, and the subject became taboo. Instead we talked about philosophy, politics, religion, literature, films, music, and eventually about ourselves. I learned about Ellen's Welsh village, stained permanently black with coal-dust, streets so steep that hand-rails were fitted along the pavements, where jobs were few and suicides common. From me Ellen learned about the festering bigotry that rotted the minds of Belfast's young. We told one another our dreams and our fears and our past histories. We poured out our souls. The only boundary to our conversation was what went on between Ellen and Aubery when their bedroom door closed.

I helped Ellen with one of her assignments and she bought me a book as a present. I can see its spine from where I am sitting now.

My friendship with Ellen made everything in my life infinitely better. A spring came into my step, I started eating properly and paying attention to my appearance, and made other friends at the University without even trying.

All of this time, Aubery virtually ignored me. I tried to be friendly but I could seldom think of anything to say. Even Ellen seemed to have little to say to him while I was present. Every night they would disappear into their bedroom, and there, I assumed, was where they opened-up to one another.

Then one morning Aubery appeared alone at breakfast, ate hastily and hurried off, telling me gruffly that Ellen "wasn't well". I waited until he had gone and tapped gently on her bedroom door.

She came out, wrapped in a gown, and with vivid red and purple bruises below her left eye.

I couldn't believe what I was seeing. Without a word I opened my arms and embraced her. She hugged me back and we stood there silently for several minutes.

I have never experienced such murderous anger, before or since. But Ellen pacified me. She had provoked him, she claimed. Cruel things had been said. She didn't want to talk about it, they would sort it out between themselves.

Skipping lectures, I spent all that day at home with Ellen. Towards midday she had a little cry in my arms and gave me one fleeting kiss on the lips and told me that I was very sweet. I treasured that kiss and longed for more but I knew that the time was not right.

In bed that night, I strained to hear what was going on in their room, but the separating walls were thick, and although I thought I could hear occasional raised voices it was difficult to be certain.

As I drifted off to sleep I heard Ellen's timid tapping on my bedroom door. This time there was a little trickle of blood running down her face, caused, I later learned, by Aubery's heavy signet ring. She collapsed, crying, into my arms, and I led her gently to my bed and held her tenderly for the remainder of the night. Without the need for words we both knew that this was now Ellen's bedroom as well as mine.

Aubery accepted the new situation more readily than I would have expected. I told him at breakfast that Ellen and I would be leaving and that if he touched her again he would be sorry he had ever been born. I don't know what I would really have done because I had never hit anybody in my life, but I was a great deal bigger than Aubery and he didn't put my threat to the test.

To an outside observer, surprisingly little would have changed. Ellen and I still walked to University together, but now we held hands or linked arms. Aubery caught the same morning train and returned at the same erratic hours. But internally, the dynamics of the flat had altered beyond all recognition.

Both Aubery and I underwent a personality change. With Ellen as my lover as well as my friend, I felt ten feet tall: my essay grades soared and I am convinced that I even looked different. Aubery on the other hand seemed to shrink into the background, scratching around unobtrusively like a mouse in a larder.

With the exams and the long summer holidays only a few weeks away, Ellen and I made plans. I would buy one of the old motor-caravans that homeward-bound Australians and New Zealanders sold on the Earls Court Road, and in this we would visit Ellen's village in Wales, then return east for the car-ferry to France, then south towards the Mediterranean, earning money by grape-picking or however we could as we travelled down.

The vehicle was purchased, and I breezed through my exams, elated by how good life had become. Nobody could ask for a nicer girlfriend than Ellen, and I would have her all to myself the whole summer long!

The day drew near. Aubery announced that he had put down a deposit on a flat of his own in a more fashionable part of London and would be moving on. I paid little attention.

Ellen and I planned to leave immediately after the last of our exams. We would meet outside the flat, packed and ready to go.

On the morning of the great day, Ellen seemed slightly preoccupied but I put it down to pre-examination nerves. I galloped through my "Ethics I" and left the examination hall before the time was up.

When I arrived back at the flat I noticed that Aubery's car had already gone, and the front door was locked. My rucksack had been loaded into the van, no doubt by Ellen, but hers was nowhere to be seen, and neither was she.

Then I found the note under the windscreen-wiper. I still have it, folded inside the cover of that book. It reads:

My Darling David,

You have been so sweet and treated me better than I have ever been treated before and I will never forget you. But you do not love me and you do not need me. You are strong and Aubery is weak. I always knew that. I can not leave him the way he is now.

Aubery is going to change. I am going to be okay. Please find a nice girl who deserves you. I envy her already, whoever she is.

Forgive me David and please try to understand.
God bless.
Ellen.

I never saw either of them again.

I am a great deal older now. I have never seen Ellen's village and I have never gone grape-picking in the South of France. Although in my dreams I have done both, many times.

"Are ye a man or a mouse?" The Rainbow Man demanded. "Are ye goin' te tell her how ye feel or are ye goin' te wait until the two of yez is dead and buried and tell her in the next life?"

The Oracle at the Adelphi

It was only when Satan Coil died that any of us discovered that Satan hadn't been his real name. He died in 1956, the year that the Russian tanks rolled into Budapest to crush the Hungarian Revolution. Of course the Hungarian Revolution was of no concern to me, I was nine years old and what I cared about was my new black Raleigh Junior bicycle, the TV set with the huge mahogany cabinet and the minuscule, blurry and often rolling black-and-white picture, and the Glenalough Adelphi, the local cinema that was owned and managed by Satan, where my friends and I spent every Saturday afternoon, transported to other lands, other times and other lives by the magic of the flickering screen.

The idea of a cinema being owned and operated by Satan was one that must have appealed mightily to the local Roman Catholic hierarchy, it may even have been them who gave him the nick-name, but I suspect that it emerged more from his habit of running up and down the cinema aisles during the Saturday matinees when the building was taken over by hordes of runny-nosed pre-teenage youngsters intent on admitting their friends without tickets through the fire-doors, while brandishing a high-powered flashlight and screaming at them in his thick Galway accent to "Sate in yer sates!". It was but a short step from "Sate-in" to the popular familiar name for the Prince of Darkness. And the Prince of Darkness, in a manner of speaking, is exactly what he was.

Satan was not a well man during the time that I knew him. He had been tall, and may even have been handsome in his earlier years, but by the beginning of my cinema-going career he had become unnaturally lean and bent-over, wore a permanent hang-dog scowl on his scrawny pallid face, and seemed always to have last shaved a couple of days prior to any encounter. He spoke in little short bursts, punctuated by attempts to catch his breath, each of which resulted in a cough-like gulp from somewhere at the back of his throat. One could chart from Saturday to Saturday the decline in his ability to climb the stairs to the projection room.

Looking back across the decades to those distant Glenalough days, things become obvious that were far from obvious at the time. I could make a good stab now at putting a name to the condition from which Satan suffered, but more importantly perhaps I can see some of the underlying causes for the slow atrophy of his will to continue. Satan had originally come to Glenalough and purchased the Adelphi in order to be close to Dilly Morgan, the Widow Morgan, as we knew her, Sean Morgan's mother. Sean Morgan was a couple of years older than me, a street-wise thick-set ginger-headed boy with a penchant for bullying, whom nobody liked but many secretly admired at the coarse Christian Brothers Primary School at the south end of the town. Whether the Widow Morgan was really a widow, or whether this was a courtesy title awarded to any woman who found herself alone with a child in the hypocritical and moralistic society of 1950s Ireland is anyone's guess. There were even rumors that Satan Coil might have been Sean's father, but we discounted that theory on the simple grounds that everyone knew that the Coils were Protestants, and the idea of a romantic liaison between a Catholic woman and an unbeliever was even more unthinkable than the notion of fornication itself. More likely Sean was the result of some ill-fated affair in Ms. Morgan's teenage years, and Satan, whose devotion to Dilly was perfectly genuine, hoped that despite his apparent disqualification on religious grounds he might still merit consideration as a suitor to a Catholic woman who was, after all, somewhat damaged goods herself. In the event Dilly Morgan never, to my knowledge, showed the smallest interest in Satan's amorous advances, and drifted into middle-life in the sole company of her thuggish son, the two of them living in one of the smallest cottages within the town boundaries of Glenalough, on the bank of an over-grown, littered and rather foul-smelling stream that only flowed if there had been a few days of heavy rain in the mountains. The cottage was called "Riversdale House".

As well as being unlucky in love, the value of Satan's business investment and the income that it generated declined rapidly and steeply during his years in Glenalough. He often complained that it was the Roman Catholic Church that had engineered his ruin, because although Glenalough was technically within the Protestant dominated and British ruled state of Northern Ireland, it was a border town and peopled predominantly by Catholics.

This Catholic/Protestant divide was enormously important in every aspect of Irish life then and still is to this day: about twelve years after Satan's death it led to the armed uprising of the Northern Catholics that is still tearing the unfortunate country apart. In fact Satan was less than honest about the part played by religious affiliations in his floundering fortunes. The truth was that the religious division functioned entirely to his advantage, since the Catholics would come to see all the slightly risqué or anti-clerical films that had been banned by the Church in the South. Indeed when he had something particularly controversial they would flood across the border in their hundreds to taste the forbidden fruit, so that whatever official line the Church may have taken about Satan's picture-house the proximity of large numbers of its members had never done his takings anything but good.

What really destroyed the Adelphi Cinema as a viable concern were factors for which nobody in particular was to blame. The world was changing. Television had taken a major hold, a lot of businesses like pubs and hotels had purchased sets for the coronation of Queen Elizabeth some four years earlier, and as the economies of both Ireland and England emerged from war-time austerity into an era of expansion and relative affluence, more and more people could afford a TV of their own, to rent if not to buy. Television meant up-to-the-minute news and live or near-live coverage of major sporting events, which the cinema news-reels could never match, as well as a good selection of films, plays, music, game-shows and all the rest that encouraged the older generation to stay in their houses. The excellent coverage of the highlights of the Melbourne Olympics, only hours after the actual events had taken place, was perhaps the final death-blow to many a small rural picture-house.

The younger generation of course still wanted to go out to the cinema: where else could you get away from the prying eyes of your parents and family to sit with your boyfriend or girlfriend for several hours in near-darkness on the pretext of attending a respectable and socially-sanctioned mass-entertainment? But car-ownership or (for the more adventurous young) motorbike ownership was becoming widespread, and the fifteen or twenty mile drive to Belleek or Sligo to attend one of the bigger and flashier cinemas was becoming part of the Saturday evening ritual. No self-respecting teenager who was in a job would invite a girl to the local flea-pit: he would make an event of it, drive her to the county town, include a snack in one of the newly mushrooming coffee-bars, and maybe park up for a while on the way home and make sure that he got value for his evening's investment. At the same time the standards of sexual explicitness permitted by the British Board of Film Censors and the Roman Catholic Church began to draw closer together, so that the occasional suggestive piece of dialogue, lingering kiss, or even the fleeting glimpse of an exposed female nipple was no longer sufficient to curb a film's distribution in the Irish Republic.

In addition to all of this, an era in which patrons would accept almost any double feature that the cinema manager was able to hire was giving way to one in which people expected to be able to see whatever Hollywood's latest offering happened to be. Three-or-four-year-old circuit faithfuls, of which there were many, were no longer acceptable to the cinema industry's younger customers, and new films cost so much to hire that effectively they were only available to the larger chained outlets. The role for cinemas like the Glenalough Adelphi was simply melting away, and there was nothing that Satan Coil could do to change that.

Satan became a bitter man, and the bitterness showed in his features and sounded in his voice when he spoke. The young projectionist that he had trained-up, Alfie McCormack, left to join the RUC in Belfast and, some thirteen years later, acquired momentary fame as the first Northern Ireland police officer to be killed by sniper-fire on the streets of Dundalk.

For a while, Satan tried to run the cinema almost single-handed. He arranged for the distributors to send a projectionist from Sligo along with the film reels themselves four nights a week plus Saturday afternoons and drive back when the show was done. On Tuesdays, Wednesdays and Thursdays there was no program. He hired a girl for the box office, sometimes sold the tickets himself, and usually showed people to their seats wielding his famous high-powered flashlight. In the daytime he could be found inside the darkened theatre clearing the litter out from between the rows of seats, or outside attaching the letters that made-up the title of the evening's program to the illuminated display-board over the front entrance. The Saturday matinees when the children got in for half a crown to watch a cowboy film, a few cartoons and an episode of "Flash Gordon Conquers the Universe" or Bella Lugosi's "Phantom Creeps" show were always his most profitable sessions, and his stern commands to "Sate in yer sates" sprang from a well-founded neurosis that he was losing a significant proportion of his takings because of gatecrashers entering through the fire-exits at each side of the screen. He tried locking the fire-exits and received an immediate and strongly-worded rebuke from the Town Hall threatening to withdraw his entertainment license if he ever did it again.

Satan was effectively a cornered man, his economic future and whatever capital he had taken with him from Galway were tied up in a venture that was obviously nose-diving, his physical condition was deteriorating at an approximately parallel rate, and his hopes for a future with Dilly had long ago crumbled to dust and drifted away on the breeze. There came a point at which Satan realized that he had nothing left to look forward to, whereupon he turned to the traditional self-medication for depression that comes in bottles and is sold at all corner-stores everywhere. From that point onwards, things became dismally predictable.

The summer that Satan Coil died was one of the hottest that we had ever had in Glenalough. A shimmering haze softened the outline of the distant Sligo hills and the stream outside Dilly Morgan's back door turned into a desiccated white roadway with a surface hardness approaching that of concrete, in which old packing-crates, tar drums, bicycle-frames and iron bedsteads had been artistically half submerged. My friends and I didn't have a great deal to do in the long school holidays so we took to hanging around the cinema and annoying Satan as he went about his daily tasks.

Between Satan and the local schoolchildren there existed a powerful and subtle relationship based on fear, fascination, irritation, admiration, distaste and probably a lot of other elements as well. There was something of the bogey-man about him, especially when he shouted at you in the darkened theatre, but deep-down you knew that he wasn't going to do anything to you, unlike the Christian Brothers who would give you a clip around the ear as quick as look at you. He filled the same role as fairytale ogres and giants and horror-film monsters: you could enjoy the thrill of being scared of him in perfect confidence that the threat was unreal. For the braver among us it was fun to tease him and mimic his Galway accent, to chant "sate in yer sates!" as he walked down the road, but he had learned that the best way to deal with this was not to react at all, and that caused us to lose interest fairly quickly. The nick-name "Satan" was an important part of his image for the local schoolchildren. Steeped as we were in religious superstitions of all kinds, we had no difficulty in accepting that he was indeed the embodiment of all that was evil and corrupt, and that when he was not in the cinema he was somewhere in the deepest pits of Hell prodding with a long three-pronged fork the roasting souls of people who had died in mortal sin. Mothers would say to their wayward infants: "If you don't come in here this minute I'll send for Satan Coil and get him to take you away!" At another level of course we knew that he was just a lonely old man trying to make a living out of a run-down country picture-house, but children have no diffi-culty in simultaneously accepting contradictory beliefs. That was one of the topics that Satan and I used to talk about. If you wanted to make it sound impressive you might call it the extent to which art is real and to which reality is art.

I was one of the least boisterous of the local swarm of school-age brats, and because I was an only-child living with my father I got to stay out later than most of the others, and sometimes managed to see the more expensive evening programs intended for adult consumption. Satan took an obvious interest in the fact that I attended these and if he found me on my own would open the conversation with a question like: "What did ye think o' thon fill-em last night then?". The word "film" is pronounced by most Irish people as though it has two syllables.

In a one-to-one conversational setting there was noth-ing scary about Satan Coil. In fact I began to realize that he was an intelligent and sensitive man, who was able to guide me into seeing a lot of things in "fill-ems" that I would otherwise have missed.

"What did ye think 'o the scene where the two of them was up in the air in the big wheel," he would probe, "an Harry looks down at the people the size of ants and says what would it matter if one 'o them ants stopped moving?"

"I don't remember that bit," I would say, "I liked the shooting in the caves at the end."

"They weren't caves," he would explain patiently, "them was sewers. Th' sewers of Vienna. What is it that you find in sewers?"

"Rats?"

"Rats. Aye. Rats. Harry was a rat. Anybody that doesn't care about one 'o them ants stopping moving, that's a rat. Harry was an evil man, but he was th' other fella's friend. The fella' that shot him in the sewer."

"You mean he shot his friend?"

"Aye. But if your friend's a rat, what should ye do? Should ye stick by him, or should ye do the right thing?"

And so it would go on. Satan Coil had the skill of a true educator, the ability to lead his pupil to a critical under-standing of a work of art, and the forbearance never to force his own conclusion on his student. All that he lacked was the trained academic's facility with words: he was not an articulate man, and perhaps that had been his undoing with Dilly. Through the few conversations that I had with him that brief summer I began to realize quite a lot about why some films were better than others. For example, one mark of a really good film is that it is possible to look at the story in more than one way. I began to understand that not every-thing in a good story, and maybe not everything in a person or in life itself, is sitting right there on the surface for you to see at the first glance. Satan Coil was my first real teacher, the one who showed me how to take the first step along the bridge that links childhood to maturity.

It was the Monday of the last week of our summer holiday when we heard that Satan was in serious trouble. He hadn't bothered to put up the title of the Monday night show over the front entrance, and in the early evening the projec-tionist arrived in his car from Sligo and pasted a notice on the glass door saying that there would be no more perfor-mances at the Adelphi until further notice. A couple of us were there on our bikes and saw him arrive, so we asked him what was going on.

"None 'o your business," he told us brusquely, but he stopped off at Flannigan's pub on the way back and within about twenty minutes the news had reached us that Coil owed them so much money they were refusing to rent him any more films until it was paid. Even at nine I could see the illogicality of this, for if he couldn't show films how was he going to pay his debts, but I could see no way into the circle. Evidently, neither could Satan. At about eight o'clock that evening, the time when the film would have been starting, the rumor reached us from the Police Station that Satan Coil had been found dead in his rooming-house by the landlady, who had come to collect back rent. He had taken a cocktail of prescription sleeping-pills and Old Bushmills Whiskey, whether deliberately or accidentally there was no way to be sure.

Satan Coil's funeral was a far bigger event than any of us would have expected. A brother of his that none of us had ever heard tell of came up from Galway in a big black Austin car and paid for the funeral, with a fine mahogany coffin and a horse-drawn hearse and a plot at the top end of the Protestant graveyard where it didn't flood in the winter. I wondered why the brother couldn't have done something for him while he was still alive. Before I'd had those talks with Satan something like that would never have occurred to me. A huge number of people came to that funeral, even though it was in the Protestant church: nearly all the children in the town, as well as the most of the older folk, and, to my great surprise, Dilly Morgan and Sean. I saw Dilly shed a few tears when they finally lowered the big dark wooden coffin into the hole, and I wondered the same thing about her that I had wondered about Satan's brother.

As you can imagine, we were a bit subdued in the couple of days that followed the funeral. We hung around outside the cinema on our bikes and talked in low tones about Satan's death, and whether or not he had gone to Hell, which seemed pretty inevitable, having a name like that, and being a Protestant. It was Friday, and we had no Saturday matinee to look forward to, and school would be starting again on Monday. I think that secretly a lot of us were feeling bad about the way that we had treated Satan: even the business about getting in without paying to the Saturday matinees seemed a bit mean and unfair now. We were beginning to discover that as well as religion with all its random rules and regulations about not eating meat on a Friday and never taking the name of God in vain and all the rest of it there was a genuine moral order in life which was based on kindness and justice. It mattered how you treated other people.

About sundown, when we were thinking about heading home for our tea, Sean Morgan arrived on his bicycle with that sly expression on his face that generally meant he had a scam of some kind on his mind. Being older than us and due to move up to the big school at the end of the term he wouldn't have bothered to talk to us unless he had.

"Have yez ever heard of a séance?" he asked, pronouncing the silent "e" at the end of the word. Of course we hadn't. "It's when you all gather around and call-up the ghost of a dead person," he explained. "Why don't we go to the Adelphi tonight and call up the ghost of Satan Coil? I'll show yez how to do it."

We protested that the cinema was shut and we couldn't get in, but Sean assured us that the green fire-exit would be open at midnight for anybody with enough guts to come along. It was the kind of challenge a nine-year-old boy couldn't really refuse.

I think there had been six of us leaning on our bikes when Sean had issued the challenge, but only three of us showed up at midnight. That wasn't particularly surprising, considering that it involved getting dressed and sneaking out of the house without being heard or seen. I had put my trousers on over my pajama bottoms and slipped my bare feet into my sandals before sneaking out through the bedroom window and climbing down into the back garden by way of the flat extension roof and the water-barrel.

Ernie, the butcher's son, had a watch, and we waited until 12.15 in case anybody else was going to come. Then with racing hearts, we gently pulled open the fire-exit and peered into the empty theatre.

The huge inner space was in total darkness except for two yellowish flickering lights right at the back, high up on the wall near the projection room. We tip-toed in and soundlessly ascended the sloping aisle towards the back of the cinema.

As our eyes became accustomed to the dark we saw that the light was coming from behind the two projection slots high up on the wall. Someone had been busy with a paintbrush and had sketched-in the shape of two enormous eyes around them, the fiery projection slots forming their glowing slit-like pupils. I felt myself enter into that complicity in make-believe that participation in theatre or performance of any kind requires. Part of me knew that the giant eyes had been painted on the wall by Sean, that the eerie light was coming from candles that he had positioned behind the projection slots, and that he was in the projection room right now getting ready to give us the "meeting with the dead" that he had obviously planned; but another part of me was completely willing to accept the reality of the supernatural dimension, eager to believe that the blazing eyes drew their light from the deepest recesses of the Inferno, from which the ghost of Satan Coil would soon address us.

We stopped before the weird apparition and sought each other's hands for reassurance. Ernie the butcher's son was the first one to speak. "Is that you, Mr Coil?" he inquired with a meek politeness that he would never have proffered the living Satan.

"Sate in yer Sates!" thundered a voice from behind the projection slots, in a somewhat forced bass register and a very passable Galway accent. It was such a shock that we literally fell over one another, tumbling to the floor in a tangle of startled bodies, not knowing whether to laugh or scream. No sooner had we fallen in front of the mighty idol than a piercing white beam shot from one of its eyes to light up part of the screen behind us. It was a good touch. This time, at least one of us screamed. The scream seemed to break the tension and from the middle of the little huddle of bodies I looked up in time to see the beam cut and the flickering firelight replace its brilliance.

"Are ye.... Are ye in Hell, Mr Coil?" Ernie piped-up nervously, entering completely into the spirit of the occasion.

"Aye, I'm in Hell sure enough," came the blood-curdling imitation of Satan Coil's voice. At the same moment there was the clatter of a falling object and one of the eyes lost its flickering inner light. We heard the faint sound of someone shuffling around on the floor of the projection room.

"Are ye.... Are ye burnin' up, Mr Coil?" Ernie probed anxiously.

There was no immediate reply but the quality of the light issuing from the two projection slots seemed to change. It seemed to become noticeably redder and also brighter. Ernie repeated his question. There was still no answer. We stood up almost simultaneously, keen to see what change was taking place inside the imagined head of the fiery-eyed monster. The light from the slots became brighter still and we fancied that we could smell something like burning plastic. Within a few moments the smell had become completely unmistakable and there was smoke issuing from the two holes in the wall. We could hear the crackling of material catching light and as we watched flames began to snake outwards from the projection slots, lighting-up the whole scene like a bonfire in a dark forest, staining the wall above the slots black in their path, bending and thrusting to touch the high ceiling. Behind us our three shadows danced insanely as we backed away instinctively towards the aisle and the safety of the fire-door.

"God almighty! I'm out of here!" I heard one of the others announce, and the two of them were gone in the wink of an eye.

But as for me, I found myself transfixed like a rabbit in the headlight beam of a car, unable to avert my gaze from the gathering inferno, hovering somewhere in the hinterland between two realities. The smell was becoming unbearable and the intensity of the heat made me back further away involuntarily, but something inside me told me that it was not yet time to leave, that this night still had something more to teach me. And so it proved.

With a single exception which I will presently explain, I have never spoken to anyone of the things that took place in the Adelphi that night. Neither have any of the others. Sean must have been able to get out in time when he knocked over the candle, because he appeared at school at the appointed hour on the Monday, and there was never the least suggestion of his having had any part to play in the cinema burning down. The destruction was so complete that the fire officers were unable to say what had started it. It occurred to me afterwards that if Satan had still been alive the insurance money might have been his salvation. But as far as our midnight séance was concerned, it was simply an event that had never taken place.

So what was it, you may be wondering, that happened between the time the others fled and the time that I made my own escape? Well, I don't expect you to believe this: I'm not sure that I believe it myself. After all, I was a nine-year-old boy with a highly active imagination, and the night's events had put me in the ideal frame of mind for accepting the incredible. But if I were standing this moment before God himself and had sworn to tell the truth or forfeit my immortal soul, I would have to announce that the voice of Satan Coil spoke to me one more time that night. It spoke quietly and calmly and it sounded nothing whatever like Sean Morgan's adolescent mimicry. It asked me to pass on a message, which, for what it is worth, I have since done. It spoke to me politely, as a friend requesting a favor.

"Would ye do something for me?" it gently entreated from somewhere within the flames. "Would ye tell Dilly Morgan thanks for comin' to the funeral?"

"Now you answer me this, St. Peter," The Rainbow Man demanded, "are ye goin' te open the pearly gates for a man who left the world no better than he found it?"

The Dragon Slayer

When the doctor first told me about this thing I tried to argue with him, ended up being quite offensive. I phoned him up afterwards and apologized of course. It was a ridiculous attitude to adopt, as if it were his fault.

I tried to force him to tell me how long I had left. You hear all these stories about people who were given three months and are still there years later. It's almost a cliché. But he wouldn't give me a figure like that. All he would say was months rather than years. And that I would probably continue to feel reasonably well until close to the end. Not an exact science, he said.

He and I were the only ones who knew about it for the first few weeks. Unless some of my friends guessed. There was one time when I caught myself telling someone that I live on a slope leading down to a cemetery. Such a powerful image, but I said it completely unconsciously. It stopped me in my tracks, reduced me to total silence.

The first few days were the worst, as you might expect. I didn't sleep very much at the beginning. But in fairness to myself I don't think that I coped with it too badly. I didn't crack up. I didn't break down and cry or rush off to find a counselor. I didn't run amok and smash everything. I just sat very quietly in my darkened room and did a great deal of thinking.

The Company owed me quite a bit of annual leave so I took it, stayed at home in the cottage. I lay there when I couldn't sleep and fantasized about what I should do with those remaining months, however long it was going to be.

My ideas became very grandiose. I thought about what might have happened if someone had walked up to Adolf Hitler in 1935 or 1936 and blown his brains out. Would the world have been a better place? Would that have been the best thing anyone could have done with an expendable life? Who knows? Hitler wasn't the only Nazi. Somebody else would have come to power. But it's hard to believe that whoever it was could have been quite such a monster. Maybe there are turning points like that in human history where one man can make a difference. Before I knew about my condition, such thoughts would have seemed like madness. But now they seemed to make sense. I had been given a kind of gift, a chance to do something worthwhile with the time left to me. It didn't have to be dramatic, but there had to be something that would give meaning to it all – to all those pointless years of sucking up to the boss and people being promoted over my head, trying to be the perfect husband and the perfect father and ending up alone in that little cottage with a rotten divorce settlement and children I never saw, who didn't want to talk to me any more – never getting anything in return but kicks in the teeth. I suppose it hadn't struck me so powerfully before because I had always told myself that things would get better, that there was time to change it all. Now I knew that there wasn't.

But maybe I wasn't destined to be a nonentity after all. Maybe there was something I could do in the world, some mighty task that would make them all turn around and say, "You know, we misjudged him. There was more to him than we ever knew…"

I started to buy four morning newspapers and to subscribe to all the news channels on satellite TV. I bought lots of writing paper and a few big loose-leaf binders and I started to take notes on what was going on in all the trouble spots of the world. Tin-pot dictators manufacturing biological weapons and hydrogen bombs. Arab suicide bombers blowing themselves up in crowded restaurants. South American drug barons with private armies and more income than the annual budgets of the countries they lived in. White slave traders smuggling women and young girls out of central Europe and the Far East to live lives of misery and exploitation in the hidden brothels of the rich West. African villagers cutting one another to pieces with machetes and burning each other alive in locked churches. Women and children starving to death because some war lord wanted to use their destruction as a weapon in his fight for power.

I began to wonder which of us was ill, me or the world out there. The trouble was there was only one of me. It wasn't enough. There seemed to be so little that I could actually do. In the fairytale world there was always just one dragon to slay and one knight to do the slaying; in the real world there were a million dragons but the knight was still on his own. I would have to change the scale of my operation.

I started subscribing to the local newspapers covering the villages within about twenty miles of where I lived. Stories about agricultural shows and new supermarkets and young girls competing for the title of Queen of the May. I seemed to have gone from one extreme to the other. That wasn't where I was going to find my dragon.

I had become a bit fixated on the idea that there had to be a dragon, an enemy of some kind to slay. Maybe that was the wrong model. Who had really made a difference in the world, I asked myself, those who had killed in a noble cause, or those who had died in one? Socrates. Jesus Christ. Thomas Moore. Mahatma Gandhi. Martin Luther King.

President Kennedy. But of course the dying had only been part of it, it had been the living that had really counted, and I wasn't going to have time for that. But maybe I could turn myself into a sacrificial lamb, like the student who had stood in front of the advancing tanks in Tiananmen Square, or the young boy who had handed out pro-democracy leaflets in full view of the troops in the streets of Burma, only weeks after his release from a Burmese prison on exactly the same charge. I wouldn't be a real moral giant of course, only a pretend one, but I doubted if the cameras would be able to tell the difference.

The details of my new plan seemed even harder to work out than with my old one. Where precisely should I go to seek this martyrdom? I had a mental picture of myself standing straight and tall on a cratered battlefield between two advancing armies, arms outstretched, shells exploding all around me, press reporters peering out from a nearby bunker. But it was a total fantasy. To make an impact like that you had to be in the right place at the right time. Circumstances had to play into your hand. It wasn't the kind of thing you could stage manage.

I felt myself sinking into a depression. Precious days were slipping by. The churchyard down the hill from my little cottage seemed to be moving closer. There was no way to make a difference, or if there was I simply wasn't clever enough to think of it.

Despite what the doctor had said I could feel my physical condition deteriorating too. I seemed to have less and less energy, less desire to eat, a queasiness in my stomach that would not go away. I phoned the Company and told them that I was unwell, that I would send a medical certificate. I knew that I would never be going back.

Early the next morning I forced myself to get dressed, pack a few things into a weekend bag, draw out some money from my Post Office savings account, and take the first train to London. I don't know what I was hoping to find there but I knew that there was nothing worthwhile I could do in the village.

I staggered from Victoria Station just before eight o'clock, feeling as though I might throw up at any moment, a stabbing pain hitting the back of my eyes with every step that I took. I walked very slowly, steadying myself against the wall as I went, the weekend bag swinging like a limp pendulum, threatening to rob me of what little balance I had left. A gnawing dread formed at the back of my mind that I had left it too late. I wasn't going to have enough strength left to change anything, the end was rushing towards me and I had done nothing.

As I felt my way along like a blind man I saw that my path was blocked by somebody who was sitting down and leaning his back against the wall. He looked up at me, an inquiring, interested look. He had an unkempt ginger beard and his jacket was torn. Nevertheless he was not old, probably no more than thirty, and had pleasant regular features.

"Yer lookin' a wee bit rough mate," he said in a thick Scottish accent, "are ye okay?"

"Not too good," I said quietly, and felt myself slump down by his side. We looked into each other's eyes. "I'm afraid I'm dying," I said very quietly, seeing no point in trying to conceal it.

"Yer lucky mate. I wish tae hell I could die."

I looked at him, shocked. "Do you have the least idea what you're talking about?"

He ignored the question.

"Have ye got a drink, mate?"

113

"You just said that you wished you could die. What did you mean by that?"

Alex, for that was his name, told me what he meant. A lot of it I could have guessed. A marriage that had started out no different to any other, a young daughter, a decent enough job in an industry that looked safe, redundancy that came from nowhere like thunder on a summer's day, redundancy money and no hope of another job, nothing to spend it on but drink; then the inevitable move to London on his own to find work. The months turning to years, the wrong kind of company, the landlady turning nasty, the drift into a rootless life dominated by the quest for the next bottle of spirits.

He wasn't a very articulate man. It took him a long time to tell his story. I somehow expected a familiar, well-rehearsed account that he would have told many times, but I was wrong. Nobody had ever asked Alex for his story before. Nobody else had spared the time to listen. The early morning commuter traffic had passed by the time he finished. The roads around Victoria had become quiet again, few pedestrians, just the steady rumble of the heavy lorries down Vauxhall Bridge Road.

"Tell me Alex," I said to him, "if you could have your wildest dream, something to make life worth living again, what would it be?"

He drew in his breath and shrugged cynically. "My wildest dream? A place tae live with Jeanie an' the wean. A job tae go tae. A fresh clean shirt every morning an' a decent pair a shoes on mae feet. A'm no a pig, ye know. I dinnae want tae live like this."

I felt one of those moments of sudden insight that come to people only once or twice in a lifetime. Alex had shown me something that I hadn't understood before. All my imaginings had been about me, about what would make me look good, about noble gestures that would win me attention, about pathetic self-glorification. That was not a proper basis for making the world a better place. It was bullshit, a total illusion, the whimpering of an ego complaining of long neglect.

"Okay, Alex," I said very quietly, "I think I can help you. But there are going to be conditions."

Jeanie is cooking something for me now as I lie here. A bit of scrambled egg. It's about as much as I can eat these days. Their daughter is starting at the village school today, both Jeanie and Alex went down to introduce her and get her settled in. I think she'll like it there. She'll be made very welcome too. We haven't very many young children in the village any more, it's turned into a bit of a commuter town for the likes of me, or at least the person I used to be.

Alex is going to see Bill Kinnear this afternoon, the man who owns the big market gardening operation on the far side of the valley. I went to school with Bill, and I've had a quiet word with him. Alex will be okay for a job there. What he makes of it will be up to him. I've had a quiet word with Jeanie as well and she knows the score. She knows he has to deal with the drinking. She's got him to detox and rehab as he calls it already. She's a good sensible woman. He's a lucky man to have her. A very lucky man.

It's a bit of a squeeze in the bungalow at the moment. We just have the two bedrooms, but I'm better off in the sitting room anyhow, on the couch, where I don't have to get up to go to bed. I don't seem to be able to move around very much at all any more. Alex and Jeanie know that they'll soon have plenty of room.

I look forward to wakening up and seeing each new day. I appreciate what it means to be alive, for the first time ever I think. It's wonderful to see the two of them on such a high, making a new start. Maybe it will go wrong again, I'm not God, I can't control other people's lives. But I'm very hopeful. Both of them have seen enough of what the world is like when you're down to understand the value of what they've got now.

So there isn't much more to tell. My life ends, but it kick starts the lives of three other people. It's their turn now, their responsibility to make something out of it if they can. I haven't changed the course of history. But maybe I've made the world a better place. Just one tiny corner of it. But it's enough so that I don't feel that it was all pointless any more. And I really don't care whether anybody ever finds out about it or what anybody else thinks. I know what I think, that's all I care about. It's a very good feeling. The name for this feeling might be freedom.

"Oh, ye think yer smart, don't ye?" The Rainbow Man taunted, "A lot a' good yer fancy talkin'll do ye when the bullets start flyin'. A lot a' good it'll do ye then!"

The Battlefield Philosopher

It wouldn't be entirely true to say that I had arrived at this airport by chance. There were many routes that I could have chosen to get home to London from the Far East, stop-overs at Bucharest or Abbu Dhabi, Vienna or Cairo, but I had chosen this obscure little Central European capital because as soon as I had seen its name I had remembered my old friend of University days, Oliver McClure. Oliver had been my favourite teacher, a charming and eccentric Irish ex-priest, not a great deal older than his students, who lectured to the trainee teachers on the esoteric subject of "Philosophy of Education". I had never forgotten his answer to a young girl's question in the very first lecture that he had given to my group: it was an answer that had seized my attention and led me into an obsession with philosophy which came to rule my life. "Will studying philosophy make it any easier for us in the classroom?" she had asked. "Only if I fail," Oliver had answered without an instant's hesitation, "if I succeed it will make it infinitely more difficult."

The lesson that Oliver had been trying to impart had been nothing less than the central imperative of Western philosophy since Socrates: Question everything. It doesn't make classroom teaching easier any more than it makes life itself easier, that isn't it's point, it makes both of them infinitely more difficult and infinitely more worthwhile. My detour therefore was to renew my acquaintance with a hero of my late 'teens, the man who had convinced me that the unexamined life is not worth living, the unexamined doctrine unworthy of acceptance.

I left the cold grey concourse of the crumbling airport terminal with just a light rucksack slung over my shoulder, having been assured in broken English by the clerk in the transit lounge that my luggage would be transferred to the connecting flight the following afternoon. Outside the terminal a cluster of ugly and functional windowless buildings, clad with corrugated iron and disfigured by rust streaks and the dents and scrapes of decades of tight manoeuvres by clumsy truck drivers, formed a large oblong courtyard in which half-a-dozen State-owned taxis, all painted regulation grey and bearing a motif of the national flag on their front door panels, waited apathetically to carry arriving passengers on their onward journeys. They stood on a yellow taxi rank one behind the other, spaced out with military precision. I went to the one at the head of the line and tapped on the driver's window. He wound it down with that air of grim resignation that state control of industry is so good at producing and waited blankly for me to name a destination.

"Can you take me to Grundhof Farm in Latvihasse?" I asked with exaggerated clarity, hoping that he would be able to make sense of my murdering of the place-names. To my relief his whole countenance lit up and he motioned towards the rear doors, plainly inviting me to get in. "You know Grundhof Farm?" I asked, mainly for reassurance, as I tossed my rucksack on to the back seat and made myself comfortable beside it.

"I know," he returned in a deep bass as he started the engine. I rolled down my window a fraction to make the odour of stale tobacco-smoke a bit less intense.

Although this was notionally the international airport of the capital city, the road out of the terminal looked entirely rural, twisting its way through dormant ploughed potato fields, the troughs choked with compacted snow, the landscape dotted with the roofless skeletons of primitive farm buildings and the shells of abandoned gutted vehicles, everything falling to ruins and beginning to blend in with the snow amid the random clumps of winter-naked birch trees.

"Civil war," the driver explained in his booming voice, adopting the role of tour guide, "many people die, many farms destroyed. Now all owned by Government. Still no good. Still grow no crops."

It sounded like dangerous talk. I nodded sagely.

Oliver had left his lecturing post at the London University Institute of Education under circumstances that had seemed at the time heartrendingly romantic. He had fallen in love with Eva, a young palely beautiful student from this godforsaken Central European cess-pit who had been admitted to study abroad under some obscure United Nations bursary for gifted scholars from bankrupt and despotic hell-holes. She had been chosen from among more than ten thousand applicants. That was a perfectly realistic measure of how gifted she was. For the first time in his career Oliver had been given the charge of a student every bit his intellectual equal, with the looks of an angel and the sad serious eyes of a motherless fawn. I said that Oliver fell in love with her, in fact every male that she had ever met had fallen in love with her, but in Oliver's case there had been some degree of reciprocation. Then (without meaning to sound melodramatic) came the revolution. The tanks rolled over the fields her father and her father's fathers had ploughed since human beings had known how to grow crops. It was only a couple of months before Eva's final examinations but there was no way that she would sit in a comfortable seminar room in London while her parents waited for the 4.00 AM knock on the door, or the explosion of the mortar shell that would end her family line forever. And of course against all the dictates of common sense and the strongest possible urgings of the Foreign Office Travel Advice Centre, Oliver had gone with her.

We rounded a bend and came upon a group of parked military trucks where uniformed and heavily armed soldiers stood around in groups, chatting and smoking with the same bored resignation that I had seen in the faces of the waiting taxi-drivers. One of them signalled us to stop and the driver wound down his window with the same unhurried detachment with which he had wound it down for me. "Soldiers," he explained, rather redundantly. They exchanged a few curt words in their own language. I heard the word "passport". The driver leaned back and repeated it to me. I handed the dog-eared document through the open window. As the soldier turned its pages he continued his conversation with the driver. Eventually the driver turned around to address me in a deep quiet undertone. "I tell him you want to go Nazzibrink, not Latvihasse," he explained. "Is better. Okay?"

For the first time, I felt a shot of unease. What had looked like the picturesque eccentricities of a foreign way of life suddenly took on a menacing importance. Why did we need to lie to the soldiers? I nodded and swallowed hard. This wasn't the time to start an argument.

Within a few moments my passport had been returned and we were on our way again. I considered asking the driver for more explanation, but somehow I couldn't bring myself to do it. It seemed such a natural reaction to him, to question it might have seemed naïve. We came to a place where the road forked and the driver took the right-hand track, the narrower and less travelled of the two. We started to ascend into wooded, snow-covered hills. The road seemed icy, but he maintained a brisk speed. For the second time in that journey I felt apprehension for my personal safety. The driver seemed to have slipped out of his tour-guide role and for the remainder of the trip he remained stonily silent. I hoped that he was concentrating on his driving.

The forest became more dense as we rose higher, and soon we were moving through a tunnel of trees that over-hung the narrow track and seemed to close over above it. The trees also seemed to serve an insulating function and the road surface became less obviously lethal.

Oliver's leaving the University had been the biggest gossip topic of my student days. He had been a popular and lively tutor, an approachable man, who attended student parties when invited, and took part in the Union Society debates, and drank regularly in the Students' Union Bar. A little circle of disciples had grown up around him, myself promi-nent among them, and more than once we had talked-in the dawn sitting cross-legged on the floor of some student rooming house, solving the problems of the world and probing the mysteries of existence with that intensity of purpose that for the great bulk of us seems to melt away in the first couple of weeks following Graduation Day.

He sent us a total of three letters after he left, all of them hurried, uncharacteristically brief and direct, friendly in their way, but (perhaps understandably) preoccupied with matters more weighty than we could readily understand. Yes, he was all right and Eva and her family were all right – so far. The fighting was still a few miles from the farm. Her older brother was in the mountains with the Freedom Fighters, her younger brother was still at home. One of their farm workers had been killed in an ambush. They had planted nothing this year, and there would be nothing to feed the cattle in the coming winter. There was no diesel fuel for the generator, and nobody came to empty the sceptic tank any more. And so it went on. By the time the second letter arrived, Eva knew that her older brother was dead, and her father was finding it harder and harder to keep the younger one at home. There were soldiers of fourteen out there now, Axel was sixteen, there was no excuse. This might have to be the last letter, it was too dangerous to ask people to smuggle them out and post them abroad. But no, there was one more letter. What a change of mood! The Freedom Fighters had won the day! They had marched into the capital, shelled the Presidential Palace, set up a Provisional Government! Eva's younger brother had come back alive, a hero of the revolution, with medals and citations, but (sadly) without his left foot. Her family could start to rebuild now. The future was bright, Oliver wished us all a life as happy as the one he was having with his adored Eva.

His three letters were published together as a framed single-page feature in the student newspaper. That edition sold out in about two hours.

We came to a crossroads high in the mountains. The trees had largely given way to a rocky, snow-bound plateau, the road itself had turned to a ribbon of compacted snow between two raised mounds, almost certainly the result of drain-digging. There were no skeleton buildings up here and no abandoned vehicles: just the rocks and the snow and the little twisted shrubs that pushed up through it here and there, jagged and indestructible.

We took the track to the left, down into a different valley from the one by which we had ascended. I had lost my sense of time, Oliver's farm seemed to be a very long way from the airport. "Is it a lot further?" I asked conversationally. I don't know whether he understood me or not but he did not answer. A light flutter of falling snow began to obstruct the windscreen and he switched on the wipers. Before long it had become heavier and I could see little beyond the drainage mounds at either side of the track. To my relief he slowed down and turned the windscreen wipers up to full speed. It crossed my mind that if I became snowed-in and missed my flight the following day all kinds of dire consequences would follow. I began to wonder what had possessed me to come here, without even an advance phone call to let Oliver know that I was on my way. What if they didn't live at the farm any more? What if I was being taken hostage by this strange and taciturn taxi-driver to become a pawn in some incomprehensible local power-struggle? My heart was beginning to beat at an unaccustomed pace and I had to force back an urge to demand, or more accurately beg him to turn around at once and take me back to the airport.

Suddenly we were passing through the rubble of a village. To either side of the road I could glimpse through the snow the shattered walls of houses with daylight showing through their windows, charred wooden roof beams pointing at dizzy angles towards the sky, burned-out vehicles, many of them on their sides, casually nudged on to the pavements so that fresh traffic could pass by. Nowhere could I see a human being, or evidence of recent habitation. Without needing to be told, I knew that this was Latvihasse.

A sick numbness had come into my stomach. This was a killing-field. This was what war looked like, even years after. How on earth had Eva and her family managed to survive fighting of this intensity?

Just a few hundred yards past the village, the driver slowed down and turned in through a gap in a wall where there had once been gates. We were headed for the front courtyard of what had been a sizeable farmhouse, now merely another picturesque roofless ruin.

"Grundhof Farm?" I whispered. This time the driver heard.

"I wait for you," he replied in booming acknowledgement, "You walk rest of way. Keep hands out from sides. Show you have no gun. Okay?"

Okay? Delightful, I almost answered. Instead I said nothing but pulled myself out into the stinging snow and started to plod my way towards the freezing corpse of the old stone building. I held my hands out in plain view as the driver had advised, even though the snow made them tingle and the ruins looked like they would provide scant shelter for a rat let alone a gunman.

What on earth was I doing here, I asked myself, what on earth did I suppose I was going to learn from it? What kind of trap was I walking into?

My attention had been on the old building and its tragic state, but as I approached it I suddenly noticed through the snow something else entirely. Parked over to my right, where the corner of a partly demolished stone wall provided a bit of shelter, was a rusting military truck about the size of a small furniture removal van, its rear end facing me. The wheels were missing and concrete blocks had been used to stabilize the chassis underneath. There was also a large galvanized water tank on the roof that seemed to be connected up to pipes of some kind, and alongside the vehicle was a series of butane gas cylinders with orange flexible tubes disappearing beneath. The final proof of human habitation was a gently sloping wooden ramp leading up to an improvised metal front door whose frame had been welded into position in the bottom part of the original huge rear door panel. The top half of the door was made of glass, and behind it, just discernible through the falling snow, a seated figure was watching me.

At the sight of the crude shelter and its mystery occupant my spirits took a momentary upward bound. They really were all right! They had lost the farmhouse but they were clinging to some kind of existence, the same as everyone else who had come through the country's recent inferno.

Throwing off all caution I quickened my pace and waved to the man whom I was now almost certain was Oliver. Then, as I got to the foot of the ramp, I saw something that hit me like a physical blow and almost stopped my heart. My whole body went numb and my arms fell to my sides. Between the truck and the wall, in a space that was well sheltered from the snow, three small wooden crosses had been driven into the ground. They had been there for some time and the neatly painted names had begun to flake, but they were perfectly legible. One of them I did not recognize. The other two were Axel and Eva.

I don't know how long I stood there staring at them as the snow fluttered past my eyes and melted into little rivulets that trickled down my face and the back of my neck.

It was the once so familiar voice of Oliver McClure, his Dublin brogue now oddly overlaid with the local accent, that brought me back to my senses.

"You shouldn't have come," he said very quietly. I looked up. The door was open and a disturbing pale effigy of Oliver McClure was looking down at me from a battered wheelchair just inside. His once round and ever-cheerful face had become gaunt and drawn, his bright ginger hair thin, wispy and almost entirely grey. Beneath his joyless eyes yellowish drooping bags spoke of years of strain and insomnia.. Had I met him in other circumstances I might have wondered if this was Oliver McClure's father – but no, there was no real question, this was Oliver.

"You had better come in," he said in that same resigned monotone that seemed to be the badge of this country.

He reversed the chair soundlessly into the dark interior and I followed and pulled the crude door shut behind me. I stood and looked down at him. For almost a minute neither of us spoke. He must have seen the shock and disbelief in my eyes.

"I'm afraid what I said in my third letter wasn't entirely true," he began at last in that strangely Europeanised brogue. He motioned me to sit and I found a plain wooden chair. Stunned into a foolish silence, my surroundings made no impression. He spoke very quietly. He seemed to find the English language quite difficult, you could tell that he didn't think in English any more.

"They came here... it was early evening. Broad daylight. Not like now. Warm. Summer time. They killed all of them. Axel. Eva. Her father. They didn't kill me. That was a very big mistake. They broke my legs and held me so that I couldn't move, but they didn't kill me. They made me watch. They thought it was very funny. I don't know why they didn't kill me. Maybe it was because I was a foreigner. I don't think you want to know what they did to Eva before they killed her. They shot Axel in the stomach. It took him a long time to die. But not as long as the man who shot him. It took him three days to die. I was very inventive. Come to think of it he got off fairly lightly. One of them took five and a half days. I had my technique almost perfected by then. You see, broken legs heal again."

I stood transfixed, as if in a nightmare. I tried to speak. Oliver was in no hurry. He waited for me to get the words out. "So it was all lies," I whispered almost to myself, "the glorious revolution. The glorious future. None of it was real. Why? What made you do it Oliver? Why did you lie to us?"

"It isn't the way it's supp to end," he said quietly, "the young starry-eyed revolutionary doesn't end up a stinking cripple in a wheelchair. He doesn't become a torturer and a sick killer like me. He gets the girl and they live happily ever after. They rebuild democracy and prosperity in their shattered homeland and bring their children up to love freedom and justice and treat every man as their brother. The meek inherit the earth. We have it all on very good authority. Those students back in London... those children, because that's all they are really... what would it have done to their dreams, their idealism... if I had told them the way it had really turned-out?"

I realized at that moment that I was one of them, that I couldn't bear to let go of the fairytale. That I wanted to reject the evidence of my own eyes. "Wasn't any of it real, Oliver," I pleaded, "any of it?"

He shrugged. "The rebels won. That bit was true. There's a new socialist President and if you look closely enough you might be able to find some difference between him and the one we executed, though I can't see it myself. But we did win. And I did fight with the rebels. In fact I became a very dangerous man. A man who doesn't care whether he lives or dies. A man like that is a formidable soldier. I set myself the task that I would kill ten state soldiers for every one that had raped Eva. That came to forty. In fact I reached a score of fifty-one, a bonus of eleven. I was very pleased with that."

"You make it sound... like a game," I whispered.

"Oh it is. It's our national sport. Every few years we wipe out half the country's population in a competition to determine which dictator we want to live under. It gives us something to do in the long winter evenings. I understand we're almost ready for the next one. There's an armed movement starting up again, against the new President… whoever he is. Difficult to remember." He paused. "But anyway, I've retired now. Just waiting to die. I took a good many wounds, finally took one through the spine. I'm a sort of a national hero, you know. I have a military pension to live on… not much, but more than a lot of people around here."

"This is… insane," I rasped lamely.

"Yes. Completely insane. I couldn't agree more. So I want you to promise me something." His tone became more serious. "I want you to promise me that when you get back to London you won't say anything about this. This isn't real. You're having a bad dream. Reality is the place where the good guys win, where young idealists make the world a better place. Where all the clichés come true. Tell them I said so. They'll believe you if you tell them I said so."

"A' course I know ye!" The Rainbow Man protested loud-
ly. "I know ye better than I know meself. But then, I sup-
pose I know everybody better than I know meself."

Cinderella's Slipper

The mourners have left my mother's house. I stare for a
while at the debris of beer cans and uneaten sandwiches and
the little stack of condolence telegrams on the kitchen table,
the coffee mugs and glasses piled in the sink, then walk
through to the lounge. Tasteful floral remembrance cards
with black borders are arranged along the mantelpiece and
on the table a bouquet of white lilies still tight in its presen-
tation wrapper waits to be put in water. I select my mother's
finest chair, the one reserved for important guests, and sit
back to think.

I find it hard to reach my own feelings. In the morning
I must return to England and my other life. How many years
has it been since I even visited here, the back-street Belfast
house where I was born and passed the first two decades of
my life?

My mind is dragged to the practicalities. Death Certifi-
cates and Letters of Administration. Disposal of her house
and her modest savings. Making sure everybody has been
informed. Is there anything I have forgotten? I try to pull
myself back to where I am, to what I am feeling right now.

This doesn't seem like a part of me any more. For over
twenty years I have worked on becoming somebody else,
somebody educated, middle class, a speaker of standard
English, able to move amongst the intelligentsia of
London's self appointed artistic elite. I remember the times
when I have tried to steer the conversation away from

everything that this house represents. I belong in this chair now. It is where my mother would have asked me to sit. I feel like a traitor to my own roots, an impostor attending my mother's funeral in disguise, with a false beard and a patch over one eye. Which of them is really me, I wonder? Have I become that which I have aped?

I make my way upstairs, to the room that was once my bedroom. Dust particles dance in the narrow shaft of sunlight streaming in where the heavy curtains don't quite meet. In the bottom of the wardrobe is a cardboard box filled with the things I owned when I left home, things my mother would never throw out. The bric-a-brac of my teenage years. I pull it out now and lift the objects on to the bed one by one.

Copies of the school magazine, photographs, a penknife, an Airfix model of a Russian Mig fighter, a plastic telescope, a pile of old vinyl records, a box containing medals won for the high jump at the school Sports Day. I was light and had very long legs back then. A single blue plastic beach shoe. How strange, I've no memory of it, I'm certain I didn't put it there. It isn't very big – it would never have fitted me. Where did it come from? What on earth would I have kept it for? Suddenly a numbness enters my stomach and the memories leap up before me.

I am leaning on the railing of the deck of The Manxman, a barely seaworthy rusting passenger vessel that operates a shuttle service for holidaymakers between Belfast and Douglas, Isle of Man. It is a glorious July morning and the little Manx seaport is rising up before me, sparkling in the sunlight like an illustration from a book of fairytales. I am vaguely apprehensive because this time I have come alone, and the Isle of Man seems almost "abroad", a place of limitless potential without parents or teachers or busybodys who know me to report back if I step out of line. Coming here is a brave, perhaps reckless thing to do. I feel a welling up of a sense of freedom and infinite possibilities. I seem to be standing for the first time on the brink of the adult world. Behind me families push forward, eager to watch the tying-up at the quay, eager to be among the first to disembark, dispose of bags and suitcases and stake out their spot on the beach. Children chatter excitedly to their parents, try to elicit promises of visits to the fairground or the Witches' Museum or boat trips in the days to come.

I turn around and find myself looking straight into the face of a girl slightly younger than myself with long straight black hair. She is wearing a skimpy almost see-through yellow summer dress and has a small rucksack over one shoulder. She smiles back at me. I feel my heart flutter and a lump come to the back of my throat. A great wave of tenderness passes through my body. In my sixteen years on the planet I have never seen a human face as beautiful as this, have never been affected by somebody in this way. I stare, tongue-tied and motionless. She is with her parents, seemingly she is their only daughter, and, horror of horrors, her father is wearing a clerical dog-collar. She giggles at me and I drag my eyes away from hers. I discover that I am shaking and my vision has become a little blurred. Also that a purpose has entered my life.

Time has passed. I am lying on a thin foam-rubber mattress inside a small ridge tent pitched in a sandy hollow a little way back from the beach at Ramsey on the north east coast of the island. The girl with the long back hair is in my arms and the skimpy yellow dress is by our feet, together with a pair of blue plastic beach sandals. It has been the most amazing day of my life and I am exhausted and totally besotted. My head is swimming and I am fighting to retain consciousness. "You've never done that before," she whispers, "have you?"

"What? Of course I..." there seems no point in the lie. "No. Never. It was fantastic. Unbelievable. We can do it again, can't we? I never want you to go away. For the rest of my life. You'll always be with me... Won't you?"

She seems to consider the question. "The rest of your life? That sounds like a long time."

"I don't want anybody but you... Ever. I don't care if you're pregnant or..."

"Pregnant! Do you think I'm a fool?" She strokes my face. "Listen, you're nice, okay? Really nice. But I'm going home tomorrow, and I've already got a boyfriend. He would make mincemeat out of you if he knew what we've been up to."

My eyes widen. This just can't be happening. She's even younger than I am, how can she have a boyfriend? How can she make love to me like that, drive me insane with pleasure, if she hasn't the same feelings for me that I have for her? How could somebody so beautiful and loving and wonderful hurt me like this?

I sit up and watch in numbed silence as she dresses. She slips on her swimming costume and bundles her dress and the rest of her things into her beach bag. "I've got to go now," she says cheerfully, "Dad might get suspicious. Maybe I'll see you again before we leave."

Suddenly the tent is empty. In my shocked state I haven't even said goodbye. I sit there for a long time before I rummage around for my own clothes and start to put them on. As I clear up the groundsheet of the tent I find that single plastic beach sandal. Its owner I never find again.

In those few moments, without knowing it, I have learned several profound lessons. Expectations and long term patterns of behaviour have been laid down. I have learned that my love for women is fated to be unrequited. I am acceptable for a short term holiday fling or its equivalent but as long term boyfriend material I have been tried and found wanting. A real boyfriend would make mincemeat out of me. I will always occupy second place or lower in the affections of the beautiful. I should be grateful to make the list at all. My status is assigned as that of lightweight summer diversion. I must make no demands, I must be grateful for any crumbs that may come my way. In the romantic stakes I categorize myself as an also-ran.

As I remember that summer day so long ago, I have a daydream. Superimposed on the face of the girl in the yellow dress, one by one, I see the face of every woman I have ever thought that I loved.

As I sit on my old bed in my mother's house I try to remember what I did with the sandal, so much time has passed it is an enormous effort of memory. I have a dim recollection of my mother coming across it in my luggage as we unpack. A half remembered conversation.

"Whose shoe is this?"

"Nobody's Mum. Throw it in the bin." She looks at me, says nothing, takes the shoe away.

"Your parting gift to me, Mother," I whisper, turning it over in my hand. The crystal slipper of Cinderella. Whomsoever this slipper fits... I put my fingers inside it. A spell seems to have been broken. I smile without knowing why. There seems to be somebody else in the room.

"The false beard and the eye patch never did fool you, did they Mother?"

"Personally I prefer the broadsheets to the tabloids," The Rainbow Man explained. "A single sheet a' one a' them'll wrap right around ye, from yer front to yer back."

Services to the Community

"Didn't work out for you in Dublin, then?"

She winced at the old man's negativity. "Dublin was fine, Mr Singer. Great. But I was there to train. To get my degree. I wasn't there to work. You don't just walk straight into a job on a national daily..." As you know better than I do, she almost added, but stopped herself in time.

"Damn right you don't. Thirty-eight years I've been in this profession, come April, and I'm still on the same paper I started on, even if I am the editor. So you'd like to come and slum it for a while, back in your old home town. Use *The Eagle* as a stepping stone to greater things."

"I didn't say that, Mr Singer. I don't know where I'll be in the future. I just know that I need a job in the industry right now."

He stopped fidgeting with the microphone of his ancient dictating machine and looked her straight in the eye. "You seem like a sensible enough girl. And young people aren't exactly queuing up to work on *The Eagle*."

"You'll give me a job then, Sir?"

"I'll give you a chance. I'll take you on for one week, let you try one assignment. That was the way I started myself on *The Eagle*. The way we all started. When I see what you can do, then we'll have a serious talk. I'll pay you for the week, win or lose, so to speak. Does that sound fair?" She nodded her approval. "You see, Evi, working on a paper like this, it isn't a degree in Media Studies that you need. It's

135

other things. If I was to ask you what those other things might be, what would you say?"

She thought for a moment. "I would say that what you need most of all is to know who you're writing for. What their interests and concerns are."

"Damn good answer, Evi! Took me a long time to learn that. You might have a future in this profession after all."

He rifled through the papers on his desk and fished out a large brown envelope with the name "Dr Liam Merryfield" scribbled on the front. "Do you know Dr Merryfield?" he asked as he handed it to her.

"Oh yes. He was our family doctor all my life. I think he delivered me."

"Well, old Merryfield is retiring at the end of next week. There's going to be a ceremony at the Town Hall, the Mayor is going to present him with something or other. Now Merryfield is exactly what you said, he's a local personality, somebody people know and care about. I want to run a special feature on him to mark his retirement. I don't just want a CV, where he qualified and what year he got married and all that. I've got that already, it's in the envelope. I want to know who Liam Merryfield really is. Do you know what I'm talking about?"

"Yes, Sir. I think so."

"All right. Prove it. You've got twenty column inches. That's just under twelve hundred words. I want it on my desk by eleven AM this day week. Think you can do it?"

"I know I can do it."

"Okay. There's just one other thing. I don't want Merryfield to know this is coming out. I want it to be a surprise. So if you talk to him, don't let him know what you're up to."

At the newsagent's shop across the road from her mother's house, Evi bought a school exercise book. She chose one that fitted comfortably inside the brown envelope. On its cover she wrote the words: "Dr Liam Merryfield" and underneath, on impulse "Services to the Community". That would keep her mind on the theme she wanted for her article. She drove her ageing blue Fiesta the few hundred yards that she would normally have walked to the other side of the town square and parked across the road from the front entrance to Dr Merryfield's surgery. She felt a little thrill of excitement as she pulled on the handbrake. She was a reporter, and she was working under cover. It was what she had always dreamed about. Maybe this wasn't the most glamorous assignment she could have imagined for herself but it was a beginning.

She watched his surgery door silently for a few minutes. It was a rented business premises, she knew. Dr Merryfield's private residence was many miles beyond the town boundary, among pleasant meadows on the fringe of the National Park. But today he was at work, as the half open doorway announced, and the somewhat dusty black Mercedes parked nearby confirmed.

She watched as a young woman with a baby in a pushchair arrived and vanished through the doorway. Evi had already thought of a good excuse to see him. The doctor at the Student Medical Centre in Dublin had put her on the birth control pill and now that she was home she would need a prescription from her own doctor to continue with it. The Pill was still a sensitive issue in Ireland and Dr Merryfield's attitude to such a request could be quite revealing.

Merryfield was still writing up the notes for the previous patient as she entered his dark little office and sat down. He bundled the sheets back into their manila envelope and smiled up at her with obvious pleasure, fixing her with a keen eye-contact that was almost embarrassing . "Hello Evi.

You haven't been to see me for a long time. Are you back with us for good?" Enthusiastic though the greeting was she could sense beneath his smile an underlying strain. She hadn't seen him for a long time, he looked older than she had expected, but there was a reassuring quality about his face that she remembered from her early childhood.

"Well, yes. For the time being. I've got a job on *The Eagle*. Or I might have"

"Working for Tom Singer? I don't envy you that. What can I do for you then?"

She felt guilty as she explained to him about the University doctor and the prescription for the Pill. It wasn't embarrassment about the topic of birth control, but about the mild deception she was perpetrating. Merryfield just nodded as she finished her speech and asked her to roll up her left sleeve. "The contraceptive pill isn't recommended if you have raised blood pressure," he explained pleasantly. He held her wrist almost tenderly, she thought, as he operated his old-fashioned measuring instrument.

So that was it. No moral lecture. No questions about did she or didn't she have a boyfriend. He gave her the prescription without demur and said that he hoped her mother and family were all well. She left feeling something of a fraud, but warmly disp towards the subject of her investigations. As she passed the receptionist's desk she noted the surgery closing time: six o'clock.

Sitting in the car she took out the exercise book and wrote: "Dr Merryfield enjoys the confidence of his younger patients thanks to his tolerant and non-judgmental approach to the diversity of present-day lifestyles." If it turned out to be wrong she could always change it later.

To kill the time until six o'clock Evi went back to the offices of *The Eagle*, and, feeling every inch the professional, started going through the archives to see what the paper had said about Merryfield in the past. Mr Singer emerged from his office once during the afternoon, glanced at what she was doing and nodded his approval.

Time dragged. There was nothing of any significance in the archives as far as she could tell. She made a few notes: he played golf in his spare time, he went to the Mullingar races. His wife had left him many years ago, his family was grown-up. There didn't seem to be a woman in his life, although he had been pictured with someone at a charity dinner. Evi took a note of her name. It was almost three years ago, if there had ever been a relationship it might well be over, but at least it was something. It hinted at the notion that the man was three dimensional, that he had some kind of existence beyond the doors of his surgery.

It was to these doors that Evi returned just before six o'clock, parking in the same spot to watch him leave carrying a small traditional black medical bag. He seemed to be deep in thought as he made his way to the dusty old Mercedes. Although he glanced once in her direction she was fairly sure he hadn't suspected anything. She waited for his car to move off and followed at a discreet distance.

Dr Merryfield drove slowly and soberly to his impressive country home and parked in the spacious driveway. Evi knew that she needed to be careful if she wanted to avoid arousing suspicion so she continued past the house and parked around the next corner, returning quickly on foot to a vantage point in the darkness of the tall hedge that lined the road opposite his gates. The daylight had almost faded and the chances that he would notice her slight figure in the shadows seemed remote.

She had no difficulty seeing where he was because all the front curtains were open and the lights were on. He had gone to an upper room which looked like an office or den of some kind, and she saw him lift an object on to a small table and sit motionless for a long time, staring at it. She wasn't certain, but it seemed to be the medical bag. After what felt like an age he got up, turned and pulled the curtains. As he did this he seemed to look straight in her direction and she feared that he might have seen her, then the curtains were across and the instant had passed.

"Poor old Merryfield," Aiden joked on the slightly fractured cell phone link from Dublin, "can't even sit down and rest after a hard day's work without a prowler doing the peeping tom bit."

"No, honestly, Aiden, this was nothing normal. You don't just sit in a chair and stare at a bag for hours on end. It was totally creepy."

"How do you know he was staring at the bag? How do you know he was on his own? He might have been having a conversation with a visitor. He might have been playing chess. He might be a classical music buff, listening to a symphony on the hi-fi. You've no idea what was going on. You just saw a man sitting on a chair. Big deal."

"I thought you would be interested, Aiden. I thought you would be supportive. I thought you would be a bit more help than this."

"Aw, come on sweetheart! Don't be mad at me. I'm just trying to bring you back to earth. You've got your first assignment and you want drama. The job isn't like that. There isn't any drama. It's hard slog, talking to people, finding things out. Little by little, inch by inch. Building up the story, one brick at a time. You're doing fine. Talk to the people who know him next. What about his ex-wife? His receptionist maybe? The woman at the charity dinner? The guys at the golf club? You're only beginning, Evi. You haven't got anything yet. Don't kid yourself. Okay?"

She sighed. "Okay Aiden. When are you coming down then?"

"That's more like my Evi. Not this weekend but maybe next. Best I can do."

"We can go to this retirement ceremony together then."

"You're obsessed, you know that? Great to be young and keen. You'll go far."

Evi slipped in quietly by the front door and found her Mum sitting alone in the lounge, her head bowed in a reflective reverie that seemed an eerie echo of Dr Merryfield's motionless pose of the night before. "Are you okay, Mum?" she asked anxiously.

"Of course I am, dear, I was just having a little rest... and thinking." She smiled self-consciously, as though to set her daughter's mind at rest.

"Do you do that often? I mean, just sit on your own and think?"

"What a strange question..."

"It's just that I saw Merryfield do that. Just sit and sit... and it reminded me of Dad... before the end..."

"Goodness, what morbid thoughts you have Evi. I was just resting, I'd been doing a bit of ironing in the kitchen. What made you think of your father?"

"It's this assignment. Dr Merryfield. I have a bad feeling about him. I can't get it out of my head."

"Because you saw him sitting down and thinking? Goodness dear, he's just coming up to retirement. He's probably in that frame of mind where you sit down and look back at your life and wonder where all the years went, and why you let so many opportunities slip by. You wouldn't understand, Evi. You aren't old enough."

She felt foolish and smiled. "Yes, I suppose so. There isn't anything you can tell me about him, is there?"

She considered the question. "We've never been personal friends. Didn't move in the same circles. But any time I had any dealings with him he was very pleasant and kind. He went out of his way to see that I was alright when your father... died."

Evi nodded. "That's what everybody says about him. That he's very kind and pleasant."

"Then maybe it's true. There was just one little thing..."

"Yes, Mum?"

"Well, this is probably me being foolish, but once or twice, I thought he... well, that he didn't quite keep his professional distance like you would expect him to. No, forget that, it's just my imagination."

Evi smiled. "Come on Mum. I'm a news hound now. I need every little thing you can tell me."

"Oh, it's silly, but when I was going through all that awful stuff with your father, he sort of comforted me a few times. Held my hand. Patted me on the back. It was probably what I needed but it felt... a little bit odd, somehow..."

"I think he's a bit clumsy socially. That was what the woman at the charity dinner said. She only went out with him once and she felt awkward all evening. The men at the golf club didn't have much to say either. His receptionist was even worse, she wouldn't say anything, as if she was being protective or something. Everybody speaks quite highly of him but nobody seems to know him any better than you do."

"He's probably just a quiet man who keeps himself to himself. Not everyone wants to surround themselves with other people and socialise. Some people like their own company. There probably isn't very much to say about him. That's going to make your job very hard, isn't it?"

Evi shook her head. "I don't believe that anybody is that simple and straightforward. I certainly don't believe that *he* is. I'll get there. I'll find out who he really is."

"I'm sure you will, dear. Poor Dr Merryfield!"

"Aiden? Good news, I think. We might be able to get together this weekend after all. I have to go up to Dublin today. I'm just getting a few things packed in a bag right now."

"How come?"

"Merryfield's ex-wife lives there, and she's agreed to see me."

"Still on the Merryfield thing then. Have you got anything worth printing yet?"

"Not really, but his wife should be a good contact. My mum agrees with you about that sitting and staring business. Says I'm daft."

"A very intelligent woman."

Mrs Brewster, formerly Mrs Merryfield, sipped her lemon tea at the dimly-lit corner table of Bewleys Cafe in Grafton Street and smiled pleasantly at Evi. "You want to know what he was like?" She seemed amused by the question.

"If you don't mind me being... inquisitive," Evi urged.

"Och, I don't mind at all. He was a quiet, hidden sort of man. Very bound up in his job, and very good at it I think. You never really knew what was going on with him when he was away from the house. He loved his work. It seemed to be all that he thought about... He was okay as a father... a bit distant... I don't know what to tell you about him really."

"Would you say, he was more involved with his patients than with his home life?"

"Involved with his patients? There's two ways you could take that, isn't there?"

Evi could see that she had struck a nerve. Instinctively she said nothing but waited for the woman to go on.

"There's something I could tell you woman to woman," she said quietly, "but you would have to promise not to print it."

"On my word of honour."

"It's just that... he used to have fantasies... about women. Nothing nasty or anything, but he used to get obsessed with a woman every now and again... the woman who served him in the Post Office maybe, or somebody he saw on TV, or even a patient. That was really the thing I couldn't stand about him. He would sing the praises of other women to me, as if I should be interested, or pleased even. It was all inside his head, nothing ever came of it, but I had to put up with it, pretend I didn't mind... I felt... degraded by it. It was unnatural. Beyond the pale. A kind of teenage infatuation thing that he used to go through... but it didn't get better as he got older. It got much worse. There. I've told you now. I didn't think I would, but it's good to tell someone. I've never told a soul, and my own family used to try to blame me and make me feel guilty for leaving him. As if I was walking out on some kind of plaster saint. Liam Merryfield was no saint. Not inside his head he wasn't."

"We couldn't print something like that anyway," Evi said quietly, "but it was kind of you to tell me. I feel I know him a lot better now. I'm only doing a light piece. A kind of tribute on his retirement."

"Retirement?"

"Yes. Didn't you know he was retiring?"

"Why would he do that?"

"Why would he do it? Sorry, I don't follow you. Isn't he retirement age?"

"Well, no... not for two or three years, I think."

Evi stared. "Are you sure about that?"

"Well, I was married to him for fifteen years. I do know his date of birth!"

"Aiden? It's me. Listen, I think I may be on to something at last. Why would a doctor retire three years before he had to? One that loved his job?"

"Is this a trick question? Well... maybe because his own health was breaking down. Or maybe... because... oh, I don't know. Maybe because he was up on some criminal charge... or some professional disciplinary thing. You're in Dublin, why don't you go and scratch around at the Irish Medical Associationl offices in Rathmines Road, see if you can come up with something there."

Evi turned her charm to full power and blinked in a helpless female sort of way at the polished young clerk across the desk. "I understand that the Medical Register exists for the protection of patients, not doctors."

"That's perfectly true, Miss."

"And all I'm asking is, do you think it's a good idea to remain in his care? Is there anything I should know about him?"

"I'm not trying to be evasive, but I really have told you all that is permissible... ethically, I mean. His papers have been temporarily removed from the files. All that I've got is a place-keeper card, as we call them, telling me that he is at present registered with us and entitled to practice medicine in the Republic of Ireland. It would be completely unethical for me to speculate about why papers have been removed. And you shouldn't jump to any conclusions yourself. Papers are removed for all kinds of reasons. It might be nothing more than a change of address that he's recently reported or any other kind of minor correction or updating. And even if there were some kind of disciplinary proceedings in the pipeline it would be very wrong to make an assumption that the complaint or complaints were going to be upheld. In many cases complaints turn out to be completely groundless, and the doctor involved is entirely exonerated. The last thing you want to do, Miss, is start jumping to conclusions."

She flicked her long eyelashes again. "Look, I'm just asking you off the record... as the nice kind man that I can see you are... do you think I should stay on his list?"

He lowered his voice and smiled awkwardly. "If there is another practitioner nearby, and it's no inconvenience, maybe you should look elsewhere..."

She lowered her tone to match his. "Can I ask you one more question? Something completely hypothetical?" She gave him her sweetest smile and he returned it awkwardly. "If a doctor retired, would they bother continuing with a disciplinary hearing?"

"Oh, very much so. Retirement doesn't mean a thing. A doctor could retire today and come out of retirement again tomorrow. Or he could keep on some private patients after he retired. Most of them do. We are here to assess a man's suitability and competence to practice medicine. Like you said, we represent the interests of patients. Retirement doesn't enter into it."

"So you would go ahead with the case. No matter what."

"If he was alive at all, we would go ahead with the case."

"If... he was alive at all..." A terrible image suddenly entered Evi's mind. Old Dr Merryfield sitting on the chair staring at the medical bag. Then he reaches out and opens it...

Evi's heart was pounding as she came to the end of her mad dash from Dublin and drew level with the gates of Liam Merryfield's country house. The front courtyard was blocked by two white-and-orange Garda cars and there was an emergency ambulance parked clumsily awry across the driveway. She slowed the Fiesta to a walking pace and drew to a momentary stop beside the young officer who stood sentry at the gate. She wound down the window and said: "I'm Evi, the one who phoned the Guards. My hunch was right, wasn't it?"

He came close before he replied so as not to shout it out. "I'm afraid so, Miss. It looks like some kind of drug overdose."

"Were they... in time?"

The officer shook his head. "We'll need you to make a statement..."

"Later," she cut him off and accelerated onwards towards the town.

Closing time had long gone and there was only one person still working at *The Eagle*. She threw open the door of Tom Singer's office and flung the brown envelope down on top of what he was writing. "You used me," she spat out in a voice that surprised even herself, "You harassed a good man to death, and you used me to do it!"

He moved the envelope to one side and looked up. "Sit down, Evi," he said quietly. She remained standing.

"You knew exactly how he was going to react when I started poking around. You drove a man to suicide and you used me to do it. You're a monster. You're a monster and I don't know why you did it!"

Singer paused to consider his words. "It's true. I did use you in a way. I used you to get a message across to Liam Merryfield. You see, Evi, I may not have a degree in Media Studies but I do understand the media. Merryfield didn't understand the kind of world he was living in. He thought he could retire, go and live in Dublin or Cork or god-knows-where and nobody would be any the wiser. But he was wrong."

The old newsman pulled himself stiffly to his feet and motioned Evi to join him at the tiny dirty window that looked out over the town square. "Look out there. You think you see a quiet little Irish town where nobody knows what's going on in the next parish let alone the next continent. But that's not true. What's out there is an ocean, Evi. An ocean of information. Data-bases, fax machines, e-mail, the Internet, mobile phones, surveillance cameras, satellite communications... there is no such thing as a secret any more. If somebody wants to find something out, they will. Every two-bit newsman on every little backwater rag like this one has contacts. Even you. Your boyfriend is Aiden Kerr of *The Irish Chronicle*. You didn't think I knew that, did you? The point is, in this business everybody knows everything that they want to know. We're all swimming in the same ocean."

He turned from the window. "Liam Merryfield made one mistake. A moment of weakness and stupidity with a female patient. From that point onward it didn't matter what he did or where he went. Even if the complaint wasn't upheld, his whole lifetime of service to this community became worthless, was turned into nothing in those few seconds. All that I did," he looked her in the eye, "and yes, I did it through you, was to show him that he had a choice." He sat down again and she waited for him to go on. "I won't say I knew Liam Merryfield, I don't think anybody did, but I understood him. Because we weren't as different as you might think. There was only one thing that he ever wanted to do, only one thing that ever mattered to him. He wanted to be a good doctor. That was all, nothing more. And if that was going to be taken away and his whole life ridiculed and dragged through the gutter, then maybe he would prefer to take the only other option that he had. All that I did was to make the position clear. It was his choice, not yours and not mine, and I believe that a man ought to have that choice. I don't apologize for what I did."

Evi's voice when she spoke had become reduced to a whisper. "So you've saved him from himself. You've turned him into a saint. A dead saint. I don't think I want to be a member of your profession, Mr Singer."

"How do you think he would want to be remembered, Evi? How would you want to be remembered if you were in his place? As a man who devoted himself selflessly to this community for thirty-three years and took his own life in a moment of depression, or as a man who made a pass at the wrong woman patient and then tried to run away and cover it up? I know which I would choose." He motioned Evi to sit down and this time she did, her jaw trembling and her eyes beginning to mist up with unshed tears. "What I did wasn't irresponsible journalism. What would have been irresponsible would have been for me to print everything I knew. I could have crucified Merryfield. I didn't do that because there are other considerations in this profession besides feeding people's lowest curiosity. We create and maintain this community's picture of itself. That means something."

Evi opened her mouth to speak but the words wouldn't come.

"Now stop talking about leaving this profession. You couldn't anyway, even if you tried. I can see it in your eyes. It's like looking into a mirror. Take a clean sheet of paper and help me to write Liam Merryfield's obituary."

"Ye know your trouble?" The Rainbow Man offered help-fully. "Ye don't take yer chances when ye get them. If ye don't take yer chances when ye get them ye'v nobody to blame but yerself."

Muskie's Big Break

It was so early in the morning that the only creatures awake on Euston Road were the pigeons, the trench-coated traffic wardens, and a small group of Japanese tourists who had misunderstood the time difference between Osaka and London Heathrow. Standing now in total bewilderment on the frosty pavement, they rubbed the backs of their hands to keep them from turning blue and made futile attempts to button-up wholly inadequate overcoats that were already as tightly buttoned-up as they would go.

Muskie spread out his blanket under the poster that had come to dominate his thoughts in recent weeks: ten feet tall and twenty long, the image of the most beautiful girl in the world straddled the full width of the steel archway above the northern entrance to Euston Underground. Reclining on the grass amid a tumult of multi-coloured flowers, her long straight raven-black hair poured over her bare shoulders with a calculated casualness. Her soft, vulnerable, totally adorable dark brown eyes peered down at him with an expression of tenderness and a willingness to please that made his knees buckle if he looked at her face for more than a few seconds. Her flimsy cream dress offered only a token concealment to the perfection of the curves that formed her flawless slim figure. This was Muskie's goddess, the earthly manifestation of the cosmic principle of beauty itself. It made his heart ache to remember that in the distant past he had many times held her in his arms, and she had satisfied the full hurricane of his passion throughout endless blissful nights of soft endearments and sweaty copulation. Who would ever believe it now? He was not sure that he believed it himself. And yet it had happened.

Muskie stepped out into the street to read for the millionth time the words beneath the picture : "Clare Hanson's new album *Songs of Innocence* – Available in shops from October 25th – Clare Hanson's UK tour begins November 29th – see her in London, Manchester, Newcastle..." The list went on and on, and in small print beside each venue was a set of dates. London, the first one on the list, had been allocated a two-week slot, which started in two day's time.

Turning around and forcing his gaze away from the poster, nodding to the shivering tourists who were still loitering uncertainly near the station exit, he carefully positioned the upturned trilby hat on the pavement beside him and pulled the cloth cover off his guitar. He had staked out his position for the morning. After blowing into his fists with a breath rendered perfectly visible by the frosty air, he performed his ritual cold-weather finger-exercise which involved bending and flexing every joint in a rhythmic, wave-like pattern to get the blood flowing. Content that he was receiving some neural feedback from these extremities he struck-up his first tune of the day. Muskie never planned his programme of songs, he just let his fingers choose, or at least that was the explanation he always gave if anybody asked. This time his fingers chose a rather depressing Appalachian folk song of doomed love. He let the story seep into his thoughts, the faultless beauty of the young girl, the tenderness and purity of the love he bore her, followed by the disbelief at her cruel betrayal:

Way down in yonder shady grove
A man of high degree
Conversing with my Flora there –
It seemed so strange to me.
And the answer that she gave to him
it sore did me oppress.
I was betrayed by Flora –
The lily of the West...

He didn't make it to the knife-play, the trial and the love that still persisted as the doomed man brooded in the condemned cell. Muskie's eyes filled with tears. He stopped playing and leaned the guitar on the wall beside him. Two of the Japanese tourists applauded politely. Stupid fingers, he thought, imagine choosing something like that.

The first trickle of early-morning commuters began to spill out of the station exit. One or two of them cast him odd sidewise glances as they passed. Muskie dried his eyes discreetly on the backs of his hands, rubbed his fingers together briskly to bring them back to life, and retrieved the guitar. This time his fingers had the good sense to choose something more distanced from his personal situation. It was the solo guitar version of "California Dreaming".

As the flow of early commuters from the station increased slightly he continued through the more cheerful part of his repertoire, never daring to settle on anything by Leonard Cohen or the younger Paul Simon, and most definitely nothing that he had written himself since the ghost of his poster-girl haunted all of those. John Lennon's "Imagine" was the most sentimental number that he was willing to risk. Before too long he had completely regained his composure and prised his mind off the past. Now all that he was experiencing was the familiar illusion of invisibility as the endless line of shop and office workers hurried by seemingly oblivious of his existence. The hat remained stubbornly empty.

After the particularly demanding virtuoso ending of "House of the Rising Sun" he paused and indulged in a moment of self-pity. He was getting too old for this kind of thing, he told himself, it wasn't working out. It was high time he did something with his life. Something. But what?

As he thought these thoughts with bowed head he became aware that he was staring down at a particularly well-polished pair of black leather business-shoes, above which the legs of a very clean and elegantly-tailored pair of dark blue trousers rose upwards and out of shot. He lifted his head and found that he was looking into the face of a Man of Importance. You could tell that he was important from the fact that his shirt was light blue and clean and crisp and his tie coordinated with it perfectly in a tasteful pattern of interlocking blue and grey chevrons. From the fact that he had dark well-tended sideburns and a tiny goatee beard at the bottom of his immaculately shaved chin you could tell that he had half-formed Bohemian aspirations and was almost certainly connected in some way with the entertainment industry. He was staring at Muskie in a way that was difficult to interpret. It seemed to contain elements of curiosity, disgust, and most notably, superiority. He met Muskie's eyes for a substantial fraction of a minute before he said anything.

"Are you the one they call the Musk-Rat?" he inquired, obviously trying hard to conceal his distaste.

"Friends call me Muskie."

"Indeed. I have a communication for you." The man took a sealed letter from his inside jacket pocket and flicked it casually into Muskie's empty hat. The contempt contained in the gesture was not lost on Muskie. "I suggest you read it…" he was obviously about to add "If you *can* read" but thought better of it. "You might find something in it to your advantage."

Without another word the man turned and disappeared back into Euston Underground. Muskie watched him out of sight before he lifted the hat and its contents. He lowered himself into a seated position on the blanket and picked up the envelope. It was a delicate pastel yellow in colour, and to his considerable surprise it appeared to be scented. The scent was familiar, but he hadn't smelled it for a very long time.

Muskie hovered nervously along with the wives, girlfriends and children in the anteroom to the prison-visiting suite. He seemed to be the only adult male visitor in the group. It made him feel conspicuous and started him worrying about whether or not he was respectably dressed. Muskie possessed two pairs of jeans, one pair of grey trousers, two long-sleeved T-shirts and two short-sleeved ones, so he did not have a wide choice of apparel for the more formal occasions. The room was over-heated by a large old-fashioned steel radiator and lacked ventilation so that little rivulets of condensed moisture ran down the insides of the windows and obscured the fields outside. The air smelled stale and carried traces of a mixture of perfumes and ill-concealed body odours. He was pleased when the metal inner door was opened by a stern-faced uniformed guard.

"You've got forty minutes," he announced without emotion, "you will be told when the last five minutes begins. Please leave the visiting area promptly when requested to do so."

They filed in and Muskie took his place where an enormous overweight man with perfectly round brass-rimmed spectacles and a stubbly blond beard perched uncomfortably on the edge of a metal chair too small to hold him. He waved his hand in salute as Muskie came up to the grille. "Muskie, man, good to see you!"

"Good to see you too, Elk, How've you been keeping?"

"Okay. Putting on a bit of weight. Keeping my contacts active. Trying to hold the business together from in here. It ain't easy, you know, Muskie."

"No, I don't suppose it is," Muskie mused.

"Have you brought me anything, Muskie?" he asked in a more subdued tone.

"Sort of," Muskie confided, taking a printed flyer out of his coat pocket and carefully unfolding it. He took it over to the window where the guard sat and asked him to hand it along to the Elk, which he did. The Elk looked down at it and his eyes seemed to mist over. "Remember Angel?" Muskie asked softly.

"Remember Angel? Are you kidding? What do you think goes through my head all the time in here? Do I remember Angel!" He looked at the picture and read the words on the little pamphlet. "Holy cow! She's as beautiful as ever, isn't she Muskie?"

"She'll always be beautiful. It comes from inside."

"Wise words, Muskie, wise words. I'd give a lot to get to one of those concerts, you know that? A lot."

"I know. But I think it's going to be a bit difficult, don't you? If I get to talk to her I'll make your apologies, tell her you had a previous engagement."

The Elk looked serious. "You might get to talk to her? Gee! That would be really something. Really something." His expression became serious. "Muskie, I hope you didn't feel bad about the nights Angel spent with me. It didn't mean that she loved you any less, you know that, don't you? She just had… carnal needs. That was it. Unusual carnal needs."

Muskie considered the theory. "Yeah. Guess so. It wasn't so much that the needs themselves were unusual, she just seemed to have more of them than a lot of other people."

"Yeah. That's it. I'm glad you don't feel bad about it. You shouldn't, you know. She wasn't just banging me, that would have been infidelity. She was banging her two flat mates, the TV repair guy, the grocery clerk at the end of the road, the Asian guy in the petrol-filling station..."

"Yeah, yeah, you don't have to go on. I know all that. It didn't bother me. Not really. But when she became the mascot for that Canadian hockey team and wanted to spend the winter in Calgary, well I began to think, is this really a meaningful relationship that I've got with this lady? I mean, that was pushing the envelope a bit, don't you think?"

"Oh yeah. Those guys. I remember them. The trainer didn't want her to go, you know. Said the guys were getting exhausted and skipping training. Last I heard they were still sending her free season-tickets every year..."

"Elk, I don't want to go over all that again. It still hurts a bit, you know? I want to get your advice about something else."

The Elk looked serious, and, in so far as he was able, paternal.

"Any time, Muskie, what can I do for you?"

Muskie took Angel's letter out of the same coat pocket, smoothed it out very carefully and sniffed the envelope one more time before he handed it to the guard. "I'm supposed to read this before I pass it on," the guard announced with an air of mild boredom.

"Can if you like," Muskie replied in a similar tone. It was the right answer. The guard instantly passed the letter down to the Elk, who read it avidly.

"That's bloody brilliant!" the Elk declared, "bloody brilliant! You're one lucky son-of-a-bitch!"

"You think I should go then?"

"You're kidding me! Of course you should go! Why on earth would you not go?"

"Well, I don't know, Elk. It could open up a lot of old wounds. I mean, I never stopped… thinking about her…and feeling things for her… I don't know how I would be if I had to meet her again and talk to her…"

"Muskie, you're crazy! This is your big break. It might never happen again. You've got an interview on national radio, a chance to sing two songs (both of which you will be paid for) a chance to get your name publicly linked with Clare Hanson… Do you know how many copies her albums sell?"

"Yeah. I guess. But you know me better than anybody else, Elk. Do you think I can do it? Do you think I have enough control not to break down in a situation like that? Be honest."

The Elk looked him squarely in the eyes. "Muskie, you and me, life hasn't treated us all that well, has it? We've tried, real hard. We've been kicked down and we've fought our way up again, because there was nothing else for us to do. But every time we get kicked down it's just that little bit harder to stand up again, ain't it? You know what I mean? Of course you do. But now you've been given a chance. A real, solid chance to make something of yourself. National radio. TV people listening. Clare Hanson's agent and guys from her recording company sitting right there in the studio listening to every note you play. And you want to know if you should go through with it? Muskie, this is it. This is your moment. You have to give it every last thing that you've got, and then some. I'm going to be listening, Muskie, and I want you to make me proud of you. Will you do that for me?"

Muskie had polished his black shoes and attempted, with limited success, to iron his only pair of grey trousers. He wore his best long-sleeved T-shirt, the blue one with the trendy circular collar-hole, covered-up at present by the heavy black waterproof jacket he had obtained for a fraction of its original price in a Stamford Hill charity-shop. He had showered, shaved, and splashed on to his face some perfumed astringent that he had been given as a Christmas present in his late teens. The guitar's carrying-case had been washed in Fairy Liquid and was now a lighter shade of blue than it had ever been in the years that he had owned it. He felt elegant and presentable. He also felt like throwing-up with blind terror.

"Can I help you, Sir?" the chillingly efficient-looking receptionist inquired from behind her gleaming chromium-and-glass battlements.

"The Musk-Rat," he whispered feebly.

"I beg your pardon, Sir?"

"It's kind of like a nick name. Folks call me The Musk Rat." She looked singularly unimpressed.

"Muskie!" came a warm and familiar voice from behind him, "You look fantastic!"

He turned around and there she was, stepping out of the lift in a long, flowing low-cut cream dress like the one she had worn the first day he had laid eyes on her. Behind her stood goatee-beard-man, sneering. Muskie's knees weakened. She didn't look a day older. Her eyes had exactly the same irresistible vulnerable softness. Her beauty was be-

yond description. He just wanted to take her in his arms...
He did.

"Muskie," she urged, dabbing at his eyes with a piece of
tissue that goatee-beard-man had supplied, as the lift
whisked them silently upwards towards the studio, "You've
got to stop crying. You can't do a broadcast in this state."

"I'm fine," he mumbled, "absolutely fine. It was just...
seeing you again like that..."

"I know, Muskie. I've missed you too. I've thought
about you a lot. We had good times together, didn't we?"

"Good times?" He thought about the phrase. It seemed
inadequate. "It wasn't just good times. You were... the best
thing that ever happened to me, Angel..." Goatee-beard-
man's sneer intensified.

"Are you sure the format of this interview is going to
work?" he asked with an air of detached superiority.

"It'll be just fine," Angel assured him. "Muskie, you've
got to be clear what's going to come up here. You've got to
listen to Ambrose. Okay?"

"Ambrose? Is that really his name? Ambrose?"

"Yes," the other curtly confirmed, "now here's what
we're going to do." The lift had reached the correct floor and
the door slid silently open. Angel and Ambrose got out and
started to stroll towards a door marked "Studio 9 Pre-Pro-
duction". Ambrose continued to talk as they pushed the door
open and lowered themselves into the soft and comfortable
chairs that had been arranged around a coffee table.

"The interview has been completely agreed with regard
to format. It won't be scripted, we won't know exactly how
each question is going to be phrased, but we will know
exactly the territory that's going to be covered. I've sorted it
out with Molly Ray, the woman who will be asking the

questions. The interview won't be live so there will be a chance to edit out any major clangers or inaccuracies, but we won't have direct control over the editing. If you were to say something... inappropriate, it is possible that the producer could leave it in, despite our objections. At the end of the day, this isn't our interview. We don't have editorial control. Do I make myself clear?"

"Sort of," Muskie ventured hesitantly.

"What Ambrose is trying to say," Angel explained patiently, "is that making the right impression on the audience is very important. You understand that in professional show-business, performers have to be careful about what image they project. Of course you do, you're a performer too. Now my album is called "Songs of Innocence", and that's how I've got to come across. Innocent. Pure. Okay?"

Muskie considered this notion. "Innocent. Pure. Like an angel."

"Like a virgin," Ambrose put in more bluntly.

"A virgin? You want people to think you're a virgin?"

"What Miss Hanson and I are saying," Ambrose tried to explain, "is that references to any alleged sexual history that you and she may have had together, or to any other alleged episodes of a sexual nature in Miss Hanson's early life, would be highly inappropriate. Is that completely clear?"

"Well, yes, but it doesn't leave very much to talk about, does it?" For the first time ever Muskie thought that Angel seemed to show the faintest trace of embarrassment. "Don't worry, Angel," he assured her, "I won't say the wrong thing. Scout's honour."

She smiled and kissed him lightly on the cheek. "You're sweet," she whispered. Muskie reached out and tried to hold her face against his for as long as he possibly could. Sweet. Was that how he wanted her to think of him?

His head was reeling. He was becoming less and less sure that he could carry off this interview.

"Suppose I totally screw-up," he whispered, "I mean totally?"

"Don't be silly, Muskie," she assured him, "you're not going to do that. And if you did, we could cancel the whole thing, couldn't we Ambrose? Back out of the contract?"

"As a last resort. It wouldn't be cheap. There's a nasty penalty clause. Don't even think about it."

Like so many things in life, the reality of the interview was nowhere near as traumatic as the anticipation. Molly Ray turned out to be a perfectly charming and mild-mannered motherly sort of woman in early middle age whose inter-viewing style was to take a back seat, provide the necessary jumping-off points to get a conversation going and then keep out of it until her input seemed to be needed again. For most of the time, Muskie and Angel talked to one another as though there was nobody else present. They explained how they had met, leaving out the fact that Angel had sought-out Muskie in order to get an introduction to the local LSD dealer, and told Molly that the first song that Angel had ever performed in public had been a duet with Muskie at the bottom of the escalator in Paddington Underground Station. Molly asked if they could remember what it was. This was a planted question. Muskie and Angel had already rehearsed the song, "Wayfaring Stranger", and gave a flawless fake impromptu performance accompanied by Muskie on his faithful guitar. Angel's voice and delivery were even better than he had remembered them. She was so good, he reflect-ed, that she actually made him sound good, far better than he really was. If only he could be as good a musician without Angel as he was with her. For he knew in his heart of hearts that it would be a long time before he would sing another duet with the world-renowned Clare Hanson.

Talking about their time together without mentioning or even hinting at anything sexual made it a lot easier for Muskie to cope. He managed to convey a picture of a brother-and-sister relationship, two penniless musicians wandering the streets of London together, offering each other support, encouragement, friendship and artistic inspiration. As the end of the allotted time drew near, Muskie was proud of himself. He knew that he had carried it off. His account had been engaging and entertaining. He had said nothing that might reflect badly on himself or any of his friends. Angel's virginity remained unchallenged.

And now the final item was at hand. In response to another planted question, Muskie replied that before they had parted he had written a song about Clare, his Angel Clare as he always thought of her, and their time together. On cue, Molly Ray asked if he could sing it for them. His solo moment had arrived. Even Angel had never heard the song before. There was an expectant hush in the studio as he lifted the guitar back onto his lap. He played the lead-in and began to sing:

I was strumming my blues in the subway
When an angel came down from the sky.
I was the one with the music
But she was the one who could fly.
Oh yes she was the one who could fly.

She said she would take me to Heaven,
If I promised I wouldn't ask why.
I was always the one with the questions
But she was the one who could fly.
Oh yes she was the one who could fly.

For angels have many commitments,
To love the whole world they must try:
I was the one with the theories
But she was the one who could fly.
Oh yes she was the one who could fly.

I asked far too much of my angel
I asked her to never more fly.
But angels must soar with the eagles
And the mortals who love them must cry.
Yes the mortals who love them must cry.

As the final chord died away Muskie could sense a change in the atmosphere of the little studio. Everyone was looking at him but nobody was saying anything. Was it incredibly good or incredibly bad? Muskie had no idea.

At last a distorted voice from a loudspeaker broke the silence. It was Ambrose talking through a microphone from the control-room next door. "That can't go out," he said bluntly and firmly.

"That goes out," said Molly Ray, quietly but every bit as firmly, "or this interview doesn't air."

The Elk sat up in his chair and waved to Muskie as he entered the visitors' room.

"Hey! Man! Two visits in a row! That's pretty cool!"

Muskie sat down before he answered. "Needed to explain. About the broadcast," he said conspiratorially.

The Elk's face grew serious. "Yeah? I wondered about it. They did somebody else this week. I thought maybe they would put it out next week."

"No, not next week. Not ever." Muskie quietly explained how everything had gone perfectly up to that last song. And about the row the song had caused between Angel's goon and Molly Ray.

The Elk shook his head. "You screwed-up again kid," he concluded sadly.

"No, not really." Muskie was actually smiling. The Elk couldn't understand why he seemed not to be upset.

"What do you mean? Did they pay you?"

"Only my travel expenses to Euston Tower."

"But you could walk to Euston Tower in ten minutes."

"Yeah. Right. I didn't put in a claim."

"So what do you mean you didn't screw-up."

Muskie drew a little closer to the grille. "The song, Elk. Angel loved the song. When they had all gone she gave me a fantastic kiss and said she loved the song." He raised his voice slightly. "And that's who it was for really. That song wasn't for anybody else. It was for Angel. And she loved it."

The Elk shook his head in exasperation. "What can anybody do with a guy like you?" he asked hopelessly. "Didn't you get anything at all out of it? Anything except a kiss?"

Muskie shrugged. "Two tickets to her Albert Hall concert tomorrow night. Me and a friend. I thought I would take Shaggy Welsh, the guy who plays the mouth-organ, and we could work the queue before we went in. Should raise a pound or two that way."

*"Mr Rainbow Man," a little girl asked when he had fin-
ished his story, "the people in your stories always live
happily ever after. Are you living happily ever after?"*

*The Rainbow Man frowned and thought for a moment.
It was a difficult question. "I'm not sure," he admitted. "I
suppose I'll have to wait until forever comes to an end and
then I'll be able to look back and decide."*

The Summer of Dust

With a pang of envy I leave my wife still sleeping and
shower and dress silently, skipping breakfast so that I can
arrive early to work as planned. The list of new students
should be in today. There's going to be a lot of administration before I can give any thought to my opening lecture.

I log in to the University e-mail system. Yes, the list is
there. But before I click on it I notice another e-mail from
someone with the first name Baljit. Seeing the name gives
me a little jolt – like a shot of electricity going through my
body. Ridiculous, I tell myself, after all these years. It's
probably a very common name in the Punjab. My finger
hovers above the left-hand button on the mouse but does not
descend. I lift my eyes and see the dust motes drifting in the
shaft of light from beneath the window blind. The empty
office fades from my vision. I am lost in a reverie, back in
that tatty two-bedroom flat in Southall almost forty years
ago…

I was a student, not long off the boat from Belfast, away
from home for the first time, adrift in a culture that I had

only seen on television, crippled by deep-seated feelings of provincial inferiority.

My place of study, an imposing Victorian building near Richmond-on-Thames, had been built by the last heiress of a fabulously wealthy family of slave traders as a sop to her conscience. Everything about it was pretentious and over-blown: the pseudo-Grecian pillared entrance hall festooned with portraits of the great and the good who had passed through it, the oak panelled corridors, the dimly-lit class-rooms and laboratories with high windows so that nothing distracting could be seen, the huge semi-circular lecture hall with stepped terraces of polished wooden seating descend-ing to the formal dais and entire wall of blackboards and screens at the front. What this building said to me was: You aren't good enough to be here. This institution is not for the likes of you. You are scum. Go away to a concrete-and-glass monstrosity in some ugly industrial city. That's where you belong.

I tried not to listen.

In our first year we were allowed to live on campus, in one of the Halls of Residence – five storey red brick out-buildings, tastefully positioned behind high trees so that their bland functionality would not detract from the grace of the main building. Inside, female floors and male floors were alternated as in a layer cake, each Hall overseen by a constitutionally grumpy resident warden whose main task was to prevent leakage between the layers. Nevertheless, such mixing was rife.

Friendless at first, I gravitated towards those I saw as fellow outcasts – the Jamaicans, the half dozen or so stu-dents from the black Commonwealth, fellow Celts from Scotland and Wales, and of course the largest outcast group of all, the second generation children of the immigrants from the Indian subcontinent.

I became obsessed with one Indian girl in particular: bright, energetic, sociable, with flawless features and a smile that at first reduced me to an inarticulate wreck, but also with an underlying sadness about her that never fully went away. I stalked her shamelessly for the whole spring term, changing my study options so that I could sit in the same classes, following her to the canteen, carrying her tray, offering to help her with her essays and assignments, leaving single red roses in her pigeon hole, telling her that I thought she looked fabulous and wanted her to have my babies. By the beginning of the long summer holidays I had more or less broken down her resistance.

The College rules said that in the second year each student had to find his or her own accommodation off the campus, and my beautiful Baljit agreed that we should look for somewhere together. It wasn't a declaration of love or even of intimacy, but I think we both understood the direction in which things were going. I knew nothing of her community or her religion – what the rules were for contact between men and women – to me she simply seemed unimaginably exotic, and I felt like the luckiest man in the world to have got as far as I had. But beyond that she might as well have been a Martian. It became a joke between us – me calling her huge extended family the Martians.

The speed with which Baljit came up with somewhere to live was amazing. She had an uncle (indeed she seemed to have an infinite supply of uncles) who was in the property letting business. His name was Raj but he preferred to be known by the English translation, King. King Estate Agency notice boards were planted in the front gardens of a huge number of run-down terrace houses in the Southall and Greenford areas. They included the phrase "DHSS welcome", an invitation to those on state benefit and a clear indication of the socioeconomic group of King's customer base.

This landscape was familiar to me. This was simply another Belfast, one in which the people had brown faces. They were all Martians in disguise of course, but it was easy to forget.

King was a big blustering man with a laugh to make the windows rattle. He wore Western dress, but with an impressive white beard combed upwards and disappearing into a bulging cream turban. He extended a huge hand to Baljit when he first met us outside the agreed address, down a back street behind Southall Railway Station. "How is my cleverest niece today?" he boomed, shaking her hand vigorously. "And you too," he added, grasping mine and squeezing it with painful force. "Danny, isn't it? Welcome to Southall!" He unlocked the front door and ushered us in through a hallway strewn with flyers and circulars for kebab houses and Indian sweetshops, up a short carpetless staircase and through a landing door that separated the upstairs flat from the rest of the building.

"This is a very fine flat," he assured us with unnecessary loudness. "All it needs is a little bit of paint and a new carpet. Maybe one or two very minor repairs. But we can come to an agreement about all that. There are two good-sized bedrooms, and you're right beside the railway station. You can be in College in fifteen minutes, door to door." I thought that was an exaggeration but let it go.

The sight that greeted us was one of squalor and neglect. The carpet was worn through and filthy beyond description, one of the bedroom doors looked as though it had been kicked in, and there were great areas of plaster missing from the walls and ceiling, revealing the ancient wooden laths underneath. Worst of all there was a filthy mattress almost filling the floor of the tiny kitchen alongside a pile of decaying garbage and empty bottles where one or more tramps had obviously created a home at some time in the past. "There were squatters for a few months," King explained jovially, "but we got them out. It's just a bit of surface dirt. Half an hour's work and you won't know the place."

I could hold back no longer. "You don't really expect us to live here, do you Mr King? To pay rent and live here?"

His smile broadened. "No – I won't ask for rent. Not for the moment anyhow. All I ask is that you put a little bit of work into the place. A little bit of tender loving care. It won't cost either of you a penny," he continued with regal aplomb. "Everything will be provided. Paint. Plaster. Carpets. Underlay. Nails. Filler. Even kitchen units and basic furniture. Anything you need. By the end of the summer you can have this place like a palace, all at my expense, and it won't have cost you a thing. The least I can do for my favourite niece."

My instincts about King's deal were not good, but whatever the future held for us it was at least a future that included Baljit, and that was enough to make everything alright. I had no special handyman skills but I could learn. We could do it – we could make this work. I caught her eye and gave her a wink. The exquisite goddess smile flickered across her face for a moment and we both knew that the decision had been made.

We moved in that same evening. The first thing we had to do was buy some light bulbs at the corner shop, because all of them had been removed. Only one of the rooms looked even remotely habitable. We spoke little as we cleared out as much of the junk as we could onto the paved front yard, ready for throwing in the skip that King had promised would arrive "in just a day or two". Everything we tried to do created suffocating clouds of dust, so that even though the flat began to look superficially cleaner the air thickened to the point where we had to go out into the front yard ourselves to keep from choking.

We stood there, linking arms in the failing light, our clothes and hair covered in dust, our hands and faces filthy, the flat still nothing short of disgusting, no bath plug even if we could get the bath clean enough to use, the kettle and gas stove in the kitchen our only source of hot water for a wash. And what I felt was elation, perfect happiness, a sense of closeness to Baljit and of shared destiny that might have taken months to achieve without this massive common task to draw us together. Baljit relaxed into my arms and I kissed her very lightly on the lips. I felt her tense-up but she did not resist.

There was one serviceable double mattress and we lay on it together that night, fully clothed, with rolled-up overcoats as pillows. After a little while Baljit snuggled up to me and I embraced her very gently until I fell asleep. I couldn't have been happier. It was only when the sun came up that I saw the tracks of the tears down her dusty face. I felt an overwhelming tenderness but I couldn't think of anything to say. Of course I wanted to ask her what was wrong, was it me or was it the dust, or was it something else entirely? But what if it *was* me? What if she told me the very thing I couldn't bear to hear? Cowardice won out and I just let it go and told her I would try to make breakfast.

I determined that I would get to know her better first, find out what to do or say to make her happy – the truth is that I never did. But at least for a time things got a lot better.

We spent the next few days emulating the slaves whose labour had paid for our College, getting the absolute basics into place. We bought a bath plug and managed to get the gas boiler to light and give us hot water. We borrowed a vacuum cleaner from Baljit's younger girlfriend and un-specified relation Surinder who lived nearby, and paid several visits to King at his estate agency premises with lists of the other things we needed. He was quick to promise but painfully slow to deliver. There was always "just a small problem" that meant it would take a day or two longer to get the paint, or the chairs or the curtain rails or whatever it was that we asked for. On the other hand he was very keen to know how much progress we had made with the clean-up. Had we lifted the carpet in the bedroom yet? Had we made a start on the damaged plaster? Had we got the door of the smaller bedroom to close properly? Had we done anything with the wash-hand-basin that had come away from the bathroom wall? The truth was we had done very little except clean the place up to the extent that you didn't get dirt on your hands every time you touched anything. Our priorities were not the same as King's. For one thing we were almost out of money. One or other of us needed to get a job. Rent might be free but food wasn't.

Sleeping on the double mattress together, more or less fully clothed, became part of our routine. When Baljit washed or dressed she did it very modestly, wrapping enormous lengths of colourful sari material around herself, always closing and bolting the door of the smaller bedroom where she dressed and kept her personal things. I could feel my frustration building, I knew that sooner or later my almost unbearable lust was going to become an issue.

But on the day that she got her job, Baljit surprised me. Maybe I mean that she shocked me. Yes, that's closer to the truth.

I was attempting to plaster over one of the big sections of exposed laths on the corridor wall, and the wretched stuff just kept falling off again on to the dirt-coloured remains of the carpet. I had obviously made the mixture too wet. Baljit came running up the stairs, through the open door at the top, and flung her arms around me as she had never done before. "I've got a job," she announced proudly. "I'm a receptionist in a travel agency run by one of my uncles. Tell me I'm a clever girl."

"You're a clever girl," I laughed. "Just how many uncles have you got?"

"All Martians are officially my uncles. And I have even better news." She produced something small and silvery from her shoulder bag. "Do you know what these are?"

I looked at them and could hardly believe what I was seeing. "Those are...well, I think they're birth control pills..."

"That's right. And you may notice that I've already taken the first five. As from now, I am officially On the Pill. I want to seduce you. Wash your hands first – and your teeth. I'll wait for you in the bedroom."

It was one of those moments when you need to pinch yourself to make sure you're not dreaming. I wasn't. She's a Martian, I thought to myself. Got to be a Martian.

For the remainder of that summer I had very little to complain about. I could put it more strongly and say that those were probably the happiest few weeks of my life. Baljit exceeded all my fantasies as a lover. There was no limit to the pleasure she could give to both of us, or to the depth of the tenderness that she left me with when I was utterly spent. Just the memory of lying with her in my arms afterwards, and feeling her heartbeat next to my skin, can still bring tears to my eyes when I think about it. In the daytime I wanted to hold her hand all the time, to maintain physical contact, touch any part of her that was available. I really couldn't leave her alone. I don't think I've ever been like that with anybody else.

I got through the work very quickly. After a bit of experimentation I became a minimally competent plasterer. My greatest triumph was getting the beastly stuff to stick to the ceiling, against all the laws of Newton and Einstein. The trick was to do it in very thin layers, allowing each to almost dry before applying the next. I got a book out from the library that explained how to get a proper flat surface. My work wasn't perfect but it was acceptable and I was immensely proud of it.

We did all the making-good and decorating before lifting the carpets, so that plaster and paint could be free to drip to their heart's content. King supplied industrial-size buckets of a paint called "Magnolia", which he wanted on every plastered surface, be it wall or ceiling. He said that it looked clean and tidy and prospective tenants found it inoffensive. It reminded me that our time in the flat would one day run out.

Beneath the carpets the rubber underlay had metamorphosed into a dry black dust that got everywhere. I shovelled it into bin-bags while Surinder's vacuum cleaner ran continuously to keep the airborne particles to a minimum. Baljit's job kept her busy for the whole working day, including Saturdays, so I did most of the work alone and tried to have the place habitable in time for her return each evening.

Surinder visited often, and she and Baljit chatted in their own language. I found this a little bit excluding but I didn't comment. I could tell that they were very close – I think I even felt a slight pang of jealousy. King visited occasionally too, to see how the work was going. He was loud and domineering and laughed a lot, but I sensed that he liked Baljit and wouldn't let her come to any harm. Baljit treated him respectfully – he seemed to be an important man in the Sikh community.

As we entered the last week of our summer recess, with most of the work complete and the place looking very respectable, I noticed that Baljit was opening up to me less and less. We were still talking, but our conversation had somehow become superficial. The sadness seemed to have surfaced once again, and the balance in our sex life shifted towards the tender holding rather than anything more active.

I told myself it was the stress of having to go back to College, books to be read, summer assignments to be written-up and handed in, new routines to be established – a return to the pressures of academic work. But in my heart I think I knew that wasn't it. Something else was wrong. Something that Baljit couldn't or wouldn't talk about.

Anxiously, my hand shaking slightly, I lower my finger and click the mouse. The e-mail opens and I begin to read:

Hello Danny. Sorry, I suppose I should call you Professor Conroy. I got your e-mail address off the College website. Your picture was there too so I knew it was you. I have to tell you though, you have changed a bit. So have I. I'm glad my picture isn't on any website.

It's been a long time, hasn't it?

I think the most upsetting aspect was that Baljit didn't tell me herself, she left it to Surinder, who made a special afternoon visit so as to get me on my own – although of course I would have been devastated however the news had been delivered. I can't remember much of what she said because my mind went numb and stopped processing information after her first couple of sentences. I just remember that she asked me to sit down and her opening words were: "There's been a change of plan."

A change of plan? Whose plan? Who makes these plans? The whole family I suppose. The whole damn Sikh community in secret conclave. The Martian Council.

Surinder and Baljit had the entire event choreographed. Baljit walked through the door just as Surinder finished her speech. They sat down side by side on the second-hand sofa that King had given us, and for a long time nobody said a word.

"I'm sorry," Baljit said at last.

Sorry? Was that all she was going to say? I couldn't take it in. My head was reeling. "You're going back to India to marry somebody that you haven't even met?" She didn't answer. "Which of us is crazy? Is it me or you?"

"Our families are different," Surinder said very quietly. "Things aren't like they are in England. It's all...different."

I looked Baljit straight in the eye. She didn't flinch. "Okay, maybe I'm not very important to you. A pleasant little summer diversion. But you've completed one year of a three year degree course. You have far better grades than me, you can have a great future here. You can do anything you want to. The world is at your bloody feet. Who is this man who's worth throwing it all away for? Tell me about him."

Surinder hesitantly answered for her. "He's just a man. His family is good, but poor."

"What does he do for a living?" I couldn't believe that I was being so cool and rational. I don't think I was feeling anything much at that moment. My emotions had temporarily shut down. They would open for business again later.

"He's just a worker." Baljit answered this time. "A worker in the building trade. An honest man."

"You've got four 'A' levels," I whispered. "You're probably in the top three or four students in your whole year group. You're headed for a first. And he works in the building trade?"

This time I saw tears beginning to form in the corners of Baljit's eyes. There was nothing there but the sadness now, everything else was gone.

Baljit didn't say any more. She stood up and left the room. She didn't even say goodbye. Surinder took over the conversation. "It isn't like England," she repeated, as though that made everything clear.

"How can a builder be good enough for an honours student like Baljit? Tell me. How?"

It took Surinder a long time to reply. When she did her voice was so faint I could barely make out the words. "Baljit...isn't a virgin."

That was something I could certainly confirm. "And that matters, does it? That makes a difference?"

"Yes. In our culture it makes a big difference."

Although I can't have been thinking very straight I could see right away that there was something skewed about all this. Something that didn't make sense. "Are you blaming me? Did Baljit tell you that she was a virgin before she met me? Is that what she said?"

"No. Baljit hasn't been a virgin for a long time...I don't think I should be talking about this."

"Don't you? Well I think I have a right to some kind of explanation."

"I'm sorry but that's all I can tell you. May I go now?"

"No, you damn well may not! I think I'm beginning to see what's going on here. I'm actually part of this plan, aren't I? King wouldn't have put the two of us together in this place if he thought...That's it, isn't it? I'm the evil white man who seduced the poor little innocent Indian girl and stole her virginity. I probably took it by force. There was nothing she could do about it, was there?"

Surinder did not answer but I could see that she understood what I was saying.

"What really happened? Who was it? Was it somebody in the family? How long ago? Tell me the real story, Surinder. I can take it. I'm doing the goddamned family a favour. I think I have a right to know, don't you?"

"You've got it completely wrong," she said quietly. For a long time we just looked at one another. It was obvious that she wasn't going to tell me anything more.

"And what about you?" I asked, as calmly and gently as I could. "Are you going to marry a builder's labourer in some godforsaken Punjabi village when they tell you to? Is that all you have to look forward to?"

"I am not like Baljit," she whispered.

"What does that mean? Hymen intact? Undamaged goods? Hoping for a doctor or a lawyer…or maybe an estate agent? Top caste totty. They could auction you off at the Lahore cattle market. Never know what you might fetch."

She stood up to go. I didn't try to stop her. "Why don't you put up a fight?" She turned away from me and walked towards the door. "Why don't you do something? Why do you let them treat you this way?" I realised that I was shouting and lowered my voice a little. "Even your name sounds like 'surrender'."

My anger was spent. I turned back to the empty couch. "Martians," I blurted out in a voice that was now choking up. "Bloody Martians, the whole damned lot of them."

I remained in the chair after she had gone, watching the dust motes slowly descending through the shaft of sunlight from the kitchen window. Then I realised I was not alone. King had presumably been waiting on the landing. I stood up and turned to face him in total disbelief. He closed and locked the door and motioned me to sit down. I opened my mouth to speak but no words came.

"Mr Danny," he began, speaking more quietly than I had ever heard him speak before, "I don't normally discuss family business with anybody, but I believe that you are a good man, and out of respect I will try to answer your questions."

I sank back into my seat and he flopped onto the centre of the couch, his bulk almost filling it.

"Nobody has forced Baljit to do anything," he began. "This marriage is a way of giving her back her good name. It restores her respectability. It means she becomes a member of this community again. I'm talking about other people now, in my eyes Baljit has never been anything but a wonderful girl."

At last I found my voice. "I want you to tell me," I said coldly. "I want to know…" I couldn't use the word but King knew what I meant.

"How she lost her virginity? You think very badly of us, Mr Danny. No, it wasn't anybody in the family. In her early teens she went a little bit wild. Yes, just like any other teenager. Just like a *British* teenager. Pop music and discos and strong drink. Contraception on demand even if you're under age. All-night parties and god knows what kind of drugs getting handed around. Our community is no better at coping with those things than yours is, Danny. Does that surprise you?"

"I…suppose it shouldn't…"

"No, it shouldn't. Everything is coming apart, the whole world is changing for everybody. Maybe good things will come out of it, I don't know. Maybe there *will* be love and peace. Maybe your generation won't have to fight a World War like my generation did. I can't see into the future. All I can do is try to hold things together right now, while we're waiting, and try to stop people from getting hurt."

"And...you say that Baljit really chose this marriage...I can't believe that. How could such a thing be?"

"This way, Baljit keeps her options open. If she wants to turn her back on this community in the future she can. We won't try to stop her. We're not Martians, Danny – or monsters. Bad things do happen in our community and sometimes we're stubborn and bigoted, but we don't treat our women like cattle. You're wrong about that."

"I'm sorry," I stammered, "I shouldn't have said that." He dismissed it with a wave.

I tried to understand the enormity of what had happened. "She could come back to England with this husband, couldn't she?"

"Of course she could, if that's what they decide to do."

I watched him closely. "But you don't think that's going to happen, do you?"

"Anything could happen. They might divorce. Or they might live perfectly happily in India. The point is, now she has the choice. She can decide whether she wants the Western ways, or our ways. The time is coming when we'll all have to make that choice. All I did was lay out the options, as honestly as I could."

He paused but I could think of nothing to say.

"About your rent – there is none. Our arrangement continues until you want to move on. Don't thank me for that. It was Baljit's idea. We can't refuse her anything, either of us, can we?"

You must know by now that you were my last little fling before I settled down. Every girl is allowed one of those, isn't she? At least that was what I wanted it to be, but it got a little bit out of control.

I'm really sorry for hurting you. I know that I did. I don't think I realised back then that men have feelings too. Even Western men. What chance has a Martian of understanding an earthling?

I can tell you about my life in a couple of sentences. It has been very simple, very ordinary. I still have the same husband and we have three girls. It's funny, most Indian men want boys, but my husband only ever wanted girls, and that's what we've got. King was right, he's a good man, an honest man. And his plastering is a little bit better than yours.

I never finished my degree. I suppose I could have, but other things just got in the way and I never did.

And that brings me to my reason for writing. My youngest daughter is going to your College to study Information Technology. It's the big thing over here, everybody wants to get qualified. Her name is Asha. She's very like I was back then, so I wanted to ask you not to seduce her.

Only joking – I want to ask you to look after her, like King looked after me. Will you do that for me, Uncle Danny?

I was going to end with 'love' but that wouldn't be appropriate for a respectable married Indian lady, would it? So I'll just say that not one day of my life has gone by without thinking about you, and I don't suppose one ever will.

Your Baljit.

The Rainbow Man opened the cardboard shoe box and released a grateful pigeon, which fluttered joyously skyward. "Be sure to write me a letter as soon as ye get there to let me know that yer safe!" he shouted after it.

Letter to Mammy

Dear Mammy,

Here I am in London! What do you think of that?

I'll start by saying sorry that I didn't write sooner. I started a couple of letters but what I was saying seemed like such (word scratched out) nonsense that I just threw them away. It took me a few days to get the hang of the way they do things over here.

Anyway I arrived at Liverpool safe and sound and got the train down to London. It went at a hell of a speed and even though it's hundreds of miles I was there by teatime. Finbar met me at the station. He's looking well but he's a lot quieter now than when we used to know him. At least it was me that did the most of the talking. He carried the big case for me and took me on a bus to the house he's living in.

I couldn't believe how big London is. We were on that bus for the best part of an hour and even then we were nowhere near the end of London. It's as if they took a whole county and built houses all over it. Even if you sit in the attic and look out of the roof-light you can't see a field or a hill as far as the horizon. Just houses made of red brick and joined together in rows, and they all look exactly the same as one another. I was afraid to go out at all the first day in case I got lost.

Finbar's house is big but it wasn't the best of the ones we saw when we were on the bus. It has a few broken windows and there's a couple of places where the roof leaks. I said he should get on to the landlord, but he said there was no landlord, so that's good at least I suppose. He and Eva seem to be living rent-free.

I must tell you about Eva. She's a foreigner, from somewhere in Europe. It seems there was a revolution or something and her country came to an end, and everybody ran away. She told me something very sad. She said that her mother and father and her sister were all dead and the only reason that she's still alive is because she was able to run faster than them. I don't think she was joking. Isn't it a hell of a world we're living in?

Eva has two bedrooms. There's the one she and Finbar have together and then there's another one she has just for herself. The one she has for herself is the best room in the whole house – there's a huge big double bed and a drinks cabinet and long mirrors on the wall. Finbar got her the big bed and put up all the mirrors and things because she isn't well, and she has to spend a lot of time in bed.

My room is downstairs at the back of the house. It used to be a kind of kitchen/diner but Finbar and Eva don't do any cooking in the house any more. Just make tea in their bedroom with an electric kettle. Finbar brings home fish and chips after work, or sometimes foreign food that burns your mouth, and Eva hardly eats anything at all. No wonder she's thin.

Finbar works at London Airport. When he told me I thought he was a pilot, flying the planes, but no, he's one of the luggage men. They put your suitcases on big trolleys and load them on and off the planes. He works very funny hours, but it's a good job, and sometimes he comes home with things for Eva. He's allowed to take home all the lost property, it seems, if it isn't claimed. He's got loads of cameras and little computers and mobile phones, and sometimes he gets jewellery and perfume and bottles of expensive booze and god knows what. He keeps some of it and sells the rest to a friend of his. It was at the airport that he met Eva. Finbar's going to see if he can get me a job at the airport too.

When Finbar's at work I get the chance to talk to Eva sometimes. She's a beautiful girl, and very well-mannered. Talks with a funny accent, but then they all do over here. You would like her, Mammy. Finbar is a very lucky man to have a girlfriend like that. I hope maybe you'll meet her and Finbar some day.

I was sorry for Eva at first because she's in bed so much of the time, but she has a lot of friends and gets loads of callers. They all look very respectable and I know that a lot of them give her presents. If they call while I'm here I just send them straight up to her room like she told me to.

Finbar told me that Eva needs very expensive injections every day, and that's one of the reasons that he has to do so much night work at the airport. I suppose some of the men who come to see her must be doctors. I'm sorry about Eva being sick because she's such a lovely girl.

I asked Eva if there was any way she could get cured so that she didn't need the injections any more and could maybe get a job herself. She said there might be a way but she was scared to go to the special hospital where they do the cure. I think she was scared in case it would hurt and also because there's some problem with her passport or something and she mightn't be allowed to stay in the country. Isn't that strange? Imagine sending somebody back to a country where all her family were murdered because they couldn't run fast enough? I don't think even the English could be that bad.

I asked Eva if she would show me where the special hospital was and she took me over there the other day. I said: "You're here now, why don't you go in and talk to them? Maybe they don't need to see your passport at all." But she wouldn't go in. She went back to the house – I think she was expecting one of her friends – and so I went in myself and I talked to the woman at the desk. She was very nice, even though she was English, and she said that there was no question of asking anybody for their passport, or even their address. If they needed treating, that was all that mattered. She said I ought to talk to Eva and get her to come along.

So I did talk to Eva, this morning after Finbar had gone to work. I said the life she was living was no life for a beautiful lady like her and she owed it to her mother and her father and her sister who were murdered to get herself cured and to live the kind of life that would have made them proud of her. She cried and I gave her a hug. I felt very guilty because I enjoyed hugging her and she's really Finbar's girl.

It took a bit of time but after a while Eva agreed to go to the special hospital and we walked over to it together. She asked if I would wait for her, and visit her sometimes if she had to stay for a while, and of course I promised her I would. That's where I am now actually, writing this letter. I'm in a kind of waiting room and Eva is being seen by the doctors and they're going to examine her and see if they can make her better.

I left a note for Finbar in case he comes home and wonders where the two of us are. It'll be great if this works out because then Finbar won't have to work so hard, and maybe we can all have a go at fixing the windows and the roof or maybe even move to a better house.

So it's true what they say about England, Mammy, it's the land of opportunities. When Eva's better and we're all a bit more settled maybe you can come over and visit us. You can stay in the room with the big bed, Eva won't need it any more when she's better.

I'd better go now. I can hear Eva's voice with one of the doctors, I think they're coming back.

Goodbye and God bless.
Declan.

"Now isn't that a daft question?" The Rainbow Man scoffed. *"Sure the only one who can tell you whether you've done right or done wrong is yerself. Any fool knows that."*

Imbalance

Lou heard his wife come in the front door and glanced at the bedside clock. It was almost half-past-two in the morning. Could have been worse, he supposed. She'd warned him it would be a long session. He couldn't be the one to talk, he'd only just got over the headache from old Barrington's retirement party. He waited in a pleasant state of semi-consciousness for the sound of her feet on the stairs, water running in the bathroom, the rustle of undressing, the shock of cold air as she pulled back the duvet to climb in beside him.

But as the drowsy minutes slipped by there was no further sound from downstairs. Maybe she was making herself a cup of coffee to clear her head. Those hen parties could be pretty wild affairs, he had been told. He opened his eyes and glanced at the clock again. Forty minutes had passed. He became fully awake. Forty minutes? It doesn't take forty minutes to make a cup of coffee.

He sat up and listened hard, but all he could hear was the breeze in the tree outside the bedroom window. He switched on the bedside lamp, got out of bed and put his dressing gown over his shoulders as he passed the door.

"Sylvie? Are you all right down there?" She was sitting in the lounge with the light off. He switched it on as he approached. "Sylvie? I heard you come in. What's the matter, sweetheart?"

She turned around and he saw that her face was deathly pale and tears had caused her mascara to run in two faint blue lines down her cheeks. Her chin was trembling. He knelt beside her chair and took her in his arms. She buried her face in his shoulder and burst into fresh tears.

"Have you been... attacked?" he whispered. He felt her head move in a gesture of denial. "What then? Please tell me. I don't mind what it is. I promise I won't be... upset. Please tell me."

I think I've killed somebody, Lou." she said, so softly it was almost inaudible.

With Sylvie looking on, almost afraid to breathe, Lou inspected every inch of the car's nearside front with the beam of his powerful flashlight. "There's no damage, Sylvie. No blood, or clothing... nothing."

"I didn't think there would be," she said in a voice that came out as a breathy undertone, "he... or she... seemed to go straight under the wheels. I felt it... like going over a bump. Oh God..." the tears started up again. "We've got to phone the police, Lou. It's the only sensible thing to do. I'm not going to get away with it..."

"Please, Sylvie. Don't rush into anything. If you phone the police they're going to crucify you."

"Maybe I deserve to be crucified."

He switched off the flashlight. "Please don't talk like that. It'll be light soon. I'll drive along that way and see if there's anything there. I still think the whole thing sounds crazy. What would a child be doing on a country road at two o'clock in the morning?"

"I saw the child, Lou. The child was there. I don't know why but the child was there."

He put his arm around her waist. "You saw something, sweetheart. It could have been a stray dog or a fox. Maybe even a young deer, or a farm animal. Young children don't wander around on little country roads at two o'clock in the morning." He led her back indoors and sat down with her on the sofa.

"Look, I think I know what it was. Have you ever woken up when it's almost dark and thought there was somebody in the room and then realized it was just a coat hanging on the back of a door? It happens to everybody, all the time. You were driving along, a bit distracted, trying to get the CD player to work. You admit you weren't really concentrating on the road. You'd had a bit more to drink than you're used to. Then you catch some kind of movement out of the corner of your eye and your wheels go over something. You get a fright and your mind tells you it was a child. You imagine the worst possible scenario. It's exactly like the coat on the door."

"No, Lou, it wasn't like that. This was a child, a toddler, and it stumbled out from the hedge. It took a step. I saw the shape: it wasn't any kind of animal. Let's go back. Right now. I want to go there. Please."

"Sweetheart, if the police are there taking statements and we drive up to them it's going to be the tiniest bit incriminating, isn't it?"

"So you believe me. You believe that it was a child."

"I didn't say that. I think it's wildly unlikely. Where were its parents? What was it doing there? But there's nothing to gain by getting involved if there's no need to. Just think for a moment, Sylvie, please. Your career is just taking off. You're up for promotion. I'm doing well too. We've got a bit of spare money for the first time ever. We can think about starting a family soon. Can you imagine what affect a thing like this could have, on both our lives?

Even if it was just drink-driving. You work for a law firm, Sylvie, you can't be up on criminal charges. Think about it."

"Do you think I can live with this for the rest of my life and just keep quiet about it? I can't do that, Lou. If I killed that child I'm going to give myself up. Even if it means prison. I want to go back there – right now. If you won't come with me I'll go on my own..."

He drew her towards him in a gentle hug. "Okay, have it your way. Let's go. Let's put your mind at rest."

"You're completely sure it was somewhere along here?"

"Of course I am. I'm not likely to forget."

Lou pulled over to the hedge and stopped before he replied. "Well, we've been up and down half a dozen times, Sylvie. There's nothing here. Just like I expected. Do you feel better now?"

She paused before she replied. "Lou, do you think I'm going mad?"

"Don't be ridiculous. You got a fright. You made a mistake. You probably hit some wild animal and it crawled away and died somewhere else. Whatever it was there's nothing either of us can do about it now. I think we should go home and get some sleep."

"You know the worst thing about it? I never thought I would react that way if something like this happened. I used to think hit-and-run drivers were monsters. We defend them sometimes at work, and I've always despised them. I thought a decent person would face up to it no matter what they'd done. But I couldn't stop. I couldn't even look back in the mirror. I went into a sort of trance and I just drove and drove until I was back home. I behaved like the worst kind of person imaginable. How can you bear to have anything to do with me...?"

He reached out and took both her hands. "You were in shock, Sylvie. You probably still are. You've got to stop blaming yourself. Even if you had hit a child, it wouldn't have been your fault. It would have been an accident. But it didn't happen so there's nothing to blame yourself for. Let it go. It's all right, sweetheart."

"It would have been my fault, Lou. I had been drinking and I shouldn't have been driving. I couldn't have been more in the wrong, and I don't know how you can forgive me."

He held her shoulder and kissed her gently on the lips. "But I do, so stop worrying about it. I know you. I know you're a good person, and I'm proud to have you for my wife. You don't have to be Superwoman. It's not in the job description."

She held him tightly and he could feel her body shuddering. "I don't deserve you, Lou," she said tearfully, "and you certainly don't deserve me."

Lou insisted that Sylvie take the next few days off work and did the same himself. They spent a lot of time together, doing the kind of mundane tasks that they hadn't shared since before they were married: going shopping, weeding the garden, taking down the curtains and washing them, visiting Sylvie's parents in Oxfordshire, going to see a play by the local Amateur Dramatic Society. They drew closer together and Lou became publicly affectionate in a way that he hadn't been since the first few months of their relationship. Although they never mentioned Sylvie's "accident" they anxiously watched every evening's TV newscast and bought both the local papers as soon as they were available in the shops. There was no report of a hit-and-run driver, or of a missing child.

On the third evening, as an unspoken celebration of having come through unscathed, they went for a romantic dinner in the same restaurant where Lou had proposed to Sylvie almost a decade before. When they had eaten and were lingering over the remains of the wine, Lou hesitantly returned to the topic of having a child of their own. "You still want children, don't you?" he prompted gently.

"I... think so... when we're both ready."

"What happened... I mean what you imagined... didn't change how you felt, did it?"

"No... well, I don't know. It's hard to think straight at the moment... No, of course not, why should it?" She paused. "Lou, I want you to promise me something. I want you to promise me that you won't tell anybody about that night or mention it again for as long as you live. It's something I have to deal with myself, nobody else can help and I don't want them to try. Not even you. Is that a promise?"

Lou nodded. They looked into one another's eyes and a new understanding was reached.

The doorbell rang and Lou opened it with rolled-up sleeves and flour on his trousers. The young woman who greeted him giggled when she saw him. "Goodness me, aren't we domesticated! Are you baking Sylvie a cake?"

"Oddly enough, I am. Well, I'm baking *us* a cake. Come in Laura, make yourself at home. Will I get her down for you?"

"In a minute." Laura suddenly looked serious and lowered her voice. "She's not in bed again, surely?"

"She's resting. I'll let her tell you why herself."

"You know, Lou, she isn't herself these days. Haven't you noticed it? I think it's since Francie's wedding – the one she didn't go to. She's so quiet and hard to talk to lately. Aren't you worried about it?"

Lou smiled weakly. "I thought you women had some kind of intuition. Don't you know what it is? That's why I'm baking a cake. We're celebrating."

Laura's face lit up. "You don't mean...?"

"The doctor confirmed it this morning." Laura looked almost shocked. "It's hormonal, Laura. That's what the doctor said. You should know about these things. When a woman's pregnant her hormone balance changes. It can change her personality. Temporarily of course."

"Gosh. You amaze me, you two. Congratulations, Lou!"

Although the words were right Lou couldn't help feeling that Laura was holding back a lot of misgivings. "She's going to be fine," he said quietly, "really she is."

On his way home from work Lou slowed the car to a walking pace as he came to the straight piece of road with the hedges on either side. As he had done many times before he drew to a halt at the spot where they had parked on that terrible night and tried to imagine the scene she had described: the darkness, the child stumbling into the road, the lurch of the car going over the body, the tiny bones snapping. He had thought about it so often it had taken on the reality of a remembered nightmare for him too, the moment when malevolent demons had intervened to curse both their lives forever. Even the prospect of motherhood seemed to have little power to break the spell. The joy had gone out of Sylvie's life, even Laura could see it, it was silly trying to deny it any longer. Lou made up his mind to ask Dr Nelson about psychiatric help for Sylvie.

"I'm very pleased you brought up the subject yourself," Dr Nelson affirmed as he perched awkwardly on the arm of Lou's sofa, "I was going to talk about it today anyway. You see," he glanced at the stairs as though wondering if Sylvie could hear, "your wife's depression is becoming quite severe, and it seems to have taken a new turn. Staying in bed and eating too much was one thing, it's not uncommon in the early stages of pregnancy. But she's gone to the other extreme now. She's hardly eating at all, and showing quite marked symptoms of stress – and I'm beginning to get a bit concerned for the health of her baby. I think specialist help is called for here." He hesitated. "I don't suppose... I don't suppose you've got any clue yourself as to what the root of this trouble might be?"

Lou's features paled and he thought for a moment, then with a pounding heart he said that he knew nothing. She had to deal with it in her own way, she had said, and a promise is a promise. He couldn't betray her trust. He knew that she would never have betrayed his.

"Well, with your permission, I'm going to recommend that she be admitted to the psychiatric ward at St. Clements for a little while. It's a very fine facility and they have great expertise in treating this kind of thing. You see when someone is expecting a baby, tranquillisers and drug treatments are much less straightforward. We have to proceed with great caution."

Lou nodded, his whole being numb, barely able to believe that his happy party-going little Sylvie could be reduced to this.

On the day that she was admitted Lou drove her to the hospital and sat with her for a time, but Sylvie didn't want to talk and before long they were sitting side by side in silence, Sylvie staring impassively into space. He squeezed her hand, told her that he loved her, and left.

On the way home, as the sun disappeared from view behind him, he parked up at the spot where the demons lived and felt their mocking malevolence. "You aren't going to win," he told them very quietly, "you may think that you are, but you aren't."

Lou was finishing off a work project on his laptop when the doorbell sounded. He had taken to working from home a lot, finding excuses not to drive past that spot, not to face the people at the office and have to pretend to be cheerful. As soon as he opened the door and saw Laura's face he knew that something was seriously wrong.

"Lou – I've just been to visit Sylvie. The hospital was going to phone you but I said I'd come and tell you instead." He waited in silence, knowing what she was about to say. "I'm afraid Sylvie has lost the baby, Lou. I'm... well, I just can't say how sorry I am." He stood, staring blankly into her eyes. "Come in my car. You're in no condition to drive."

Lou was in a trance. Laura had to fetch his coat and help him into it, then lead him to her car like a bewildered child.

She drove unnecessarily fast, rushing innocently past the straight piece of road where the demons lived, and for once Lou felt nothing. He realised that at that moment he was probably beyond feeling anything. He remained silent until they had parked and walked to the door of the side-ward and Laura had motioned him in, remaining outside herself, closing the door discreetly behind him.

Sylvie looked weak and drawn but she was sitting up in bed and she gave Lou a faint welcoming smile. It was the last thing that he had been expecting.

"Sylvie," he began, taking her hand, "I'm so sorry... so very very sorry..."

197

"I'm sorry too Lou," she replied in a hoarse, barely audible whisper, "but it's all over now. We can start our lives again."

He wasn't sure that he understood so he didn't say anything. She looked into his eyes as though expecting that he would understand.

"The debt has been paid, Lou. The debt has been paid."

"Livin' in the past," said The Rainbow man sadly. "'Tis the tragedy of Ireland. Ye'll never get anywhere that way. Ye'll wake up dead one morning an' ye won't have lived at all."

Lettie

Lettie realized that she must have dozed off on the sofa and had woken up well rested but a little disoriented, not sure what time it was, or even what day it was. Not that it mattered a great deal. One day was pretty much the same as another. It was a long time since she had felt so refreshed and free from her usual aches and pains.

Is it daytime or nighttime she wondered? She could open the curtains and look out, but she didn't like doing that. The bright light from the street showed the dust that covered everything. They had offered her a home help, but Lettie didn't want strangers in the house, interfering, going through all her things, fussing around. This was her house and she liked it as it was. A bit of dust never killed anyone. When she was ready she would get the dusters out, and the vacuum cleaner and the sponges. It was her house. It was her business. They were a lot of interfering busybodies at Social Services. Didn't know when they weren't wanted. Didn't know when to leave a person alone.

She took the photo album with the leather binding down from the bookshelf and sat back in the sofa. She opened it at the page with the picture of Thomas in uniform, pretending to stand to attention beside his little sister, his kit bag sagging to one side on the ground in front of him. That little sister was herself, of course, Lettie at nine years old, in her frilly white dress, with the long golden blonde hair that would darken to brown a few years later. You couldn't tell what colour anything was from the picture of course, in the picture things were just different shades of sepia. She looked so happy and proud of Thomas, going off to fight the Kaiser and win lots of medals and come back a hero. The war would probably be over by Christmas, most people thought. They were wrong.

She wasn't sure if she really remembered him or not. Her mother used to talk about him so much, it was hard to be sure which bits she actually remembered herself and which bits she had been told when she was older. She knew that he used to throw her up in the air and catch her again, and call her his little princess. And that he used to read stories to her in bed before she went to sleep. He had such a lovely smile in the picture. Such a fine young man.

She wiped away a tear and turned to another page. It was her wedding picture – her best one – with herself and Cyril standing outside the church, she with the bouquet and the veil pulled back from her face, the two grinning brides-maids a couple of paces behind. That was the nicest picture that she had of herself – there was a kind of light shining out of both their faces in that picture – maybe it was some trick that the photographer had used, but it was the way she had felt that day, and the way that she had looked: radiant, like a film star. There was no point denying it, she had been beautiful in her teens and her twenties. The only thing that had spoiled the wedding had been her mother's hostility towards Cyril. Her mother had done everything in her power to stop Lettie from marrying Cyril: when all her efforts failed she had resorted to the futile gesture of boycotting the wedding. Lettie had been hurt by it. More hurt than she allowed her mother to see. But that was all over now. And her mother had been wrong about Cyril. It had been a good marriage. Or all the bits she cared to remember had been good. Cyril had been a thoroughly decent man. How lucky she had been! How few women could put their hands on their hearts and say that!

She turned one more page. Herself in the maternity ward, with little Violet in her arms. She was smiling at her newborn baby but it was a forced smile, filled with tension and unease, and Violet's eyes were closed and her head bent over to one side. For no reason that anybody could explain the infant's life was seeping away, her child would not live to see a second sunrise. Cyril had kept this picture hidden from her for years, had refused to let her see it, told her that he had thrown it out. But she always knew when he wasn't telling the truth and eventually she had persuaded him to let her see it, and then to put it in the family album. Violet was family too, after all. The only family of their own that she and Cyril would ever have. "I'm sorry, Cyril," she whispered, "I wanted to give you children. Children that would live… that would grow up… I really did. I don't know why I couldn't. I don't know why."

"Don't be silly, girl," came his cheery north country accent from the easy chair at the other side of the fireplace, "it wasn't you fault. Where did you get a daft idea like that?"

She looked across and there he was, his newspaper furled on his lap, his reading glasses dangling as ever from the string around his neck. He looked her straight in the eye. "Like as not I was the one with the problem. There's no way to tell, Lettie. And no point in greetin' about it. All over and done with now." He unfolded the paper and started to read.

Lettie felt a moment of disorientation, something not quite right, then the feeling was gone. He glanced up at her from his paper. "Happen ye'd better go upstairs and see if your mother's all right, lass," he suggested in a kind but firm tone.

She looked at him for a moment, then made her way quickly upstairs. The door of the main bedroom was open and her mother was sitting up in bed. She looked rosy-cheeked and healthy, no real reason for her to be in bed at all. "Are you okay, Mum?" she asked with concern, "Is there anything I can get you?"

"No, Lettie, nothing at all," her mother beamed. "Sit down for a moment. I want to have a talk with you." Dutifully, Lettie made herself comfortable on the edge of the bed.

"Lettie, I want to apologize to you. I tried to stop you from marrying Cyril, and I was wrong. I shouldn't have interfered."

Lettie smiled. "Don't be silly, Mum. That was ever so long ago, and it didn't exactly stop me, did it?"

"I was angry with you, Lettie. I thought you were a headstrong and selfish young woman. I thought he was going to turn out the same way as your father, and I was wrong. That was prejudice and stupidity on my part. And fear. I was frightened because my health was beginning to break down and I didn't want you to leave me."

"But we didn't leave you, Mother, did we?"

"No, Lettie. You stayed with me right to the end, and you couldn't have been nicer to me, either of you. Cyril was as good a son to me as... well, as Thomas could ever have been if he'd come back from the war. And I never thanked either of you... and I feel bad about that."

She grinned broadly. "Don't be silly Mum. You didn't have to thank us. We liked having you here. And we knew how you felt. Cyril knew perfectly well how you felt about him. I always knew you would like him when you got to know him. Everybody liked Cyril, unless there was something wrong with them. You had been hurt by Dad. We understood that."

"Did you Lettie? Did you really?"

"Of course we did. Don't give it another thought."

The doorbell sounded, making Lettie start. "You'd better go and see who it is," her mother urged.

From the top of the stairs she saw that Cyril was already opening the front door. She hurried down to see who it was. Cyril continued to open it, with an exaggerated slowness and then stood to one side, smiling back at Lettie. There were two people at the door. One was a tall elegant young man in a brown army uniform and a brown private's cap. There were medals on his chest, two bright rows of them, and he carried a canvas kit bag over his shoulder, and in his free hand an old fashioned Lee Enfield rifle with the bayonet fixed. The kit bag and the rifle were brown too. Even his skin had an odd sepia tint, like a very inferior brand of artificial sun-tan cream. Standing in front of him, smiling in an excited sort of way, was a very sweet young girl of about nine in a white frilly dress. She had long golden blonde hair and was clinging to a fold of the soldier's uniform with one hand, as though she were afraid that she might lose him.

Lettie began to feel disoriented again. "Thomas?" she whispered. He beamed a painfully handsome smile in her direction and stepped forward to greet her, lowering the rifle and the kit bag as he entered, leaning them carelessly against the wall.

"Lettie?" he greeted her warmly, holding out his hand, "My little princess? Gosh, haven't you grown!"

She took his hand, felt the firm warm grip. Words would not come. "Thomas?" she whispered again, feebly.

"I've come home, Lettie," he said cheerfully, "aren't you pleased to see me?"

Feeling weak and bewildered she embraced him and felt his powerful young body take her full weight. "Do you want me to throw you up in the air, Lettie? Like I used to do? I could, you know." She shook her head, felt him lower her to the ground once again.

"Is it really you, Thomas?" she asked quietly, "is the war really over?"

"Aye, Lettie. All over. Believe me, you don't want to hear about it. Aren't you going to say hello to your daughter?"

She looked down at the little girl. "My daughter?"

"Hello Mummy," said the little girl cheerfully. "Don't you know me? I'm Violet."

The sense of unease was beginning to leave her. She met Violet's smile and returned it. "Violet? But... you've got so big..."

"Are you going to play with me Mummy? Are you going to come out to play?"

"Come out to play..." she repeated, the words oddly drained of meaning. Violet took her by the hand and pulled her excitedly towards the open door. It was sunny outside, and birds were singing, and Lettie could hear a dog barking far away. Her face tingled in the sunlight as she stepped into the front driveway. It looked different somehow, there were so many trees... and a little stream. That hadn't been there before, she was almost sure... and flowers. So many dazzling flowers... and beyond, soft rolling hills covered with such beautiful shimmering green meadows where animals grazed, the size of ants in the distance.

Violet pulled on her hand, willed her to follow along the twisting pathway, over the bridge, into the lush forest. But Lettie didn't know this landscape. Didn't know where Violet was taking her. She looked back towards the house and for a moment fancied that she could see through the open doorway the motionless figure of a frail old woman, slumped on the sofa with an open photo album on her lap. Then it was gone. Just a trick of the light, Lettie decided.

She held Violet's hand and they ran together up the winding tree-lined path towards the far off sun-drenched meadows.

"I used to be quite a religious man," The Rainbow Man explained, *"until one morning I woke up and realised that God had stopped believing in me..."*

Immaculata

The Angel of the Lord declared unto Mary
And she conceived of the Holy Ghost.

(*The Angelus*)

Immaculata's sensible flat shoes clicked along the pavement as she hurried past the open iron gates of the school hall car park. Her slight and youthful figure was respectably covered by her ample grey overcoat and a plain blue scarf held her long dark hair tight against her head. Her monthly confraternity meeting at the church had run unusually late because of a talk given by a visiting missionary father with a high pitched voice and a slow delivery: it was quite dark now, and she could hear the repetitive mechanical bass line of an undistinguished dance record playing inside the hall. The end of term disco was clearly getting under way.

The signs of the impending event barely registered in Immaculata's brain, it was not the kind of thing that interested her: for some reason she had never felt drawn to the activities of other girls of her age.

"Immaculata!"

She stopped dead in her tracks. It was Billy Sullivan, the son of the local filling station proprietor, almost two years ahead of her at school. She hadn't noticed his dark form behind the iron railings.

"You frightened me! What do you want, Billy?"

"Aren't ye comin' to the disco, Mackie?"

"I don't like discos."

He lowered his voice. "Do ye want to see somethin'?"

She eyed him suspiciously. "What?"

"Me new motorbike. Ye can have a spin on the back of 'er if ye like."

Immaculata was even less interested in motorbikes than she was in discos, but felt vaguely flattered that Billy was talking to her. He was a boy that the older girls giggled about when they thought no one could hear. He had a real leather jacket and his father had been in jail once for smashing up a bookmaker's shop in Clonmel. Immaculata's mother was on late shift at the hospital and probably wouldn't be back much before midnight. There was no pressing reason to go straight home. She hesitated for a moment, then back-tracked to the gate.

It was the first time she had ever ridden on the pillion of a motorbike, and although it had amounted to no more than an unsteady and jerky circuit of the block, by the time they arrived back in the car park her heart was racing and her head buzzing with the intoxication of danger and forbidden adventure. The unaccustomed intimacy of clinging to Billy Sullivan's waist, the growl of the engine, pitching of the seat, rush of wind against her face and the smell of Billy's deodorant spray filtered through his leather jacket all conspired to penetrate the barrier of inhibition so carefully constructed by her mother and the Roman Catholic Church. She brushed his lips lightly with hers as he helped her off the back.

"That was great, Billy."

Without saying anything Billy took her in his arms and covered her mouth with his, bending her head back and attempting to force his tongue between her lips. Completely unprepared for such an event, Immaculata took several seconds to react, by which time she could feel his hand inside the back of her coat, pulling her shirt up, touching her bare back with ice cold fingers, fumbling around for the catch of her minute teenage bra, a garment which in fact fastened at the front. An impulse of excitement surged through her body, but this time she knew things had gone too far, kissing with tongues, hands inside clothes, it all spelled SIN – the gates of Hell were opening up before her. She found a purchase on Billy's chest and pushed him away with all the strength of her two arms.

"Get off me, Billy Sullivan," she warned him, twisting her face away from his.

"What is it with you, Mackie? Nuala Molloy lets me do a lot more than that. I only wanted a bit of a feel."

"Well maybe you should go and feel Nuala Molloy then," she snapped, pushing him further away as he lowered his hands from her waist.

"Sure there's no fun at all in you, girl. Ye may as well be an auld maid of thirty."

"I've got respect for myself, Billy Sullivan. And I don't want any babies till I'm married."

"Sure a wee bit of a feel never got anybody preg-en-ant," he tripped over the pronunciation of the word, "ye've been listening to too much tripe from them auld nuns at the Convent School. Ye'll never get a boyfriend if ye'r frigid. Ye've got te relax enough to get somebody interested."

"Off you go, Billy. Nuala Molloy will be getting lonely. Maybe she's interested. I'm not."

He started to turn, then seemed to change his mind and grasped her wrists. "If there's one thing pisses me off it's a fuckin' little tease like you," he snapped.

"You let go of my wrists or I'll..." She suddenly stopped. She was looking at something or somebody over Billy's shoulder. Billy was certain it was intended as a trick, there was nobody else out at the back of the car park. He bent her forearms up to pull her face closer to his. Over his shoulder Immaculata caught a fleeting movement of something white among the parked cars. Something only she could see, something that had come to remind her of the standards she had set herself. Before there was time for another thought Immaculata's knee contacted the centre of Billy's trousers with considerable force. He squealed like a kicked animal and collapsed in a writhing heap at her feet.

"You bitch! You filthy fuckin' little bitch! I'll get you for that! I'll fuckin' get you for that...!"

Immaculata smiled contentedly and made her way back towards the gate.

An unseen shutter opened with a click behind the square mesh-covered aperture and Immaculata could see the dim silhouette of a man's face.

"Bless me Father for I have sinned," she intoned mechanically.

"How long is it since your last confession?"

"A week."

"And what sins have you committed within that week, my child?"

"I have had impure thoughts four times, told two lies at school... and... I've seen an angel."

There was a pause. "Did you say you'd seen an angel?"

"Yes, Father."

Physically, Immaculata and her mother were strikingly similar. On more than one occasion they had achieved the cliché of being mistaken for sisters. Slender, graceful and rather serious in demeanour, with pale faces, high cheek bones and large soulful brown eyes, they both wore their straight near-black hair just below shoulder length and tended to dress very conservatively. The only immediately evident differences between them were her mother's slight superiority in terms of breast development and her extra inch or so of height. Standing now outside the heavy carved door of the Bishop's house they unconsciously held hands for mutual support and waited.

After a few moments it swung soundlessly inwards to reveal a stout middle-aged woman in a practical dark business suit. She smiled down reassuringly.

"Good afternoon Mrs Sweeny and Immaculata," she greeted them with affected friendliness, "won't you come in. His Grace is expecting you."

They dipped their fingers in the small holy water font just inside the doorway and performed the mechanical ritual of blessing themselves, flicking their hands from forehead to heart, then to left and to right shoulder, before following the elegantly clad housekeeper down the corridor. As they had expected, the interior of the striking building, known to some as the Bishop's "palace", was virtually a museum of church art and ritual, crammed with religious pictures and marble statues on plinths, ancient-looking leather bound books in carved wooden cabinets and ceremonial clerical robes lovingly displayed in large glass cases. It even smelled of incense and sanctity, invoking in Immaculata and her mother the familiar involuntary surge of awe and timidity.

The Bishop's study was large and book-lined and only fractionally less formal than the rest of the building, an effect mainly achieved by the inclusion of a tasteful and lifelike coal-effect gas fire in the centre of the large open grate. Opulent leather armchairs of different sizes were grouped around the fireplace and two of them were occupied by middle aged men in black suits and clerical collars who insisted on standing to greet the newcomers, their stiff courtesy merely adding to their guests' discomfiture.

"Good afternoon ladies," the older and more distinguished looking of the two began with a smile that held no warmth, "I'm glad you were able to come. This is Monsignor Cunningham from the Tullamore Seminary. I asked him to join us to give us the benefit of his expertise in the matters you have come to discuss. I hope you have no objection."

"No, Sir. Your Grace," Mrs Sweeny replied meekly.

"'Father' shall be perfectly adequate. For both of us. Won't you please sit down?" He motioned towards an out-size sofa and they all sat down, the newcomers somewhat self-consciously. "A little tea?" he asked politely, and gestured to his housekeeper who was still watching from the door. There was a click as she closed it and went to comply with his request.

The Bishop fixed Mrs Sweeny with a polite gaze, then turned uncertainly towards Immaculata. He paused for a few moments, uncertain as to how he should begin. "You are still a very young girl, aren't you Immaculata?" he said at last, "Fourteen, I believe?"

"Fifteen next month," her mother put in.

"I believe I confirmed you in the faith some eighteen months ago?" Immaculata nodded. "I've spoken to your teachers, and to your Parish Priest. They speak very highly of you. I am told that you are a well behaved and respectful student at school, and an exemplary member of the Young People's Sacred Heart Confraternity at St. Joseph's Church. These things show great moral strength and maturity. They are achievements of character for which you and your mother should be justly proud, and of course thankful to almighty God."

"Yes, Father. Thank you, Father."

"But... what we're here to talk about..." he looked embarrassed, "is the angel that you say you have seen."

He stood up and leaned his back against the mantel-piece before he went on, looking straight into the young girl's face. His demeanour took on the aspect of one about to preach a sermon. "Immaculata," he said thoughtfully, "all of us, when our spiritual life is just beginning, tend to focus on the more dramatic, external aspects of the holy Church. Statues, buildings, angels, signs and miracles... things that are really only symbols of something much deeper. Take this Sacred Heart painting, for instance," he turned around and motioned towards the shrine over the fireplace, a red oil lamp burning in front of a stylised Christ image. "everybody knows Jesus didn't have a heart made of gold on the outside of his body. That's just a symbol, a representation of the love that Christ had for all of us, a love so powerful he accepted death on the cross to save us from our sins. That lamp as well, it isn't a magic lantern like the one in Aladdin: it's just a representation of our devotion to the teaching and the way of life of Jesus. It's another symbol. Devils and angels and cherubs and burning bushes and fiery chariots... they aren't ordinary objects in the world like tables and chairs... they're ways of understanding the world, of ex-plaining things when the reality is beyond the limitations of our human minds..."

"But there are angels," Immaculata protested, quietly but firmly, "I've seen one. I've talked to her."

There was a moment of uncomfortable silence which was broken by Monsignor Cunningham. His tone seemed sharp, even harsh compared to that of the Bishop.

"Immaculata, young people frequently believe that they have been favoured with visions and mystical experiences. Especially devout and holy young people such as yourself. But on closer examination they invariably discover that they have been mistaken."

At this Immaculata's mother seemed to take offence. "How can you dismiss Immaculata's vision like that? She hasn't told you anything about it yet. Are you saying that there are no such things as angels? No such things as miracles?"

"I am saying... that such things, if they exist, are so uncommon that we might expect one or two examples in a century. Not even in a generation. In fact I can hardly recall the last time the Church gave credence to a claim of this kind. My dear Mrs Sweeny, we don't live in an age of visions and miracles any more. We live in an age of hard fact, scientific objectivity, placing our fingers in the wounds, re-examining all our traditional beliefs. And the Catholic Church has been able to taken on the scientific age and to emerge strengthened. More focused on its core beliefs and values. Our belief in a loving and forgiving God and in the sanctity of human life, our devotion to such values as honesty, faithfulness, kindness, charity and tolerance towards our fellow man. Those are the things that make us Roman Catholics, not the kind of externals and trappings that His Grace spoke of."

"Now wait a minute," Mrs Sweeny protested, sensing an unfairness in the line that the Monsignor was taking with her daughter, her angry impulse overcoming her intimidation at the presence of these high ranking priests, "you didn't talk about symbols when we were at school. Immaculata and I learned from the same catechism. I can still remember it now. 'Who made the world? God made the world.' 'Who is God? God is our father in heaven, creator and lord of all things.' 'Where is God? God is everywhere but in a special sense he is present in heaven where he is seen by the angels and saints.' Where he is seen by the angels and saints, Father. That was what we were taught. That was what you told us was true. Angels and saints. Not symbols. Angels. Are you telling me that that was a lie?"

The Bishop decided to parry this one. He beamed a paternal smile in her direction. "Mrs Sweeny, the school catechism was written many decades ago, and it was written for children. It was a product of far less sophisticated times than we live in now. Even within your lifetime, which has been a lot shorter than mine, ideas and attitudes have changed within the Roman Catholic Church. We have become a lot less literal in our beliefs, as Monsignor Cunningham was trying to explain to you. We realize now that a lot of things... like angels, devils, purgatory, penances, indulgences... were merely metaphors used to explain complicated ideas to people whose lives were simple, who lacked education and scholarly attitudes. They were never important. They were never meant to represent a literal truth. They were... what shall I say, handles to allow us to grab hold of concepts that were at heart moral and philosophical."

"If you want to see a religion that has stood still for a thousand years take a look at the Islam practiced in the Middle East," Monsignor Cunningham almost snapped, touching on some personal academic preoccupation.

"Bishop, I can't argue theology with a man like you. But you taught my child and you taught me that there were angels: good angels watching over us, keeping us safe from harm. And now you're telling us that there aren't. Well, all I know is that my Immaculata says she's seen an angel, and spoken to it, and my Immaculata doesn't tell lies."

As she finished there was a polite knock on the outer door. The Bishop's housekeeper had arrived with the tea.

Mrs Sweeny could see that both priests were grateful for the interruption.

Immaculata timidly entered the doctor's surgery and closed the door carefully behind her. He beamed up at her from behind his desk, a kindly dark suited middle-aged man with a neat beard. "Take a seat, Miss Sweeny. How can I help you?"

She hesitated, tried to say something but failed: her chin trembled for a moment with the unspoken words.

"Please don't be embarrassed. I am a doctor, Immaculata, I have heard it all before. I'm here to help. I'm on your side, no matter what it is, and everything that you say to me is in total confidence."

"Doctor Ryan," she stumbled over the words, "can you tell me if I'm pregnant?"

He became more serious. "I certainly can, Immaculata." He glanced down at her notes. "But looking at your date of birth, even such the possibility of such a thing involves a serious legal issue. Are you aware of that?"

"Yes, Doctor. It's all right. I haven't had sex."

"Then I can answer your question straight off. You aren't pregnant. I'm going to get the nurse to give you a brochure..."

"No, Doctor... I mean... I would still like to have the test."

He looked at her quizzically. "In all of human history, my dear, there has only been one immaculate conception."

"I know, Doctor. I think she was about my age too."

The Bishop sat down with calm dignity and started to pour out the tea. Monsignor Cunningham seemed to take this as the signal for him to begin his questioning.

"Immaculata," he said in a friendly but businesslike tone, "when you see the angel, is it always in the same place?"

"No, father. Usually it's in my bedroom, but not always."

"And can you tell us please what it looks like?"

"It's a lady – all dressed in white. The robes cover her head, like a nun's dress, and there's a veil over her face."

"I see. And about how many times have you seen her?"

"I don't know. Ten or twelve?"

"Can you see her now?"

"No... it's usually when it's dark, or nearly dark. And when I'm on my own. Or when I'm in danger. Or when... there's a temptation..."

"I see. Has your mother ever spoken to you about angels?"

"No, I don't think so"

Her mother glanced up sharply. "May I ask what you mean by that, Father?" She demanded.

"Mrs Sweeny, there are matters which I think we need to speak about in private."

"I have no secrets from my daughter. Absolutely none. Whatever you have to say I want her to hear as well."

"As you wish." He composed himself and looked her straight in the eye. "I think we both know that..." he hesitated "that your daughter Immaculata was born outside of wedlock. In fact, there has never been a Mr Sweeny, has there?"

"Immaculata knows that. I haven't hidden anything from her. She knows that she was the result of an attack... something that happened to me when I wasn't much older than she is now."

"Quite. And you did the right thing in going through with the pregnancy, and in being open with her about her origins, and in treating her as an innocent child, free from any taint of guilt regarding the actions of her biological father. And above all in bringing her up in the holy Catholic Church, in the full light of God's love. In all this you have done a very good job, Mrs Sweeny."

"So why are you asking if I've talked to her about angels?"

"Mrs Sweeny," he glanced towards Immaculata again, obviously wishing that the girl wasn't there, "I am aware of the... attention that you attracted yourself... as a schoolgirl at the Francis Xavier Convent School in Tullamore."

She looked slightly ruffled. "I believed that I had a vocation, a special calling..."

"You believed that you saw visions, didn't you, Mrs Sweeny?"

She dropped her voice so that it was little more than a whisper. "I was visited by the Blessed Virgin in a dream. I was told that she had a special task for me, a special job. Something that I would have to do when I was a bit older. That was all."

"I see. And was she a lady in white, with a veil over her face?"

Mrs Sweeny glowed with embarrassment. Immaculata found her hand and held it. "I had a dream, Monsignor Cunningham. I was steeped in religious stories and I had a dream. That was all."

"It wasn't all, Mrs Sweeny." Monsignor Cunningham knew that he had the upper hand and pressed ahead with relish. "You very nearly founded a religious order of your own, didn't you? You had half a dozen little disciples saying special prayers and wearing special amulets and following you around. What was the basis of your private order of pre-adolescent nuns, Mrs Sweeny? What did you tell them?

Did you enjoy being the Mother Superior? The Sister Foundress?"

At these words the Bishop once more intervened, his tone pleasant and conciliatory. "I don't think that is entirely relevant to what we are here to discuss, Monsignor Cunningham. Children often go through an obsessive religious phase in their mid-teens. All children like to play games and have gangs. Let us try to keep a sense of proportion."

The monsignor's chin quivered.

"I beg your pardon, Your Grace." He shifted in his seat so that he was looking straight into the young girl's face. "Tell me about the last time that you saw the angel, Immaculata."

"I saw her yesterday, when my mother told me we had to come here. I was going to tell her that I felt ill, that I wouldn't be able to come. And then I saw the angel and I knew that she didn't want me to tell a lie, that she needed me to come here."

"Where were you when this happened?"

"In my bedroom, sitting at my desk. I'd just unpacked my bag to start my homework."

"And where was the angel?"

"I just caught a tiny glimpse. Out of the corner of my eye. That's all I see a lot of the time. She just comes for a second... to remind me that she's there."

"Just a white shape, for an instant, in the corner of your field of vision?"

"Yes, Father. But other times she stays, and lets me see her clearly, and talks to me."

He looked her straight in the eye. She met his gaze without flinching. "And what does she say to you, Immaculata?"

"That I've been chosen for a special task. A very big task. And that I don't have to agree to it unless I want to."

"Are you having trouble getting to sleep Immaculata," her mother asked, poking her head around the door of her daughter's room.

"A bit, Mum."

"Is it... something to do with the angel?" Mrs Sweeny opened the door fully and smiled down reassuringly at her daughter.

Immaculata took a few moments to reply. "She asked me something, Mother," she said hesitantly. "Something... very scary."

Her mother came into the room and stood over the bed. "What did she ask you, sweetheart?"

"I... can't tell you. I promised her I wouldn't. She said I mustn't tell anybody."

Mrs Sweeny reached out and took her daughter's hand. "You must never break a promise," she said gently. For a moment neither of them spoke.

"Let me get you something," said Mrs Sweeny at last, turning to go.

"Another sleeping pill?"

"You need it sweetheart. Your sleep is important. You're lucky you've got a nurse for a mother who can get you things like that."

"I know that we're here to talk about your daughter and not you, Mrs Sweeny," the Monsignor probed, "But there is one more area that I feel I must go into. Would I be right to suppose that it was your own pregnancy in your late teens that put an end to your plans to enter a religious order?"

"My pregnancy put an end to a lot of my plans," she said coldly. "I didn't see a great deal of that tolerance and forgiveness and kindness that the two of you were talking about a few minutes ago. The Carmelites made it pretty clear that I was no longer welcome as a postulant. The hospital where I was supposed to be going to do my training discovered they didn't have a place for me after all. I had to leave home and move to the North of Ireland and find another hospital to get away from the whispers. Nobody believed me that I'd been attacked. You know that. They saw a pregnant teenager and they could only think of one thing. But none of that matters, Father. Not any more. I finished my training, in spite of them all, and I brought Immaculata up on my own, and she didn't want for anything either. I'm not bitter about any of it, Father. I have a beautiful daughter. I have a good life."

"Mrs Sweeny, this is frankly somewhat delicate." He hesitated. "We both know perfectly well that there are certain... parallels... between Immaculata's situation now and your own at that time. Putting it plainly, we both know that Immaculata is indeed pregnant. It serves no purpose to evade that fact."

"I had no intention of evading anything, Father," said Mrs Sweeny very quietly, looking him straight in the eye.

He seemed mildly unnerved. As he watched she searched in her handbag and produced a small brown envelope which she handed to him, standing up to do so. He reached into his inside pocket for his reading glasses.

"It's the result of a pregnancy test," he announced, somewhat reluctantly, "signed by Dr Ryan in Drumcray."

"Yes, Father," said Mrs Sweeny, with a hint of something a little bit like triumph in her voice, "and now would you look at this one please." She handed him a somewhat larger white envelope. Again he opened the sheet within and read it.

"This is from the gynaecology consultant at the Mater Hospital in Dublin," he said quietly, "it says he's examined your daughter and that she is medically virgo intacto."

"Yes, Father. Now, would you look at the dates of the two tests."

Immaculata's eyes flickered between waking and sleep. It was there again, the tall white shape, but she was finding it so hard to stay awake – so very hard to keep her eyes open against the power of the drug that her mother had administered. It was speaking to her from far away, through a drifting grey fog that was trying to engulf her. She struggled to hear the words, battled with the sleep that was so hungry to claim her.

"Have you reached a decision, Immaculata?" the angel asked her gently.

"Yes," she whispered.

"Shall you bear this sacred child?"

Again she managed to whisper: "Yes."

"Then rest peacefully. It shall come to pass."

The Monsignor's eyes widened in disbelief. Without a word he passed the documents to the Bishop. The two men looked at one another, shocked into silence.

"What are you... going to do?" the Bishop managed to say at last, "you don't intend going public with this, do you?"

"Going public? Are you saying I should hide a miracle? Let people think my daughter is a slut? Let them treat her the way they treated me?"

The Bishop put his hand to his head and closed his eyes for a moment. "A virgin birth, Mrs Sweeny," he whispered.

"A virgin birth. Have you any idea what the press will do with this? What they'll do to your daughter? What it's going to be like for the two of you if this gets out?"

"I don't think it's me or Immaculata that you're worried about," she said very coldly. "Is it, Bishop?"

There was a long silence. It was Monsignor Cunningham who finally spoke. "Mrs Sweeny, as we've tried to explain to you, The Roman Catholic Church no longer bases its teaching on... miracles and conjuring tricks. If you go public with this it could have an absolutely devastating effect on the entire Church. It could set us back decades. We don't trade in this currency any more. It's going to cause splits, divisions, uprisings of ultra-traditionalist Catholics challenging the authority of the Pope himself. It could put us back almost to medieval times. Destroy our chance for the ecumenism that we all want, the unification of all the great orthodox faiths of the world. It's going to be a disaster for everything the present Holy Father is trying to achieve."

She looked him straight in the eye and there was a kind of triumph in her voice. "Then why has Almighty God sent his angel to speak to my daughter, and why has he done this thing? Do you think he might be telling you that his Church has swayed too much with fashion?"

Mrs Sweeny remained perfectly still at the end of the bed and waited until her daughter's eyes had closed and her breathing had grown slow and regular. When she was certain that the girl was deeply asleep she removed her white headgear, pulled the veil away from her face, and took off her white ward coat. Switching on the bedside lamp, she produced a black leather medical case and gently drew down Immaculata's duvet. Smiling, she looked past her daughter's prone figure to something or someone at the far end of the room. "Behold the handmaid of the Lord," she said quietly. "Thy holy will shall be done."

She opened the case and carefully unpacked a large syringe which was attached to a length of thin transparent tubing. Beside it was a silver container resembling a small thermos flask which bore the label "donor semen" and a batch code.

"I'm sure your baby is going to be very beautiful," she whispered to Immaculata. "Just like you."

"Sure most men only go with a whore to have somebody to talk to. I've never needed one meself," The Rainbow Man explained.

Personal Services

Lexie shuffled about nervously as the man in the dark suit approached. She had a fair bit of experience under her belt by now but she still found the initial approach highly embarrassing.

He looked respectable enough: neat dark suit, black shoes, hard to tell the colour of his shirt and tie by the light of the street lamp that turned everything to shades of yellow. She smiled nervously. "Got the time, Mister?" she addressed him in a tone as cheerful as she could muster.

"I've got nothing but time," he replied in a mild, cultured sort of voice.

"Oh, yes, very clever! You've got the time but have you got the inclination?" It was a pretty feeble joke but might serve its purpose. He came closer and looked her up and down. It was difficult to gauge his expression. His features were pleasant enough: early forties perhaps, tall, well-proportioned, obviously okay with regard to personal hygiene. She could do worse. He was beside her now so she could speak more quietly. "Are you interested in doing some business?"

He didn't answer right away but seemed to continue with his inspection, concentrating now on her face, staring rather unnervingly into her eyes. At last his face broke into a smile and she felt the tension ease.

"Mary Magdalene," he muttered, almost to himself.

"Well, in the same line of work I suppose." He was quite witty. She was beginning to like him. It's so much easier if they have a sense of humour.

"Are you going to wash my feet?" he asked.

"If that's what does it for you. But just so we understand each other, no kinky stuff, no anal, no kissing on the lips, and you've got to wear a rubber. Fifty for a couple of hours or I can stay all night for a hundred and fifty. Up to you. Payment in advance."

He nodded thoughtfully. "Seems very reasonable."

"Will we... say all night then?"

"Oh yes. I think we shall say all night."

He turned, clearly expecting her to follow, and walked towards the nearest front door, just next to where they were standing. "Oh, you live right here?" He nodded.

There was a pile of neglected junk mail in the hallway and the place smelled faintly of mildew and damp. The paintwork was old and scuffed and there was a payphone over the cluttered hall table. Lexie said nothing but the man clearly felt that an explanation was needed. "I've recently come out of hospital after a long illness," he explained. "This place is just temporary. I don't intend to be living here very long."

"It's fine," she lied cheerfully. "Feeling okay now I hope? What do I call you by the way?"

"Martin. And you? Mary of course, isn't it?"

"Whatever you say. Mary and Martin. M and M. Get it?" From his expression she rather thought that he didn't.

Martin's room was upstairs – the light from the street-lamp shone straight in his window. The place was a reasonable size, clean and tidy, and furnished in an old-fashioned sort of way with a wooden writing desk, a couple of tasteful landscapes on the walls, several well-stacked bookshelves and a large neatly turned-back double bed. Lexie nodded approvingly. "You keep your room very neat."

"When one's living space is restricted tidiness becomes a necessity." He took off his jacket and hung it carefully in the wardrobe.

"You read a lot, Martin?" She looked around. There was no TV.

"I am a researcher, Mary. I have conducted research all my life."

"Well, it's a nice room. Say, is it okay if we get the financial side of things out of the way first? Then we can relax."

"Of course." He sat to unlock the drawer of the desk and took out three crisp fifty-pound notes which he handed to Lexie.

"Thank you kindly, Sir!" The notes disappeared instantly into the inner recesses of her jacket. He remained seated at the desk watching her, his whole body very still, his expression neutral and unreadable. She was used to shy men but this didn't seem like shyness. "How would you feel about having a shower first?" she suggested with a twinkle in her eye, "We could have one together and I could scrub your back. It's a nice way to get acquainted."

He remained motionless. "Can we talk for a bit first? I'm best with words. That's how I like to get acquainted."

"Of course." She perched awkwardly on the bed. "Dirty talk? Do you want me to tell you what turns me on, sexually?" It was a skill at which she didn't particularly excel but if a paying client wanted it she was willing to have a go.

"No. I just want you to tell me a bit about yourself. Why you do what you do. That sort of thing."

"Martin, this is a business relationship. Of course I have a personal life, but I don't discuss it with people I don't know very well. You understand?" Writing a book, Lexie thought to herself. Bet any money he's writing a book. He'll probably prattle on all night and I'll get no sleep whatever.

He nodded. "I understand. Maybe you would like to hear a bit about me instead?"

"That would be nice, Martin." She shifted position on the bed and propped some pillows against her back for comfort. He turned his chair to face her and seemed to think for a moment before he began.

"There has been... very little love in my life, Mary. Very few friendships. I have spent far too much time alone, devoted far too much time to my work. It's been a lonely life. Not a very good life."

"But you're still young, Martin. You can have lots of lovers. Lots of friendships. Lots of fun."

"I'm not blaming the world," he went on, ignoring what she had said, "the problem is with me. I know that. I don't relate well to people. I was brought up by my father – my mother died when I was a baby. He was a very severe man. Not loving and not... approachable."

She nodded. Therapy session on the way. She'd had it all before. "What did he do?"

"He was a minister of religion. Scottish Presbyterian. He was a cruel man, an appalling man. A tyrant and a hypocrite. And worse. Sorry Mary, I have been most dreadfully unsociable. May I offer you a cup of tea, or something a little stronger?"

She smiled. "Your father wouldn't approve. Gin and tonic maybe?"

"I've only got whisky, but it's a good one."

"Whisky it is then. Got ice?"

"Ice in a single malt? Not done, Mary." He made his way to the bedside cabinet beside Lexie and opened it. To her alarm a bundle of assorted kitchen knives and hunting knives tumbled out on to the floor. Martin seemed unperturbed. "My knife collection," he started to pick them up and replace them one by one. "I need a bigger cabinet." He fished out the whisky bottle and two large whisky glasses. Lexie noticed that he hadn't put away one of the knives, a large sheathed hunting knife that he placed on top of the cabinet. Lexie estimated her distance to the door and mentally rehearsed getting to it in a hurry.

"Oh there's no need to be alarmed," he handed her the drink, "I only keep them because they wouldn't let me have anything like that while I was in hospital. You always want what you can't have, don't you? The same applies to the whisky. It's a very fine one, isn't it?"

She gulped some down and nodded. "Terrific." He took a sip from his own and sat beside her. He was between her and the door now but the knife was slightly out of his reach. "What was wrong with you... I mean, why were you in hospital, Martin?"

"I'm afraid I had a nervous breakdown. Stress, you know. Working too hard. Worrying too much."

"But not any more. I mean, you're cured now, right?"

"Oh yes. That's what they do in hospital. They cure you."

"But, it took them a long time. Right?"

"I went in to hospital when I was fourteen years old."

She was stunned. She spoke very slowly and deliberately. "You were over-working... when you were fourteen years old?"

"Examination pressures. Academic matters. My father had big ambitions for me, you see. I was a bright boy. I had a great future ahead of me. Or so everyone thought." He leaned across her to put his drink on the bedside cabinet, alongside the knife. "But it never happened. Things didn't work out."

"I'm... I'm sorry, Martin."

"There will be a reward, of course. I've done everything I was told. They never said that I would be understood in this life. That would be too much to expect."

"Who never said?" She could feel her heart pounding.

"The angels, Mary. God's angels. They're everywhere, you know, although we can't see them."

She took another mouthful of the whiskey and nodded. "Yeah. Right. God's angels."

"Everything that happens is meant to happen, you know. Your coming here tonight. My finding you beneath that street light. It's all for a purpose, Mary. We are all the instruments of God's will. Every one of us."

"I'm... sure you're right, Martin."

"Oh yes. I *am* right. Are you ready to do what you said, Mary?"

"You... want sex... right now?"

"I want you to wash my feet. And anoint them."

"Oh! Right! Sure. Why not. Got some water or something?"

"Just a moment." To her horror he picked up the knife instead of his drink and disappeared through the door by which they had entered. A few moments later he returned with a large ornate silver tray bearing a plastic bowl full of water, a towel, two bottles of toiletries, and, to her considerable alarm, the knife – all tastefully arranged like a waiter would carry them in a fancy restaurant, or a priest in some kind of religious ritual. He put down the tray for a moment, locked the door and slipped the key into his shirt lapel pocket. "We wouldn't want to be disturbed," he said quietly. Lexie's mouth fell open but she could think of nothing to say. Lifting the knife he placed the tray on the floor near to where he had been sitting. He dangled the instrument carelessly in his right hand until he sat down and placed it on his lap.

"Do we need the knife?" Lexie asked in a voice that came out as a hoarse croak.

"Oh yes. Essential. It's part of the ceremony."

Lexie felt her heart begin to race. She got to her feet unsteadily and knelt down in front of Martin. This brought her eyes level with the knife on his lap. It was a high quality item, with a dark hardwood handle and a curved blade about seven or eight inches long, sheathed in a well-made leather holster. It wasn't clipped in, it could be deployed in an instant.

She slowly untied his laces and eased the neat leather brogues off his feet. "You said you've always done what the angels told you," she probed in the most casual tone she could muster, "what kind of thing did they tell you to do?"

"They asked me to do a most terrible thing, Mary. They asked me to kill my own father."

Her hands froze in the middle of the act of removing one of Martin's socks.

"It wasn't murder, it was a cleansing. You see, Mary, my father was the Antichrist. Would you like me to put my feet in the bowl?"

"Eh? Yes. Right. In the bowl." She wondered if he could feel her hand shaking as she pulled the sock completely free. His feet were clean already, rather long and graceful, with the nails meticulously trimmed. Mechanically, she squirted a little shower-gel from one of the bottles and started to massage it into his skin. Normally she would have found the activity quite pleasant and soothing, but her whole body felt rigid and her attention remained totally focused on the knife on Martin's lap. "How did... I mean what did the angels tell you to do?"

"You mean the manner of his death? It was a sacrificial killing, in the tradition of biblical sacrifice. It's still the basis of the religious slaughter of animals throughout the Middle East. The animal is bound and one or more of the carotid arteries in its throat is severed with a single stroke. Unconsciousness follows very rapidly. It's an extremely humane form of slaughter." He noticed that she had stopped massaging his feet. "Is there a problem?"

"Oh no. Of course not. Sorry. No problem." She returned to her task with renewed vigour. For a while she worked in silence. "I think they're done now. Will I dry them?"

"Dry them and anoint them with the oil."

She looked down and saw that the other bottle contained baby oil. "The oil. Yes, of course." Carefully she lifted each of his feet out on to the towel and put the tray and the bowl to one side. She dried her hands and then started to dry his feet, slowly and almost tenderly, drawing a fold of towel gently through each of the gaps between his toes. When she had quite finished she paused.

"The oil," Martin reminded her, "just the oil now, and the ceremony is almost finished."

"Almost finished?" she queried in a breathy whisper.

"Yes, Mary. Almost finished."

Lexie hesitated. She looked up and saw that he was studying her with a serene expression like a priest conducting a service. As she watched his gaze seemed to drift down from her eyes to her throat. The knife was resting on his knee, inches from his hand. She imagined the quick thrust that would rip it from its sheath and draw it across her throat. It would require less than a second. Any sudden movement she made might become her last. He was far bigger and far stronger than she was. If she struggled she would be instantly overpowered. She glanced at the locked door. She felt the way she had when she was a little girl, paralysed with fear, helpless and abandoned, those nights when her stepfather had come home drunk and furious looking for someone to blame, someone to hurt, someone to strike out at.

Frantically she tried to think of a course of action. There was really only one and the thought of it sickened her. She doubted that she had the stomach to go through with it. Something inside her seemed to respond to the terror she was feeling and the thought entered her mind that she was not going to be a victim ever again. Forcing herself with all her will power, every inch of her body trembling, she reached out for the oil but in the middle of the slow action suddenly speeded up and grabbed the bowl of water in both hands, flinging its contents straight into Martin's face. As he lifted his hands to his eyes she grabbed the knife from his lap, lost a mind-numbing half second pulling it from its sheath, and then with all the weight of her body behind the blow, slashed it viciously through his throat.

Letting out a stifled scream of horror at the pulsating fountain of blood drenching his seated figure, she stumbled back against the writing-desk and used it to pull herself to her feet.

Martin opened his eyes and, incredibly, he seemed to smile at her. When he spoke it was with perfect clarity and calmness. "The angels, Mary. Can't you hear the angels?" His smile broadened. "To you oh God I commend my soul!" With these words his eyes seemed to glaze over, his face still fixed in its blissful grin, and he slumped back on to the bed. The fountain spurted two more times and abated

Eyes wide with terror Lexie backed towards the door. There was a strange ringing in her ears and the room seemed unnaturally bright as though her eyes were letting in too much light. Martin's body twitched once, the last feeble surge of blood swelled grotesquely over his shirt, drenching the pocket containing the key, and he became totally still.

Shocked into a semi-conscious trance, unable to take in what had happened, Lexie laid the bloody knife gently on the white towel and found herself listening intensely for a chorus of angels, surprised that none could be heard.

"Sure I don't care if you're a Hindu or a Confucian or a Zoroastrian or even a Presbyterian," The Rainbow Man declared generously, "we've all got te have somethin' te worship that's bigger than ourselves. For me it's The Rock of Gibraltar..."

Celia's Shrine

I'm glad you like the bungalow. I would like it to go to a happy young couple like you. We were always very happy here. Well, as happy as anybody ever is... you know what I mean. Why don't you sit down and I'll make the two of you a cup of tea?

This was out in the country when we first moved here you know. Fields and sheep and cows. You couldn't call it the country now, could you? Times change. The city grows. We still have the field at the back, of course. Well, we always called it a field. Just a bit of rough meadow, really. We never did very much with it. The idea was that we would have a pony when our boy got a bit bigger. We would build a stable at one end. We never did, of course.

No, it wasn't that. More that... our boy never did get big.

I don't mind talking about it. It's a very long time ago now. Emily and I married quite late in life. When Emily had Charlie she was forty-one years old. We were one of the unlucky ones. The one in twelve. Charlie was born with Down's Syndrome. They called it Mongolism back then. And they didn't have the treatments for it that they have nowadays. He had other complications as well. He didn't live very long. We always called it Charlie's Field. It sort of... kept his name alive.

The three rose bushes? Oh you noticed them did you? Yes, they do look a bit out of place. Just three rose bushes in a triangle in the middle of a field. Funny that you should call it a shrine. It is, in a manner of speaking, but it has nothing to do with Charlie. It's a much longer story, I won't waste your time with it.

Well, if you really want to hear it I suppose I could tell you while the kettle's boiling. You'll think it's very silly though. It was... oh, nearly thirty years ago.

It was late in the evening and somebody knocked at the door. He was an odd looking boy, long flowing robes, long golden blond hair with a little beard, a yellow band around his head, jewellery, open-toe sandals... Very regular features. You know the first thing I thought? It's Jesus Christ, come looking for disciples! Although I suppose Jesus would have been dark-haired. Probably didn't wear medallions either, come to think of it.

Anyway, it turned out he was travelling with his girlfriend and their van had broken down right at the end of my driveway. I was a bit suspicious at first. Could have been a trick to get into the house. Could have been anybody. But he had such a... genuine face, I couldn't not trust him. Fancy dress or not, I liked the boy as soon as I set eyes on him. I went down to see the van, and it was incredible! All painted up with scenes out of Eastern mythology. Gods, demons, dancing-girls, men in chariots, soldiers turning into falling leaves, an old man teaching children under a tree... And it was so colourful! I just couldn't describe it, really. You would need to have seen it.

I got another shock when I met his girlfriend. I could see why she hadn't come up the drive with him. Her name was Celia. She was a beautiful blonde girl, looked about fifteen but she was probably seventeen, and ready to give birth at any moment as far as I could see. She was a slight little thing apart from the bulge. Great big blue eyes. And you know the way that some pregnant women can almost radiate happiness and well-being? Well, she was like that. She sort of... lit up the inside of that little van with her own inner light, if you know what I mean. You couldn't take your eyes off her. It was like... a religious experience. I just wanted to sit there and stare at her. It seemed like such a privilege to be in her presence...

Sorry, I'm rambling now. Talking nonsense. She was just a teenage mum-to-be. That was why they had come back from India, it turned out, only the trip hadn't gone as smoothly as they had hoped, and frankly they were running out of time. Her folks lived in Bath – they still had a couple of hundred miles to go and anybody could see they weren't going to make it. She was in no condition for travelling. There was hardly room to sit down in the back of that van, it was crammed full of beads and wall-hangings and carved wood and bits of jewellery and clothes and God-knows-what.

Well, to cut a long story short, I wouldn't let them go on. I thought the least we could do was let them use Charlie's room for a few days while they sorted themselves out. I wanted to phone the local hospital and put them on stand-by, but the girl wouldn't have it. Said that she had to give birth on the earth, facing a certain direction, while some kind of incantations were read out... all kinds of stuff like that. But it was what she wanted, and this was her baby, so I did my best to go along with it. I said they could use the field at the back, but we would have to put up some kind of shelter of course. The boy said that was no problem, that he could make a teepee out of three pieces of wood and a couple of old sheets. Three pieces of wood and old sheets! Can you imagine it? It didn't look too bad actually, when they'd made it. I was quite impressed. Lucky it was spring and the weather wasn't too bad. Can you imagine giving birth on the ground in England in the winter?

I'm afraid Emily wasn't all that keen on having them in Charlie's room. I had to insist... to plead for the girl almost. It surprised me. Let me see a side of Emily that I hadn't seen before.

Yes, it seems crazy looking back on it now, but everything went quite well, all things considered. I got to know the boy quite well. He talked about love and peace and non-violence and all the things that kids used to talk about back then, and about the community they'd lived in in India. How the world was going to change for ever, no more wars or cruelty or exploitation or private property or possessiveness. How they believed that the child they were going to have together was going to be one of the seeds. One source from which this wonderful new world was going to grow.

Emily didn't like it. She said he was just trying to say it was all right to sleep around. I must admit I found her a bit... unsympathetic. She and I were more different than I had realized, I suppose.

On the second day another couple arrived in another van, friends of theirs, to see them through the birth and to try to sort out the broken-down van. They were a pretty unusual pair as well, I can tell you. But good people, you know? You could tell just by looking at them. Good through and through.

The baby arrived on the third day after the van broke down. The two men did the chanting and the other woman looked after Celia and did the practical things. Emily and I didn't interfere, just watched from the back window and waited until it was all over. Emily thought I was completely crazy to go along with it all. She seemed hostile for no reason. Said I'd turned the bungalow into a tinker camp. Said I would find myself in the court if anything happened to the girl or her baby... maybe she was right, I don't know. But it was what Celia wanted, and I couldn't see any harm in it.

When it was pretty obvious that she had had her baby, the chanting stopped and the two men came out of the tent. I thought they would be over the moon, breaking open the champagne and the cigars and all the rest of it, but they seemed a bit subdued. Her boyfriend, Martin, the one like Jesus, just stood there with his back to the tent and the other one walked up towards the van. I thought there must have been some tragedy, like Emily had said, and I lost no time in getting out there to see what was going on.

There was no tragedy, the baby was tiny and beautiful and Celia was sitting up and smiling and holding it to her breast. I think it was the most beautiful sight that I have ever seen in my life. But there was just one thing. That baby hadn't been fathered by Martin. It had light brown skin and a head of jet-black hair. When I saw that I understood everything.

I tucked back the flap of the tent and I put my hand on his shoulder. He didn't say a word, just stood there. I didn't say anything either. What was there to say? Congratulations? Bad luck? That's free love for you?

I don't think it had crossed his mind for an instant that it mightn't be his own kid. He had despised the whole notion of fidelity, attacked it in detail and at length: so what was he supposed to say now? I really felt for the boy. I suppose his whole world had just fallen to pieces. It's that whole thing about getting your heart and your head to agree. What can anybody say about it? I just went inside and poured him a stiff drink and took it out to him. He downed it in one.

Talking about drinks, I think the kettle's boiling. I'll just go and make the tea. There isn't much more to tell you anyway.

The ending? Oh there isn't one really. Their friends in the other van loaded up all the stuff out of the broken-down one and took it away. Apparently they were going to sell it at stalls at pop-festivals or something. They never got the other van going. I had to phone up to get it taken away in the end.

I drove Celia and Martin and the new baby to the train station. She gave me her address in Bath but I never looked her up. I suppose I didn't want the spell to be broken. Didn't want to hear that she was a part-time bar-maid at the local pub and her daughter was up for shoplifting or something. I wanted to go on believing that that child was going to be special. That she was going to help to change the world. That I had witnessed some kind of miracle.

Martin? Yes, I think he stayed with her, at least for a while. But he was talking about going to London to look for work. I somehow doubt if they were together for very long after that. You could tell that something had died between them. Something... changed between Emily and me too I think. I've never been able to put my finger on it, but something did.

Oh, the three rose bushes? Yes, I planted them in the holes that were left when they took out the tent-poles. So right in the middle of that triangle was where the baby was born. I've always thought of it as sacred ground, somehow.

Yes, I suppose the birth of that little baby disrupted a lot of lives in one way or another. Not the first time that a teenager having a child has done that. I seem to remember something about it in the New Testament. I wonder if that innkeeper had a wife?

"It's no good tryin' te put the evil eye on me," scoffed The Rainbow Man. "I've got a bone out of St. Patrick's own finger on a string around me neck. Yer not dealin' with an amateur here, boyo!"

Witchcraft

My sister Ita was born in the summer holidays a month before I was due to move up to the big school. I never thought I would have a sister, or a brother either, because I thought you had to have both a mother and a father if you wanted babies, and we hadn't seen my father for years. I couldn't even remember what he looked like, and my mother said she was glad he had gone and that sometimes she had nightmares about him coming back. So I was surprised when my mother told me she was going to have another baby. I thought maybe it was a changeling, one of those babies the fairies leave you when they take away a real child, or maybe the Devil's child, the kind of baby witches have. Not that my mother was a witch. But there was one living just outside the town.

Everybody in our gang knew the woman in Raven Cottage was a witch. Her name was Nellie Brooks. Sometimes you could catch a glimpse of her through the grass and the weeds that choked her front garden and grew up to where the thatch began. Everybody knew that she ate little boys if they got too close to the cottage. Boiled them up in a big black cauldron that she had dangling on a chain over the fireplace. Sometimes when you passed by you could smell them boiling. It was all you could do to keep from being sick.

241

We didn't know a lot about her except that she was about two hundred years old and she had a one-eyed black cat that was nearly as old as she was. That was her familiar. You would see it sometimes sitting on the gatepost, watching people go by on the lane with its good eye. Keeping a lookout in case any boys got too close.

On summer nights you could see her flying past the full moon on her broomstick, on her way to visit the Devil with a big sack over her shoulder, full of the souls of all the boys she had boiled and eaten. I never actually saw her myself but Billy Slevin saw her lots of times and told us all about it. He could sit up later than us because his mother was dead and his dad was usually drunk. He was lucky, he got to do a lot of good things because of that.

Of course the best time to see her was on a Saturday afternoon because that was when she took the bus in to Drumalea to do her shopping at Biddy Conlon's post office shop next to the green. We used to wait for her to get off the bus and taunt her a bit, maybe throw some earth at her, and then run off.

"Aul' Nellie Brooks! Can't catch me!" Billy would run between her and the shop and fling a handful of clay at her, "Aul' Nellie Brooks! Drinks 'er own pee!" Then I would run past from the other direction and fling some more at her as she turned around. It was a sort of a dare, to see if she would try to catch us for the pot. She never even tried.

Nellie was the ugliest woman in the whole world. Her hair was long and thin and grey and she combed it straight back off her face. Her nose was sort of rough, like the surface of the moon, and there were hairs growing out of it. She had a fork-shaped red mark on the side of her chin. Billy said that was the Devil's mark, most likely where his forked tongue had touched her. She always wore the same thin black dress down to her ankles and a black lace scarf over her head, with her hair poking out the back of it. And even though she was eating all those boys there wasn't a pick of meat on her – you could see her skeleton underneath her skin. All the lumpy bits on her spine stuck out and you could see that it had a bend in it, like the letter "S".

But the thing about Nellie was that even though she looked like a little gust of wind would blow her away, everybody knew that she had magic powers she'd got from the Devil, and she could put the evil eye on you if she wanted to.

Then Mum had the weak baby. I thought it might be my fault, for taunting Nellie Brooks. There didn't seem to be any life in the little thing. It just lay there and hardly moved at all. If we'd had the money I think my mother would have taken it to the doctor.

Anyway, somebody told my mother that I had been taunting Nellie, and she was waiting for me when I got inside the door after school. Her eyes were red like she'd been crying.

"That's all I need! A son that attacks poor old women! Don't you think I have enough to contend with? Don't you think there's enough people in that town bad-mouthing us? What in God's name did you think you were doing?"

She went on like that for ages. Most likely she thought Nellie had done something to the baby for revenge. I told her I never touched the old bat but she wouldn't hear a word of it. She wrapped Ita in a woollen shawl and told me that we were going to go and see Nellie, and if I had tried not to come she would have had me by the ear, so I shut up and tagged along.

I don't mind telling you I was scared, pushing through those big weeds up the path to Nellie Brooks' front door.

My mother had to put her hand under my arm and hold on to me to keep me from bolting. I thought she was doing a crazy thing, walking up to the door of a woman that boiled children for her dinner and gave their souls to the Devil. I couldn't stop thinking about it. But there wasn't a lot I could do. The smell from that black cauldron over the fire was terrible. I tried to pull back but I couldn't get free of my mother's grip under my arm.

Nellie came to the door and opened the top half, and smiled out at us. I'd never been that close to her before. She only had a few teeth left and that smile scared me something wicked. She seemed to be smiling at the baby. My mother didn't understand the reason she was doing it. "Mrs Brooks," my mother said, calm as you like, "I've brought my boy to apologize to you for what he did at the bus stop outside Biddy Conlon's shop."

"We were all young once, Mrs Grant" she said in a voice like one of the nuns at school. Not the kind of voice I would ever have expected of a witch. "Is that your new daughter?"

"It is, Mrs Brooks. Her name's Ita."

"A good Irish name. I've got a great granddaughter named Ita. Will you come in and have a drop of tea? I'm sorry about the smell, I'm boiling up a few lights from the butcher for the cat. I can't smell anything any more so it doesn't worry me."

Lights from the butcher? My mother seemed to believe her. We came in and took a seat at the far side of the fire. It was a clean little cottage, and inside the smell wasn't so strong, because it was going up the chimney from the pot. She started to make the tea. I wondered what we would turn into if we drank it.

"Mrs Conlon told me that your baby isn't thriving," she said as she measured out the spoonfuls of tealeaves into the pot. I looked at my mother and I could have sworn she had a tear in the corner of her eye. Nellie stopped what she was doing and came over to sit beside my mother. "May I look at your hands, dear?"

My mother held them out. She looked first at the palms, then the backs. She put her hand up to my mother's face and pulled down the skin under one of her eyes.

"What did you have for your dinner today?"

"Well... just potatoes, and a drop of tea. We can't eat the way we used to, before... before Liam went off."

She questioned my mother about everything we ate in the week. About whether we ever had an orange, or a bit of spinach, or how much milk we drank in the day. I suppose she just wanted to make conversation. She held Ita for a while and looked at her hands too, and her eyes. She was a mad old woman all right. She made my mother promise that she would pick some blackberries for the two of us, and have them boiled up with sugar and buttermilk, and buy oranges in Biddy Conlon's shop, and take a few eggs from Nellie's hens home with us, and come back for more.

You could tell she was casting a spell of some kind. I thought she was probably trying to turn the two of us into a pair of toads. And that was why I wouldn't eat any of those queer new things that my mother started to cook up. At least not at first. But when I saw that she hadn't started to turn into anything after a couple of days I thought I may as well give it a try.

Now I don't know whether it was the eggs that were magic or the tea that she gave us, or the blackberries boiled up with the sugar and the buttermilk or what, but Ita started to get a lot more lively after that, and she got bigger and fatter and started to act more like a regular baby. My mother started to go over to Nellie's place once or twice a week and before you knew it she was going in to Drumalea to do Nellie's shopping for her and earning a little bit of money by cutting Nellie's grass and feeding her hens and such like. And my mother seemed to get stronger as well, just like Ita, so that when my father showed up again, a couple of months after I moved up to the big school, she was able to chase him out of the house with the broom handle. My mother said he would never be coming back again and that would be soon enough as far as she was concerned.

So don't let anybody tell you that witches only do bad spells. They can make sick babies better and they can make your Mum strong enough to kick your dead-loss Dad out of the house for ever. So just think what a witch could do if she wanted to get mean! We don't taunt her any more if we see her in Drumalea, and I wouldn't advise you to either. If she needs to eat a little boy every now and again to keep up her strength, that's okay with me. She wouldn't do it unless they deserved it.

"Sure ye don't have te tell me how lonely it is in big cities," The Rainbow Man lamented. *"I've been to London an' Paris an' Rome an' Jupiter, an there's one worse than the other."*

The Go-Between

Having nothing else to do I simply wandered through the wet sodium-lit streets of a city as endless as the night sky, drifting aimlessly through a moving ocean of humanity that went on and on in any direction that I cared to walk. Around each crowded corner, beyond each traffic-locked junction, more shops, more lights, more houses, more people staring through me, hurrying past with a nervous glance in my direction, forever on the move, forever striving to be somewhere else. As my feet grew tired and the slow drizzle began to soak through my clothing I gravitated as always to the kind of pub that catered for the likes of me, the people with nowhere else to go. Bright lights outside, dim lights inside, unobtrusive vaguely sentimental music just loud enough to permit relaxed conversation or to cover up its absence. A seating plan that blurred the distinction between those who were on their own and those who were not. The honey smeared on the human fly-paper that gathered up the rootless.

I ordered a drink and stood with it in my hand, scanning the faces of the people at the tables, making use of that radar by which we who are alone and don't want to be can detect others like ourselves. The highest reading came from a young black woman huddled into the far corner of the room, sitting alone at a table for four, with an almost full glass by her hand. I made my way directly to where she sat.

"May I?"

She smiled and motioned towards a chair. I introduced myself and sat down. Her name, she told me, was Sammi. My opening question was easy and obvious: where was she from? It was almost all that I needed to ask. She launched, hesitantly at first, into a long and detailed account of a life that had begun in an African missionary hospital and taken her eventually to a shared apartment in the student nurses' residence of another grander hospital, thousands of miles away in west London. Between there and here she had known good times and bad, love and loss, pain and joy, children and commitment, family and the leaving of family, the hope of a dazzling future in a far off land, the slow coming to terms with a much less glamorous reality. In essence it was the story of everybody who had ever responded to the lure of the neon fairyland that was permanently just out of reach where the end of the rainbow touched the ground. When it was my turn I told my story too, beginning with my arrival as an innocent and unworldly teenager from rural Ireland, standing transfixed between my two big suitcases on the Liverpool landing stage, too scared to ask the way to the train station. I told her of the jobs that hadn't worked out, the relationships that had floundered, the dreams that had somehow slipped away as the years piled one upon another.

We were both of an age when all such things ought really to have been resolved. Apart from the shallowest of externals, I thought, there was no significant difference between us.

I was certain that neither of us wanted to be alone that night, and that each was waiting for the other to make a move of some kind. It was a situation in which I had always felt particularly clumsy and inept, but bolstering up my confidence with the cliché that I had absolutely nothing to lose I finally managed to gather enough courage to ask if I could walk her back to the nurses' residence block where she lived. We left the pub hand in hand and within a couple of hundred yards I was shielding her from the rain with my right arm and the flap of my jacket around her shoulder. We shared our first kiss in a darkened doorway beneath the awning of a shuttered pawnbroker's shop.

I could feel her eagerness, the way her lips seemed to cling to mine, her hands covering all the territory from my head and neck down to my back and my buttocks, circling around to my chest, to my tummy and my belt, and below...

I slipped my right hand beneath the end of her blouse and gently eased it out of her jeans so that I could feel the warm flesh of her back, then very slowly moved my caresses around to the front.

Breaking her lips free she whispered in my ear: "Can I ask you something?" I nodded and waited for her to find the right words.

"It's about my room-mate," she said almost apologetically.

"Your room-mate?" I was puzzled.

"My room-mate is very unhappy tonight," she explained with obvious embarrassment. "Maybe... tonight... you could make her happy instead of me?"

I took my hand out of her clothing. "Make your room-mate happy instead of you?" This was positively the weirdest situation in which I had ever found myself. "What are you talking about?"

"She is a very nice girl. A white girl. Do you like white girls too?" I nodded inanely. "Tonight, you go with Natalie. Okay? Maybe another night you go with me."

I swallowed hard. "Maybe you would like to explain to me exactly what you're talking about," I repeated weakly. Suddenly feeling rather cold and insecure I instinctively began to tuck Sammi's blouse back into her jeans.

"Natalie had a bad day today," she said quietly. "Very bad day. She had a row with her lover. She needs you more than I do. You go with Natalie tonight."

Although my head was slightly reeling I could see a kind of logic and honesty in what Sammi was saying. We weren't in love. What we had to offer one another we could get from almost anyone. Closeness. Physical pleasure. A little tenderness. A shoulder to cry on perhaps. What was the point of pretending that we were special to one another?

The traffic sped by on the big dual carriageway beside us, making a hissing sound as each set of tires traversed the wet tarmac. The headlights intermittently lit up the features of Sammi's small and elegant face. I stared into her eyes and wondered what it was that so offended me about her suggestion. It was the breaking of the illusion, I realized. It was her refusal to collude in the fiction that we cared about one another, that we had achieved some kind of contact that made us less separate, less alone.

"What makes you think that Natalie would like me, Sammi?" I asked quietly.

"I know the kind of men that Natalie likes. I always choose for her."

My puzzlement deepened. "You always choose for Natalie?"

"Natalie is shy. She... isn't very good with men."

I felt my brow wrinkle with perplexity. "If she's shy, how can she cope with... this? With you taking men back for her?"

"It's hard to explain. Come back with me. Talk to Natalie. See for yourself."

Before I could get a grip on the strange mixture of feelings that were pulling me in different directions Sammi had taken hold of my hand and was leading me briskly through the drizzling rain towards the entrance of the brooding grey nurses' residence. In the lift we said nothing, Sammi merely smiled at me reassuringly, after which her face relaxed into an expression that most resembled quiet satisfaction. Totally unfamiliar with this strange role into which I had somehow become slotted I no longer held Sammi's hand or touched her, but just stood impassively by her side, rather wishing that my ordeal might come to a speedy end.

Sammi unlocked the inner apartment door and stepped aside to let me go in first. Her room-mate, small and blonde and very pretty, had been sitting at the window looking down at the rain and the traffic. No doubt she had seen us come to the front entrance. She turned around and smiled at me and I could see that she had been crying.

I was beginning to feel a little better about the weird situation. Natalie was indeed a tempting prospect. She looked at me for a moment, then looked past me at Sammi. "He's very nice," she said quietly, "you are good to me." It was strange to be talked about by a woman with whom I was supposedly about to spend the night. A woman who had said nothing to me, not even hello.

She walked towards me, raising her arms and opening her hands, seemingly to embrace me, but continued straight past, and when I turned around she was kissing Sammi no less passionately than I had kissed her myself only minutes before.

Stunned, I watched the two of them for a moment, then instinctively drew back towards the door and the corridor leading to the lift. They made no attempt to stop me or to communicate with me in any way.

I looked back and their embrace was becoming ever more abandoned, so that I felt like a voyeur of something very private and rather beautiful. I gently closed the door and left them alone. My head reeled with incoherent emotions, a twinge of disappointment, acute embarrassment, but absolutely no bitterness, malice or resentment. I knew that I had served my purpose.

In the street below, the river of people was still on the move and the next pub was only a couple of hundred yards down the road. I buttoned up my coat and stepped back into the endless human stream, feeling its comforting anonymity close in around me.

"Man alive, I wouldn't like to owe money to the likes of you," The Rainbow Man declared. "You're the type that'd dig a corpse out of its grave for the gold teeth."

The Debt Collector

Benjamin was out of breath from forcing his way through the tangle of springy sycamore shoots and blackthorns. He could see little by the faint shards of moonlight that broke through the heavy forest canopy above him—he merely pressed blindly ahead, knowing that he would reach the clearing sooner or later, as he always did.

The first thing he saw was a slowly pulsating glow through the branches, like a distant lighthouse flashing on and off, and as he drew closer, making as little noise as possible, he could hear the whirring of some small electrical device and catch glimpses of a moving figure between himself and the light. He held his breath and slowed to a snail's pace in a desperate effort to approach undetected. He could see the source of the sound and the light now: it was an old-fashioned slide projector like the one they used at his school years ago, its internal fan buzzing and shafts of light spilling out from the horizontal slats on its battered sides. The projectionist was sitting on a low wooden chair by the table that held the machine, and lifting slides out of a large cardboard box at his feet. He inserted them one by one, to be projected on to a cheap roll-up portable screen on a rickety tripod. In the intervals between his pulling one slide from the projector and inserting another the screen became glaringly white, then dimmed again to offer a sepia-tinted image of some long forgotten moment in Benjamin's early life.

A sense of invasion, of having his territory violated, seized Benjamin. That isn't his life, he thought angrily, that's my life. What right has he got to be looking at my life? He lurched forward, snapping a branch loudly as he did so.

The projectionist instantly rose to his feet and turned around to look straight at Benjamin. Back-lighted as he was by a picture of the seven-year-old Benjamin on his first two wheeled bicycle, it was impossible to make out his features. He growled a phrase in a low voice and a thick foreign accent. It sounded like: "You or me", or perhaps it could have been: "You are me". It was meaningless to Benjamin, yet deeply disturbing. As soon as he had said this he turned and hurried off into the forest, leaving the projector running and the dim, slightly out-of-focus picture motionless on the screen.

Benjamin stepped forward tentatively for a better view. The sound of the fan stopped but the picture remained for several seconds. Then it rippled and melted grotesquely from the centre outwards, and red and yellow flames and thick black fumes spewed from the ancient projector. A foul smell of burning celluloid choked Benjamin's lungs and he woke up, coughing and retching, alone in his darkened bed-sitting-room, with sweat soaking his pillow and running in rivulets into his eyes and down his temples. He sat up and wiped his face with the sheet. Take it easy, he told himself, calm down. Just a dream. Just that stupid dream again. He placed his right hand on his heart and felt its pounding slowly subside.

It was a scene straight out of a nineteen fifties Western. Benjamin stepped into the bar and everybody stopped talking and looked at him. Just like John Wayne in the movies. Not that this was a Texas prairie-town saloon with sawdust on the floor, spittoons on the counter and a honky-tonk piano in the corner playing The Streets of Laredo. This was Benjamin's quiet local which in the last few months had gone so far as to start describing itself as a "wine bar", and its location was less than five minute's walk from the Clock Tower at Crouch End, but still the moment achieved that cliché b-movie quality of hushed anticipation.

. Benjamin's immediate impulse was to leave again. Although he traded a lot on his good looks and was used to drawing a few female glances, this was something entirely different. Their stares were curious, intrigued, eager for whatever novelty and entertainment value the developing situation might hold. Roll up! Roll up! See the freaky drunken driver who knocked the old man into eternity! First appearance at this pub since the second of February!

That was when it had happened. Monday three weeks ago. Now Benjamin's life had changed forever. He would never be the same light-hearted womanising hard-drinking rising star of Aspects Media. If the company kept him on at all it would be an act of charity, because his driving licence was one of the requirements of his job, and he wouldn't get that back for two years. He would be twenty-seven the next time he legally sat behind the steering wheel of a motor vehicle. That was old in the media industry. You needed to have made your mark in a big way by then. But more importantly his own image of himself had changed. The carefree self assured young guy who had everything wasn't there any more. Days of sitting alone in his tiny flat, too scared to face the world, nights of that crazy recurrent dream, moments when the darkest thought of all had come into his mind . He didn't really know this new person that he had become.

There were three tables partly occupied and a few more people on stools at the bar. Benjamin knew virtually all of them, at least their first names. He steeled himself to go through with it. Life had to go on. There was no other option. He selected a nearby table where two young men of his own age in smart/casual baggy sweatshirts sat either side of a pretty young blonde woman who looked vaguely uncomfortable in a blue shoulder-padded business suit.

"Okay if I join you?"

"Benjie, of course, good to see you again," one of the men enthused. Despite the welcome Benjamin could detect a faint undercurrent of unease in the voice. He pulled up a chair and took his place opposite the woman with as casual an air as he could muster.

Everyone said hello. Then the first Freudian slip. The woman, Rose by name, something at Loring Merchant Holdings and girlfriend of the man who had greeted him, asked him if he was drinking, then quickly corrected herself by asking him WHAT he was drinking. It gave Benjamin the opening he needed.

"Yes, I'm drinking, Rosie. Drinking the same as usual. Not driving tonight, you see, I can drink as much as I like. And in case any of you want to know, the old guy is still in the coma and he isn't expected to come out of it."

"Jesus, Benjie," Rose's boyfriend protested, "it could have happened to any one of us. Any one of us here tonight. I heard you were barely over the limit. Hardly been drinking at all. It was Monday night for Chris'sake!"

"It's happened, Mike," Benjamin said sadly, "nothing is going to change it now. I didn't see him step out. I just heard the crack. I don't know whether it would have been any different if I hadn't had a drink. Probably not. Even the police said that. But I'll never know. Nobody will ever know. I was over the limit and I hit somebody. That's all there is to it. Can we talk about something else now?"

The evening didn't go too badly after that. Everybody was very sympathetic, all buying him drinks, telling him: "There but for the grace of God..." Benjamin knew perfectly well that most of them had come in cars and would be driving home in them, and that wasn't lemonade they were drinking. People don't learn anything from a thing like that, he mused. Not really.

Benjamin had assumed that his easy rapport with women would have gone with his self confidence. But Rose looked straight into his eyes all evening and at closing time kissed him goodnight, full on the lips. He supposed that she was sorry for him. Maybe, he thought fleetingly, he would see her in the pub by herself some time...

In bed that night, although he'd had more than his usual two or three doubles, Benjamin found it very difficult to get to sleep. He lay flat on his back in the middle of the big mattress, gazing at the ceiling and waiting for the computer monitor to switch itself off and plunge the room into complete darkness. It functioned as a night-light on a timer for the nights that he slept alone, which, since the accident, had been every night. Usually he was asleep before the shut-down moment arrived, tonight he was not. The light died and dim swirling shapes formed before his eyes, resolving themselves slowly into the familiar dark, brooding forest landscape of his recurrent dream.

A watery moon peeping through momentary gaps in the branches lighted Benjamin's slow but purposeful walk through the forest, his feet sinking into the soft dry leaf-mould with every step, above him the heavy canopy of ancient beeches, oaks and ash trees. The spaces between the trunks were choked by the growth of the younger vigorous sycamores and blackthorns so that he had to pick his way through, bending the branches as he passed and allowing them to spring back into position behind him.

Benjamin knew what was coming next. He had been in this dream many times before. It was never exactly the same but the variations were only minor. There would be a glimmer of yellow light up ahead, barely detectable at first, then it would grow brighter. Yes, there it was. He must try to be quieter now, to approach the clearing with the absolute minimum of disturbance, not to make the intruder run off. That was how Benjamin always saw him, as an intruder, although intruding into a clearing in the middle of a moonlit forest didn't make a great deal of sense. But somehow Benjamin knew that the clearing was his own territory, his own very personal space, and the other had no right to be there.

This time the intruder was sitting at a small desk surrounded by filing cabinets, some of which had open drawers. He had his back to Benjamin's vantage point behind the branches, hunched over some papers which he was reading by the yellow circle of light from a small angle-poise lamp. Despite the care and silence of Benjamin's approach it was obvious that the intruder knew he was there. He straightened up and looked directly towards Benjamin, mumbled something that sounded like "You or me" and rose briskly from his chair, hurrying into the woods before Benjamin could disentangle himself from the thicket of branches that barred his way. In the few moments it took him to get to the desk the intruder had vanished, but not before Benjamin had got a good look at his face, the old lined and sunken Negro features, the Afro hair, thin and almost white with the ravages of age, and the peculiar series of dark horizontal scars on the cheekbones just below each eye.

"Leave my things alone," Benjamin spoke aloud as he packed the papers that the old man had been reading back into the filing cabinets, "these aren't yours. These are my

things, my memories." The words were of course completely redundant. The intruder was no longer there to hear.
Benjamin carefully filed away the picture of his mother as a
child, his first school report, the love letter from his first girl
friend, the smell of the dentist's surgery when he had an
impacted wisdom tooth removed in his first term at University...

Benjamin took the Underground train in to the West End
that morning and went to the studio for the talk that he had
been dreading with his boss Wes Bewler. He had never
really liked Wes, with his blond goatee beard, sculpted
sideburns and affected American accent, and he was convinced that Wes thoroughly enjoyed telling him, so very
politely, that legally the company owed him nothing and he
couldn't really see much "on the creative side" for a man in
Benjamin's position just at the moment. Words like
"sacked" or "fired" were never even hinted at, but it was
made perfectly clear that Benjamin's employment with the
company was at an end.

After the interview, feeling close to rock bottom, Benjamin strolled around a few West End shops in the cold
winter drizzle before re-boarding the Underground on impulse and making his way to the main Reception at the
hospital to which his victim had been taken. There was a
very pretty mixed-race girl at the desk, and the act of talking
to her cheered him up a little. When he explained who he
was and who he had come to see her face became serious
and she asked him to wait while she talked for several
minutes in a very low voice on the internal telephone.

"Mr Lojo's condition is unchanged," she said rather
formally when she put the phone down, "He hasn't regained
consciousness and the nurse in charge of Intensive Care says
that very little purpose would be served by your visiting

him. Also the official visiting hours are between two and six," she cast a sidewise glance towards the wall clock which was reading twelve twenty. Benjamin shrugged and was turning to go when she called him back. She waited until he was right back at the desk before giving him a heart-melting smile and telling him very quietly: "My lunch break begins in ten minutes".

They sat in a quiet corner of the crowded and impersonal hospital canteen and looked out at the strengthening rain. Benjamin wasn't concerned about the girl's motives in calling him back. He guessed that she had felt a little sorry for him as Rosie had the night before, that his plight had triggered some nurturing motherly instinct. Whatever her reasons he found himself pouring out his heart to the girl in a manner that was quite uncharacteristic. He told her about the way he had been feeling that night, the things that had gone wrong at work, the hurt when somebody named Debbie had rejected his advances, his decision to have just one drink and then go straight home, the way that one drink had become two and then three, the stomach-churning crack of breaking bones and the splatter of blood across the windscreen. She listened attentively and without interruption – would have listened for longer but Benjamin had questions of his own. He asked her to tell him about Lojo, the man who had been hit. Was that a West Indian name?

"He's from Trinidad originally," she explained, "I don't know how long he's been in this country but he has no family over here. His sister is here visiting him now. She's a funny old thing. Really strong Trinidad accent. She says his spirit isn't there any more, only his body. In a way she's right, the doctors think he's brain dead." Her voice softened, "Sorry, I didn't mean to upset you."

"I'd give anything in the world if I could take back those ten seconds after I drove out of the pub car park," he whispered.

"I'm really sorry about what happened," she said, taking his hand, "we all are. It was an accident. Accidents happen. All the time. Nobody can stop them happening."

He squeezed her hand gently. "Would you like to come out for a meal tonight?" he asked as casually as he could.

"Can't make tonight," she replied with what seemed genuine disappointment, "but tomorrow would be okay."

Benjamin had his usual dream that night. He told it to his lovely new companion over dinner the following evening. She listened with a quiet fascination, gazing into his eyes. Benjamin had never felt so interesting before. He didn't have to play-act or make anything up. This delightful creature whose name was Marcia really cared about his feelings and his dreams and his innermost longings. Perhaps life wasn't so cruel after all. He could feel the attraction grow, the desire to sit nearer, to touch her, to let his arm fall casually over her back...

Her head was on his shoulder and they were almost lined up for a kiss, sipping the last few drops of wine from their glasses, when he reached the part about the dark scars underneath the intruder's eyes. Marcia suddenly tensed. "Scars under his eyes? How did you know about those?"

"Know about them? What do you mean?"

"Mr Lojo has scars under his eyes. It's some kind of tribal marking. He was a voodoo priest or something back home."

"Mr Lojo..." Benjamin's strange haunted dreams suddenly began to make some kind of sense. The intruder was Mr Lojo. He hadn't seen his face on the night of the accident but he might have seen a photograph of him somewhere, in a newspaper perhaps... and yet he had no recollection of it. " I suppose it's guilt," he whispered, "those must be some kind of guilt dreams..."

Marcia put down her glass and reached over to embrace him with both her arms. "You don't have to sleep on your own tonight," she whispered, "not if you don't want to."

It was the pleasantest way of getting off to sleep known to mankind. Certainly the nicest thing that had happened to Benjamin since the accident. The exhilaration of having a pretty girl in his arms felt like the first step towards bringing the old Benjamin back to life.

Benjamin felt strong tonight. He strode through the forest snapping branches under his feet and breaking them crudely with his hands to keep them away from his face. He didn't care if the intruder ran away or not, or what happened to the trees or the memories or the filing cabinets. This was a dream, something going on inside Benjamin's mind. It couldn't do him any harm if he didn't allow it to.

The angle-poise lamp was still switched on and the intruder was still there, standing in front of the desk and the filing cabinets, back-lighted by the glow of the lamp, but Benjamin could still see him clearly, the white hair, the dark skin, the scars beneath either eye. This time the intruder did not move, did not try to run away. Benjamin walked right up to him and stopped. For a moment their eyes met in silence. Then the old man spoke, very quietly in a heavily accented voice: "You owe me".

"So that's what you've been saying," Benjamin returned in a conversational tone, "you think I owe you. Well, I suppose you're right, I do, but it's a debt you can never collect. I'm strong tonight, old man. There's nothing you can take from me tonight."

"You're wrong Benjamin," he warned quietly, "you aren't strong."

"I'm not afraid of you. Not now, and not ever again. I'm walking away from you old man. And I don't care what you do with these things. They aren't real. You aren't real. There's nothing you can do to me. Good bye old man." With these words he strode past the man and the desk and the lamp and kept on walking across the clearing to where the forest closed around him once again, but here the path was broad and well trodden. He did not need to push the branches aside any more, he could walk as quickly as he wished. Without looking back he lengthened his stride and pressed on and on towards some distant unknown goal in a part of the forest that he had never visited before...

Benjamin could hear voices in the darkness, very far away. He was waking from a deep heavy sleep. As he edged closer towards consciousness the voices grew a little more distinct. One belonged to a crisp official-sounding man who spoke in a clipped Standard English. "I know this decision has not been easy for you, Miss Lojo," he was saying with affected concern in his voice, "but I am glad that you have come to see that it is the only sensible course of action."

Benjamin struggled to concentrate and to draw nearer to full consciousness but there seemed to be something preventing him, a barrier. His eyes would not open, his body would not respond. He heard the woman's voice next, it was high-pitched and had a sort of sing-song quality as well as a heavy West Indian accent: "My brother he not here no more, Mister. He gone a someplace else."

"Quite so, Miss Lojo. I think perhaps you should leave the room now."

"I leave in a one a minute, Mister."

"As you wish. Nurse, would you switch off the artificial respirator please. And hand me the notes if you would. Time of death..."

With a superhuman effort Benjamin managed to open one eye. There was a woman's face staring down at him, an old plump black woman's face that he had never seen before. As he drew her features into focus he saw his own face reflected in the lenses of her round brass rimmed spectacles. Before the scream could reach his lips the blackness engulfed him.

Marcia, cuddled up close to his side with her head snug in the crook of his shoulder, felt a wakening twitch in the body of the man with whom she lay. She kissed him gently on the cheek. "Good morning. Did you have any bad dreams?"

He opened his eyes and beamed down at her. "Marcia darlin' that the best night's sleep of my life so far!"

"Hey! That's clever! I didn't know you could do a Trinidadian accent!"

"Have I ever seen a miracle?" The Rainbow Man turned the little girl's question over in his mind. "Well, a miracle is something that you can't explain, and now I come to think of it I've seen very little that I can explain, so the miracles are in the majority."

The Hand of God

Benny put the key in the ignition and nursed the old Ford van into reluctant life. He looked over his shoulder at the boxes and piles of clothes and books shaking in the back with the vibration of the engine. It had turned into the saddest night of his life so far. The end of his first supposedly permanent live-in relationship. He tried to comfort himself with the thought that it had really ended a long time ago, when the good bits had faded away and the bickering had turned to ugly recrimination and long dark silences. He was certain that he had not been without fault in the way that it had soured, but he deserved better than to be told to pack up and leave at ten o'clock on a rainy November night. He wished that he could be properly angry with her but in his heart he could find only this heaviness and this need to be swiftly gone. He knew that he would not be coming back.

He eased the van out into a space between two lumbering lorries on the dual carriageway and matched his speed to theirs. The regular swish of the windscreen wipers seeped into his thoughts and calmed him a little.

Across the wide grass verges tall ugly blocks of flats drifted by, yellow light flooding from some of the windows, most of them in total darkness. He passed a cemetery, the gravestones dimly and intermittently visible behind a neglected screen of winter-naked trees. Houses, more flats, a

265

school with a playing field. He seldom paid this much attention to his surroundings when he was driving, but tonight he had nowhere to go and hoped that somehow a particular place or thing would suggest itself to him as a destination.

It was a senseless exercise, he realized, it was all the same. The suburbs went on forever, there was no reason to choose any one place over another. He randomly picked a particular housing development with an accessible car park and drove into it. The blocks rose all around the central courtyard and a row of jemmied and vandalised garage doors lined the far wall. It would do as well as anywhere else. He selected a place next to the shell of an abandoned car and switched off the engine and the lights. This would not be the first night he had spent in the van, indeed he had camped two summer holidays in it, one of them alone, the other not, but he knew that tonight would be cold when the last vestiges of the engine heat died away. He climbed through the familiar gap between the front seats into the back and busied himself pulling the crude curtains across the rear windows.

By the far corner of the courtyard, near to some large black refuse bins, his eyes caught the movement of a small human figure. Instinctively he glanced at his wristwatch and confirmed that it was after midnight. It was a woman, dressed in a dark flowing dress and carrying a bulging white plastic carrier bag, but she was no bag-lady. Her movements were too graceful, her demeanour too alert. What would a woman be doing out in the rain at those refuse bins in the middle of the night? She was looking in his direction, she had heard him drive in. Was she expecting someone? He remained still and watched.

Slowly, hesitantly at first, the slight figure began to walk towards the van. Probably a drug thing, he thought. Most likely the dealers drive in here and park and the people who want to buy come up to them. Or could it be a prostitute pick-up spot? Was she going to ask him if he wanted to do business? She walked steadily towards him through the gloom. As she drew nearer he saw that she was quite young and undoubtedly Asian. Her dark dress was a traditional costume, he assumed it to be Pakistani but he was no expert. There was a separate head scarf that enclosed her hair such as many Moslem women in England seemed to wear. He dismissed his theories about drugs and prostitution.

There seemed no point in concealment so he pulled himself into the front of the van and opened the door to greet her. She was dripping wet but smiled up at him in a manner that he could only think of as radiant. "Are you... real?" she asked in a reverential, slightly foreign-sounding voice.

It was not the question that Benny had expected. "Am I real? What do you mean by that?" He felt vaguely sorry for her, standing so small and forlorn in the rain, looking up at him as though he were a pop star or a holy man.

"I know who you are," she said quietly, "you don't have to pretend."

"You do? Well, you can come in out of the rain if you like. I'm afraid I can't say the same about you." He reached out and she took his hand and allowed him to help her up the high step into the passenger seat. He closed the door gently behind her. She sat with the carrier bag on her knee, still looking at him in that wide-eyed, worshipful way. He found it downright unnerving. "What can I do for you?" he asked in a tone as conversational as he could muster.

"Save me," she said with a quiet confidence.

Benny stared at her. She was small, probably about his own age, quite pretty, evidently entirely insane. Why did he always have to get landed with the fruitcakes? "If I could save someone," he said evenly, trying not to sound harsh, because he didn't want to offend the girl, "I would save myself."

"Do you really not know who you are?" she asked calmly.

"I thought I did. Okay, who am I then?"

"You're an angel. And you have been sent to save me."

Benny sighed. Fruitcakes. The whole world was teeming with fruitcakes. European ones, Asian ones, black ones... Where did they all come from? Why did they all pick on him? "Sweetheart, you seem very nice, and if I was in the saving business I would be happy to oblige. But I am not an angel and I have not been sent by anybody to do anything. My name is Benny Harper. I study Electrical Engineering at the University of the South Bank. My parents live in Wiltshire. I haven't been to church since I was about twelve years old. Trust me, I would know if I was an angel."

She studied him even more closely. "Is it possible that you really don't know?" She seemed to struggle for the right words. "Then perhaps I must tell you. Every night, before I go to sleep in the room with my two sisters, I pray to Allah to save me from this marriage to Rehan, my second cousin. It is what my family requires, I have no choice in the matter. I know that Allah is real and that he hears my prayers, but I believe that this marriage is the will of my father, not the will of Allah. I beg Allah, if it is his sacred will, to send one of his angels to save me from this loveless and unnatural match. Rehan repels me, he is old and bad-tempered and has bad skin. I have begged them all not to make me wed this man, now there is no one left to beg except Allah himself.

But Allah knows all things and hears all things. And this night in my dream I heard the voice of Allah saying I must go outside at once, that the angel had been sent. I would see the angel arrive, all in blue. I made sure nobody saw and I came down the stairs, and as I opened the door I saw you arrive – all in blue."

"All in blue...? You mean, in a blue van?"

She nodded and smiled disarmingly.

"Sweetheart, this is terrible. I don't want to let you down, but I'm no angel and this van is no fiery chariot, and I have no power to save anybody from anything. I'm a student, damn it. And a part time nightclub bouncer. I don't do rescue missions. You've got it all wrong. See?" He turned his back momentarily. "No wings."

"Allah did not say anything about wings."

Benny felt lost. Completely out of his depth. He sat in silence for a few moments. "What can I say to you that's going to convince you you've got the wrong person?"

She thought for a moment. "Very well, Mr Benny. If you did not come for me, why did you come?"

Benny's brow furrowed as he considered the question. "I have no idea," he admitted at last.

"You do not know, but Allah knows," she assured him quietly.

He shook his head and looked at her sadly, and beyond her small trusting face at the rain that was still running in twisting rivulets down the side window. "What's your name, sweetheart?"

"Fatima."

"Fatima. Right. That's a lovely name. Look, Fatima, this is crazy. I am not an angel. I'm not even a very good man. I've just had a flaming row with my girlfriend and I was thinking pretty damned uncharitable thoughts about her just before you showed up. I don't have anything to offer you. You've got to get that straight. You shouldn't be here. I'm sorry about Rehan but there's nothing I can do about it. You shouldn't trust... people like this. You don't know anything about me."

"If the Lord of the Universe trusts you I can trust you too."

For a moment they were both silent. Benny had been in some pretty weird situations but this one took the biscuit.

"Perhaps that's all that an angel is," Fatima volunteered at last. "An ordinary man that Allah trusts."

"Well, if that's so I'm not very impressed with him as a judge of character."

Fatima smiled. Across the courtyard Benny saw more figures appear close to the refuse bins – tall, striding male figures, talking in a mixture of English and a language that Benny did not know. Two of them. They were coming straight towards the van.

"My father," Fatima explained with a commendable calmness, "and Rehan. He came to our flat to speak with my parents tonight..."

Instinctively Benny reached for the ignition. The engine was still warm and started instantly. "I kind of think maybe it's time we weren't around," he said weakly.

"Please wait. Let my father speak." She rolled down her window and a few drops of rain blew across on to Benny's face.

The men stopped a few feet from the van and stared in open-mouthed disbelief. It was Rehan who spoke first. Benny could tell by his pitted, crater-like skin, probably the legacy of childhood smallpox. "Is this the daughter you would have me wed?" he intoned in a deep sepulchral bass, "a woman who meets alone with men in a public car park when her sisters have gone to sleep?"

Her father's jaw trembled but it took him a long time to find the words. "I have never felt such shame," he whispered. "Leave us, Rehan. I ask only that you will not talk of what you have seen tonight. Leave my home in peace and friendship. There is nothing for us to discuss. I can give you only my blessing. My eldest daughter is dead." So saying he turned to go.

"I have done nothing wrong, father," she shouted after him, but he was not listening. Benny watched the two of them out of sight. Fatima rolled her window up again. When Benny looked at her the tears were streaming silently down her face.

"Fatima," he put his hand on her shoulder, "that's a terrible thing for your father to say. I know you must feel awful... but, well, isn't it the will of Allah?"

She nodded and tried to dry her tears on the backs of her hands.

"It seems to be a night for break-ups," Benny said sadly. "Put on your seat belt, Fatima. This isn't the best place for us to be."

"Where are we going?"

"Don't ask me sweetheart. I haven't the foggiest. What have you got in that bag?" As he spoke he nosed the van out of the courtyard and rejoined the dual carriageway, which was now completely deserted.

"In this?" She held it up. "My passport, my Birth Certificate. My school reports and exam results... a little bit of money... my toothbrush... everything I thought I would need."

"You and Allah planned this between you, didn't you?"

She nodded. She was almost smiling. "You are wrong about Allah," she scolded him gently, "he is a very good judge of character."

Publication History

Story	First publication
Blind Date	*E-Life* (magazine) (1996)
Collateral Damage	*Cimmplicity* (magazine) (2002)
The Lies of Sleeping Dogs	*Voices From the Web* (anthology) UKA Press (2003)
Knight Errant	*SciFiDimensions* (magazine) (2001)
Letting Go	*Franklin's Grace & Other Stories: Winners of Ireland's Fish Short Story Prize* (anthology) (2002)
The Battlefield Philosopher	*Cenotaph* (magazine) (2002)
Lettie	*Caravan* (magazine) (2000)
Witchcraft	*Voices From the Web* (anthology) UKA Press (2003)
The Go-Between	*GFO Free Press Magazine* (2003)
The Hand of God	*Voices From the Web* (anthology) UKA Press (2003)

(All other stories published for the first time in this collection)

By the same author

The Other End of the Rainbow	Companion to the present volume. Short stories. Merilang Press (2008)
SIRAT (a novel)	The dawn of electronic intelligence. The human era draws to a close. iUniverse (2000)

About the author

The son of an Irish country GP father and a former hospital nurse mother, David Gardiner has lived in England for several decades, and worked as a teacher, handyman, satellite TV installer and mental health care worker, among many other things. He has dabbled in almost everything, and wandered the planet in wide-eyed fascination at the things it contains.

David has a large website at Davidgardiner.net

Merilang Press Books

www.merilang.com/merilang-press/

You may be interested in other books from Merilang Press:

Books for Adults

Sun on the Hill
Poems from Wales by Daffni Percival

Letters from My Mill
by Alphonse Daudet, translated by Daffni Percival

The Other End of the Rainbow
Short stories by David Gardiner

Solid Gold
An anthology of the best prose from 5 years of *Gold Dust* magazine, edited by David Gardiner

Children's Books by Daffni Percival

And Thereby Hangs a Tail
Memoirs of a border collie puppy as he grows up and learns to be a 'good sheepdog' as his mother told him
1st edition (colour), 2nd edition (black & white)

A Sheepdoggerel Anthology
A collection of animal poems with a preponderance of collies

The Rainbow Pony
A bedtime story for young children – small card book

9 780955 543067